For the Love of David

For the Love of David

by Laurel Bradley

STORYTELLER

A Publisher of Quality Fiction

ISBN-13: 978-1-938833-02-1

Author Website
http://www.LaurelBradley.com

Give feedback to:
laurel@laurelbradley.com

FOR THE LOVE OF DAVID is a work of fiction. Apart from the well-known actual people, events and locales that figure in the narrative, all names, characters, places and incidents are the product of the author's imagination or are used fictitiously. Any resemblance to current events or locales, or to living persons, is entirely coincidental.

Cover photography by Kate Bradley

Cover art by Janie Bradley

Background texture by Danuta Kowalska
dreamstime.com

Storyteller Publishing
www.storytellerpublishing.com
Email: info@storytellerpublishing.com

Printed in U.S.A

ACKNOWLEDGEMENTS

Thank you:

God, for the countless blessings you've given me: faith, a fabulous husband, health, and talents among the many.

Tom, for your constant love and support.

Benjamin, Adam, Jacob, Emily and Daniel, for being patient when writing got in the way. Each of you kids is a blessing.

Erin and Janet, for helping me whip the manuscript into shape.

Mom and Dad, for being my personal booster club and selling copies of my books out of the back of their car.

Book club and Central WI Writers, for all the suggestions.

Renee Wildes, for coming up with the title.

Kate Bradley, photographer, and Lainey Bradley, model, for the baby picture.

Jamie Bradley, for the cover art.

Alan and Goldie Browning, for believing in the book.

DEDICATION

To Tom my personal "happily ever after."

The Baby Drop

Eau Claire, Wisconsin
November 3, 1980

In her hiding place seated beneath the leafless trees, Marissa Fleming clutched the beige athletic bag against her chest. She watched as a heavy-set, thirty-something woman got out of a blue Ford and walked into the grocery store.

Marissa ached everywhere, but her heart hurt the most. She'd thought long and hard about it. This was the right thing to do. The best for her, for…everyone.

Then why did it hurt so much?

The super maxi pad between her legs was warm and heavy with blood. She should change it, should lie down and rest. But not yet.

When the woman disappeared into the building, Marissa struggled to her feet and shuffled through the thick brown mat of leaves to the parking lot.

It was too early in the morning for anyone she knew to be on Water Street. Too early for much traffic at the grocery store either, but that couldn't be helped. Maybe the woman was somebody's mom rushing to pick up milk for breakfast. Marissa hoped so. But if that were true, she didn't have much time.

She urged herself forward. It didn't matter that she wished she weren't there. It didn't matter that she would rather have been in bed at the dorm or in the cafeteria at Davies Center having breakfast. Or even at the dentist having a cavity filled. She was there to do what needed to be done.

Sweat trickled down her back despite the cold autumn wind that cut through her gray sweatshirt. Her hair hung lank and uncombed around her shoulders instead of how she usually wore it, up in a perky side ponytail ala Chrissy Snow of *Three's Company*. She paused to pluck at a strand stuck to her cheek before pulling up her hood. It was appropriate she looked like crap. It was all just part of the nightmare.

She forced herself to take another step. Just one. Tears stung her eyes. She'd been over it again and again. There was no other choice. People were counting on her. She was the first girl in her family to attend college. She couldn't let them down. She had classes to take. A degree in finance to earn. She wasn't ready for this. This…mess just wasn't in her plans.

Taking a deep breath, she crossed Kerm's nearly empty parking lot. She gently placed the bag on the cold cement under a sign by the store's door.

"I'm sorry. This is for the best. It is. It really is." Her throat ached as she forced herself to turn away. She tried to swallow the painful lump, but it wouldn't move. Too many things she couldn't swallow. The enormity of what she'd done, what she was doing, almost overwhelmed her.

She stumbled back across the parking lot. Part of her wanted to run, to rejoice. She'd done it! She was free! Another part wanted to shove this memory behind the door with all the other bad dreams. A quieter part just curled into a ball and cried. Trying to hold it all together, Marissa wrapped her arms around herself. She returned to the rough woods above the river and lowered herself onto a frost-coated log to watch.

§

Inside Kerm's grocery store, Libby Armstrong brought her half-filled cart to the check out. She unloaded her groceries onto the conveyer belt and smiled at the clerk. "Pretty quiet this morning."

"Yep." The middle-aged checker smacked her gum, her fingers flying across the cash register keys. "No one seems to wanna shop this early. It'll pick up once the college kids finish class. Paper or plastic?"

"Think I'll try the plastic this time." Libby smiled as she paid for her groceries. Sometimes it seemed as if the only conversations she had were with sales clerks and patients at the clinic.

It was too early for the carryout boys to come in, so she pushed the cart to the door and paused to zip up her jacket before going outside.

Her cart rattled past a beige bag she noticed lying on the concrete outside the door. She walked on by, opened the trunk of her car and placed her purchases inside. Then returning the empty cart to the corral by the door, Libby thought she saw a slight motion out of the corner of her eye. She stopped with a jerk and stared at the athletic bag on the ground.

The cloth bag moved again and then emitted a thin cry. It sounded like a kitten. What kind of person would leave a bag of kittens on a cold sidewalk to die? Poor things. Her hands trembled as she tugged at the zipper. The bag opened slowly, almost reluctantly. Expecting a bundle of fur, Libby froze in shock. She stared at the red, wrinkled face of a newborn child.

"Oh." Her breath left in a gush.

Glancing around for the bag's owner, Libby saw no one. Who would leave a baby like this? She knew what she should do. Go in the store. Call the police. But she couldn't. They'd send the baby to foster care. It'd be passed from one family to the next while the powers that be searched for its mother. There'd be months—maybe years—of court proceedings to sever the birth mother's rights before it'd be put up for adoption. She remembered what had happened when she and Jenny were little. Remembered it too well to put an innocent baby through that kind of upheaval.

Instead, she scooped up the bag and, cradling it in her arms, walked to her car. Once safely inside the blue Ford, her heart beat a strange tattoo. She scoured the surrounding area for signs of life. Where was the mother?

She started the car, turned on the heat, and waited for it to kick in before she unwrapped the silent child, swaddled in an old towel.

Tears filled her eyes. "You're beautiful. Dear God, you are so beautiful."

The tiny boy was perfect and obviously just newly born. A light fringe of black hair stuck to his scalp with the waxy, white vernix and dried blood still present. His sweet, oval head was slightly crooked from his journey into life. Long, black lashes adorned the tightly closed eyes and pale, yellow dots topped his nose. His rosebud mouth moved slightly as he sucked on his tongue and slept.

Libby had seen her sister Jenny's babies as newborns, had raised the youngest since infancy, so she knew this baby's scrawny body and wrinkled skin were normal. The baby's umbilical cord had been clamped with a piece of string, and his little feet were folded against his shinbones.

"Why would someone leave you in a bag?" Libby asked the sleeping infant. Her heart hurt for him. She looked out the window for the mother. Where was she?

"I should turn you in," Libby acknowledged. It wasn't too late.

She could drive to the police station or the hospital, explain how she'd found him. Maybe foster care wouldn't be so bad for a newborn.

She shook her head, remembering how she'd fought to keep Jenny with her. A ten-year-old fighting the system. The old pain and helplessness rose like a specter. It seemed as if she'd always been fighting for Jenny. Fought for her even as she died. Two years of battling cancer had shrunk her vibrant sister to a shadow. Despite the stories Libby told, the kids couldn't remember what their mom had been like before she'd become sick. They'd been Libby's to love and care for.

Then six months after the funeral, Libby's brother-in-law, Mark, had remarried. He'd sold the house in Marshfield, Wisconsin, and moved to North Carolina last spring. Starting a new life, he'd called it. It was another death for Libby. An unexpected one that still made her cry at night. Now, half a continent separated her from her only remaining family. Libby was alone. Since there was nothing but painful memories left in Marshfield, she had moved a couple hundred miles to Eau Claire.

She looked again for the baby's mother. Nothing moved. The three other cars in the parking lot were empty. She stroked the newborn's cheek before gently tucking the towel around him. Her decision was made. There'd be no impersonal foster care for this little one. No. If his birth mother wanted to throw him away, Libby would take him.

Finders keepers.

Pick Up

The slam of a car door jerked Marissa awake. She must have dozed off because she was still on the log in the woods behind Kerm's grocery store. The woman she'd seen earlier stood next to the trunk of the blue Ford. She looked maternal, almost pregnant. Marissa's stomach cramped at the thought. Was she?

The shopping cart rattled as the lady pushed it back to the building. Fear stole Marissa's breath and froze her in place. From where she sat, it looked like the bag was inside the cart corral instead of next to it. If, instead of walking all the way, the woman pushed hard to propel the cart the last few feet into the corral as Marissa always did, it would hit the bag. Maybe even run it over.

But the woman didn't carelessly push the cart, and Marissa's heart began to beat again. She watched as the woman pushed it just inside the metal cage and stopped mid-stride for a moment. Marissa knew she'd seen the bag.

Marissa held completely still, peering between the bush's naked branches and praying. Take it. Please take it. The woman stood in the lot, scanning the woods. Marissa held her breath and closed her eyes as if that would help her remain camouflaged.

When she finally opened her eyes, exhaust plumed from the woman's blue Ford sedan. She slapped herself to stay awake. She was losing time, dozing off.

And then she realized that everything was okay. The bag was gone. Somewhere inside the blue four-door. She stared at the license plate, trying to read it before the car pulled out of the lot and disappeared.

LDY something.

"LaDY," she said to herself, trying to imprint the letters on her brain. "A LaDY took the baby."

Marissa should have been relieved; instead, she hung her head and sobbed.

§

Moments passed. How many? Marissa didn't know. She was too

dizzy. She wondered how much blood she had lost, but she didn't have the energy to make herself care. She continued sitting in the woods between Kerm's and the river. Her eyes rested on the small bits of trash caught in the long grass and leaves next to the parking lot. That's what she was. Flotsam. Eyes closed, she leaned against a tree and rested a bit more.

The LaDY took the baby. Tears filled her eyes, but she didn't know if they were tears of joy, regret, or exhaustion. It was too confusing. She'd sort it all out later.

Minutes passed. Cold seeped from the ground. Shivering, she opened her eyes and looked down the steep embankment to the Chippewa River. It would be easy to jump in and float away. The frigid water would soon numb her body the way leaving her son had numbed her soul. Tempting. So tempting.

She could almost feel herself stumbling down the hill, plunging into the water. It would take less effort to drown than to walk back to campus and get cleaned up. Still, it was a temptation she would ignore, at least for now.

She'd dealt with the past. She'd left her mistake behind. Now, she needed to move forward. People were counting on her. Struggling to her feet, she took an unsteady step and stopped, sweaty and cold, panting from the exertion as she looked at the dorms across the river. She'd walked that distance and more every day. It wasn't that far. Besides, if she didn't start now, she'd sink back into the grass and stay there, uncaring. And wreck everything. So, she forced herself, and she took one step and then another, beginning the seemingly endless walk back to campus.

She had already taken care of the mess. The bloody sheets were gone; she had seen to that. Putnam Hall had a garbage shoot that led down to a burner. Monday and Thursday mornings, the staff burned the trash. Not ecologically sound, but useful.

And the afterbirth was also gone. It would, Marissa thought grimly, make a meal for the stray dogs and cats that foraged along the river's edge. Or raccoons. Better a raccoon than someone's spaniel dragging half of it home or puking it all over the rug. Bile rose in her throat at the thought. The baby was safe. Nobody's dog would get the baby. She hadn't tossed it down the hill.

She swallowed hard, pushing away the image and the accompanying urge to vomit. That's all she needed. Although it would have been poetic justice, of a sort.

When the pains had started, Marissa told her roommate she had the flu. Jessie had shoved a change of clothes in her backpack and escaped to spend yet another night with her boyfriend. She wouldn't be back until that afternoon at the earliest, and then only for a change of clothes. Jessie didn't want to get whatever Marissa had.

Not much chance of that. Jessie was too smart. But then, Marissa had thought she'd been smart as well. What did it matter? She shrugged. Jessie thought she had the flu. One would think a nursing student like Jessie would be more observant or more sympathetic. Marissa sighed and dragged herself up the incline to the foot bridge. It wasn't that Jessie didn't care. She was just busy. Hospital rotations and a serious boyfriend left Jessie little time for anything else.

Marissa should feel grateful. But, oddly enough, she didn't.

Maybe if someone had noticed, she'd have…

She had hoped that thinking about Jessie would occupy her mind so she wouldn't remember. She'd hoped, but the memory of her son's face flashed before her eyes. His face was red, and his mouth open as he protested his entry into the world. She hadn't heard his cry over the music from her stereo. Still, she'd made the mistake of holding him for a few minutes.

Just to quiet him.

Yeah, right. Even *she* didn't believe *that* lie.

He'd stopped crying in the temporary safety of her arms and opened his blue-black eyes to stare back at her. He was so incredibly beautiful. He weighed next to nothing, but the reality of him was so much more than she'd imagined. And he was warm. So very warm. She shook her head savagely to clear it of the image. He was gone. It was over. What she needed now was a shower, some rest and some food.

Marissa pulled the hood of her sweatshirt over her head and trudged across the bridge back to the main campus.

§

Libby drove to Target talking sweet-talk to the sleeping baby, who was haphazardly belted into the seat next to her.

"You'll need *food* and *clothes* and *diapers*. Oh, yes you will and…." Her eyes filled with tears. She reached over and stroked his cheek. He was a part of her heart already. How could his mother have left him?

In the parking lot, she shifted into park. Her hands shook as she opened her purse and extracted an old receipt and a pen to make a list.

She needed diapers, blankets, bottles, formula...everything.

And a car seat. A crib would have to wait until later, she decided, thinking about the balance in her checking account. She picked up the athletic bag and cradled the baby in her arms. He was a warm, moist weight, like a heavy loaf of fresh baked bread.

Libby's heart ached at the thought of leaving the baby alone in the car, but she couldn't take him into the store trussed up in an athletic bag. She reassured herself he would be safe. "I'm sorry, honey, but I'll have to leave you in the car," she told him. He'd already been abandoned once whether he knew it or not, and she didn't want him to think she would abandon him as well.

"You'll be all right. I'll only be a couple of minutes."

Libby carefully placed the baby on the seat, pulled off her jacket and wrapped it around the sleeping newborn.

"I'll be as fast as I can," she reassured the child as she kissed his forehead in a gentle promise to return. She got out of the car and gently arranged him on the floor of the back seat, making certain he was tucked in and warm. She looked in her purse to be sure she had her keys before locking the car doors. It wouldn't do to lock herself out of the car and him in. She took a step away from the vehicle, hesitated, and turned back to press her forehead against the car window and look inside. It was hard to see him in the shadows of the footwell, but he was fine.

A cool wind cut through Libby's sweater as she hurried through the parking lot. He'd be all right. She just had to get what was on the list. She grabbed a cart and strode purposefully to the baby department. The store had everything a baby needed and then some. It was overwhelming. The list of things needed. The enormity of what she was doing. She took a breath to steady herself. It would be okay. It wasn't necessary to get it all now.

The list was damp and crumpled in her fist. She smoothed it out and tossed things into her cart, checking off items as she went. The pen ripped the moist paper. Formula, cloth diapers for at home, disposable diapers for going out, wipes. The cart filled quickly. Bottles, blankets, sleepers. How many did she need? How many could she afford? What size? Newborn or larger? Babies grew so fast. Pacifier, stuffed bear, car seat. The price of the car seat floored her. Oh, no. There went the savings. She put back the bear. She'd pass on the rest.

There was a line at the only open checkout. Libby fidgeted. Was he all right? Had he awakened? Was he crying? She forced her mind back to finances. Did she have enough in checking or would she need to use her charge card?

"Ooh, expecting a little one, I see," the cashier commented as Libby transferred items from cart to conveyer belt. "When are you due?"

Libby looked at her belly. She was fat. Fifty pounds overweight on a good day, and it all seemed to collect around her middle. She could pass for pregnant.

"Uh, any day now."

"Well, I wish you an easy delivery. My daughter just made me a grandma. Forty hours of hard labor. They finally had to take her C-section. Beautiful little girl, Rachel Marie."

"Congratulations," Libby said by reflex. Her mind was racing. Could she pass for pregnant? Could she really keep him? How?

Back outside, she stopped the cart next to the car and fumbled the key into the lock. In the backseat footwell the baby was lying motionless. Libby's chest tightened. She licked the tip of her left index finger and stuck it in front of his nose. She held her breath as she waited. Air puffed rhythmically from his tiny nostrils, cooling her finger as it evaporated the moisture. She breathed a sigh. Just sleeping.

She turned to the cart, tore open the car seat box, and placed the infant carrier on the back seat before lifting his small, warm weight from the footwell. "Hi, sweety. I'm back." The bottom of the athletic bag was warm and damp. She smiled. "Good thing I got diapers."

She pulled diapers, wipes, receiving blankets, and a sleeper out of the cart.

The little guy screwed his eyes tight and wailed in protest as she cleaned him up, wiping the sticky, black poop from his little bottom. Once dressed and tightly swaddled, safe and warm in Libby's arms, he quieted and opened his blue-black eyes to regard her in a slightly cross-eyed look before drifting back to sleep. She sighed and held him close. His cheek was petal-soft against her lips.

He melted against her and filled her heart. This was what Heaven felt like. She could have stayed in the backseat of the car forever, holding him while the cart sat outside the door half-full and waiting. Could, but shouldn't. She needed to get him home before he woke up and decided he was hungry. She'd bought ready-made formula with individually-sealed nipples, but the formula would be cold, and he was so young.

Reluctantly, she slid him into his new car seat and strapped him in, double checking the instructional pamphlet to make certain she had done everything correctly before buckling the seat to the car.

§

Libby pulled the car into the garage and killed the engine. The baby made small sounds in his sleep as if trying to decide if he was hungry enough to wake up.

Hurry, hurry. There was frozen food, produce and baby paraphernalia to put away. She unbuckled the car seat. *Get him inside, and then what? Groceries or baby supplies?* Pressured to do everything at once, she wasted time in indecision and ended up doing nothing for several seconds.

The newborn's grunt, spurred Libby to action. She brought the baby inside and then scrambled to empty the car, set a bottle to warm in a pan of hot tap water, and put away the groceries. Somehow, the package of Oreos was opened. She chewed, trying to decide what to do next.

The baby eventually put an end to her running around with an angry cry for food. Libby rescued him from his car seat.

He arched his tiny body and wailed. Hungry as he was, he didn't seem to know what to do with the nipple. Screaming, he pushed it out of his mouth with a stiff little tongue. Libby wiggled the nipple gently in his mouth until he finally clamped down on it and began to drink. His satisfied little sigh prompted a matching one from Libby.

It wasn't until he was back asleep with his little belly round with formula and a fresh diaper securely pinned in place that Libby remembered work with a panicked start.

It's Tuesday, she reminded herself. Her day off. Thank God. Still, her stomach turned queasy. She ate another cookie without tasting it. How was she going to explain the baby? She couldn't bring him to work with her, and he was too little for daycare. If she kept him, she'd need the job more than ever. It seemed like too much to overcome. Still, there had to be a way to make this work. She needed to talk with someone, but who? A co-worker? There was no one she could call. Her brother-in-law, Mark, was out of the question.

Tears pooled in her eyes. The baby slept unaware, small and warm and trusting in her arms. He deserved a mother who loved him. She could give him that if she could just figure out the rest. She ran several scenarios through her mind before picking one. It pained her to realize she was going to have to lie to keep him. Lie and keep on lying.

She felt like a hypocrite. How many times had she stressed honesty to Timmy, Michael and Laura? She remembered watching the old movie *Lassie Come Home* on television with them. "There's no two ways about it," the father told his son when Lassie, having been sold to the landowner, showed up on the doorstep and the boy wanted to keep her. "Honest is honest."

Libby looked at the baby in her arms and thought of her life before him—an endless cycle of work, television and Oreo cookies. There was no one to talk to and nothing to look forward to but the rare letter from Jenny's kids. Life without this baby would be more unbearably lonely than it had been before the possibility of him existed. But this wasn't about her. She pushed away the half-empty package of Oreos. This was about him. What would be best for the baby? Not languishing in foster care while the authorities looked for his birth mother. She was certain of that. Social services wouldn't terminate rights until they found his mother, and then they'd try to keep him with the birth mother. Hadn't Libby just read an article about children being returned to a drug-addicted mother? Could she let him go back to the woman who'd abandoned him? Could she hand him over to an uncertain future when she knew she had all the love he would ever need?

§

An hour later, Libby pulled her car into Gunderson Pediatric Clinic and shifted into park. Instead of getting out of the car and taking the baby inside, she sat in the car and listened to the seconds tick off. Was keeping him the best thing for the baby or just the best thing for her? She wished she could be certain.

She caught a glimpse of her pale, worried face reflected in the window.

"I can't do this." She turned around to look at the baby's small, sleeping form in the back seat. Her knee hit the keys that still hung in the ignition waiting for her to start the car and drive it to the police station.

"I don't lie. I don't steal." And this lie was so big and the theft so wrong. She couldn't, could she? She wished she'd taken the Oreos along. Somewhere in town was the woman who had given birth. The mother needed help. At this very moment, she could be in a hospital getting treatment. The doctors and police could be asking her, "Where is your baby?" And what would she tell them? "What baby?"

Oh, God. What was the right thing to do?

Clinics and hospitals were probably being put on alert to look for any suspicious newborns. If she didn't turn him in, would they arrest her at the clinic? Would he go back to his real mother? Did his birth mother really want him, or would she be forced to take him? Why had the woman abandoned him in the first place?

The Oreos churned in Libby's stomach. There was no way she could take him in for a check-up. She hid her face in her hands. She had to take him in for a check-up.

Tears trickled down her face. She looked at the infant sleeping innocently in his car seat. "I want you," she whispered. "Oh, baby. I want you so much."

Should she go in and lie, or should she tell the truth?

Perhaps the difference between a sinner and a saint was the level of temptation.

There, in the back seat, was her temptation. A family of her own. She could lie and pray she wouldn't get caught. Caught and sent to jail. Caught and out of a job. Or worse, caught and never able to see him again.

Stop thinking of yourself. Take him inside. Any mother who would abandon her newborn outside a grocery store probably hadn't taken care of herself during her pregnancy. This baby could be premature or have been born of a mother who smoked or used drugs. He was so little. He might be underweight because of fetal alcohol syndrome or other maternal abuse. She needed to get him checked out for his well-being. The devil take her own.

She opened the passenger door, unbuckled him from his car seat, and stood staring. Her stomach rolled. Claiming she'd had a baby was insane. She should go in and tell the truth. No one was going to believe he was *her* son, anyway.

The baby was heaven in her arms.

If the lie worked…Oh, please God, let it work. Because if this enormous, unbelievable lie worked, she'd get to keep him.

She closed her eyes tight and said the only prayer she could.

"Thy will be done."

Leaving the car seat strapped in the car, she carried the towel-wrapped newborn into the clinic where she worked.

§

Libby's fellow receptionist, Cheryl McCann, didn't look up until Libby stood at the counter.

"Libby?" Cheryl looked at her and laughed. "Missed us so much, you had to come in on your day off, huh?"

"Not really."

"Who do we have here?" Cheryl smiled at the baby.

Libby cleared her throat. "You're not going to believe this." Her voice shook. "I'm not sure I believe it. I…"

Cheryl's smile faded. "What's the matter, Libby? Are you all right?" Her eyes narrowed in concern, or was it disbelief? Libby's hands shook.

"I'm fine, but I…" Oh, God, here we go. "I just had a baby." She was an idiot. She was a lousy liar. Her memory wasn't good enough. There were too many risks. She could lose the baby, lose her job, lose her freedom, lose her soul.

"You *what?*" Cheryl sounded as stunned as Libby felt. "You're kidding, right?" She stared at the baby.

There was still a chance to turn back. She could laugh, make a joke of it.

Sweat stood on Libby's brow. Her stomach clenched. She hugged the baby to her chest. "No, I'm not. I didn't even know I was pregnant, and now I'm a mother."

"Oh, Libby. You need to get yourself to the hospital." Behind the desk, Cheryl was on her feet.

"I know. I will. I just wanted…I just wanted Dr. Westland to look at him first. Make sure he's all right."

"Libby, they'd do that at the emergency room."

"I—" What could she say? That she couldn't go to the emergency room because the doctors there would want to examine her, and then they'd see she hadn't given birth? That she was just having her period? "I didn't think. I just…It's all so fast and…Couldn't Dr. Westland just look at him first?"

"I'll get you right in." Cheryl left the desk.

Libby was looking for a seat in the crowded lobby when Cheryl returned, looked at the baby in Libby's arms, and gathered Libby in a hug. "I can't believe it. You were pregnant and didn't know it? I'd heard stories like that, but I never believed they were true until now. You should be in the hospital."

Libby nodded. In the *psych ward.*

"Come back with me. I'll get you in a room, and we can do the paperwork there. Are you sure you don't just want me to take you across the highway to the hospital?"

"I'm sure."

"Are you bleeding much?"

"No. Like a heavy period is all."

Cheryl stood next to an open examining room door. "Sit. I'll get the doctor."

Marsha, Dr. Westland's nurse, arrived a minute later with a clipboard in hand.

"You had a baby? You didn't know you were pregnant, and you had a baby?" Marsha regarded her with narrowed eyes.

She wasn't buying it. Libby's eyes pooled with tears. Of course she didn't buy it. "It's so stupid, I know. It's just I don't have regular periods, and I thought I was just getting fatter and…" She knew she was rambling, but she couldn't seem to stop. She hated lying. Couldn't do it.

"Oh, honey, don't cry. It doesn't happen often, but it does happen. Let's just take a look-see at your baby, make sure everything is all right."

The nurse took the baby from Libby's arms. "What's his name?"

"David," Libby answered though she'd never consciously thought of names. "David Matthew Armstrong."

"Well, David, let's have a look at you." She placed the baby on a blue pad and unwrapped the bath towel Libby had used to make her story believable. He was wearing a washcloth diaper held together with safety pins.

Her eyes met Libby's.

"I didn't have a diaper," Libby lied. She wouldn't have had one if her story were true and she'd just given birth at home and come right in. "I didn't know he was coming."

"You did a great job," Marsha told her, as she unfastened the first pin. David stretched and noisily filled the makeshift diaper. "A really good job."

Libby tried to pay attention to everything Marsha did, but she couldn't focus. The nurse poked David's heel and milked out a couple of blood samples. Libby's head swirled with fearful, hopeful thoughts, half-formed prayers, and the desire to memorize every second she spent with David so she could relive them while she rotted in prison for kidnapping.

David weighed six pounds, three ounces and was nineteen inches long—a long, lean baby. Marsha took his temperature and measured his chest and head, as well. She was handing a copy of the measurements to Libby for David's baby book when Dr. Westland knocked once and walked in.

"Well, young lady," Dr. Westland said, closing the door after the departing nurse. "You certainly surprised us."

"He surprised me."

The doctor's smile faded. "Libby, why don't you sit down."

Libby's smile froze. "Why?"

"You look a little pale. I don't want you passing out on me."

"I'm fine."

"Nevertheless, Marsha will take you to the emergency room as soon as we're done here. Should have sent the two of you right over there. Anything happens, there'll be hell to pay."

"I'm fine, really. I just wanted you to see David."

"Well, I'm here now." He picked up the chart, read what was written there, and then looked at David. "Full term by the looks of him."

"I wouldn't know," she answered, hoping she had her story straight. "I'm not very regular. My periods, I mean." Did he suspect? Was he testing her? "I thought I was just getting my period. Bad cramps and, well, then there he was."

"Hmmm." He was checking David's ears. "You're lucky. Sometimes first babies take a while."

Libby folded her hands together and squeezed tight. *Please, God, please.* David seemed fine to her, but she knew nothing of his prenatal care, nothing of his birth mother's health or history. Sweat soaked the cotton lining of her underwire bra. Dr. Westland talked while he worked, checking David's hip joints and reflexes, poking, probing and palpating to check everything. He examined David's penis and scrotal sack and was rewarded with a sudden geyser that he dodged deftly.

"Looks like the water works are functioning fine." He took the white paper towels Libby offered and dabbed the infant.

"Everything looks good."

"He's normal, healthy?" Stupid. He'd just told her that.

Dr. Westland smiled at her, clearly unfazed by her maternal jitters. "He's a healthy newborn. You did a good job, Mom."

Libby sighed but her hands remained clenched in her lap.

"Since the birth was unattended, you will need a signature for the birth certificate worksheet. I'll have Marsha fill one out for you. They rarely can find them at the emergency room."

"Thank you." Libby's heart skipped a beat. She couldn't believe her ears. *Thank you, God!* She tapped down the urge to kiss the doctor.

"We've got some free samples of formula and diapers. I think one of them even comes with a diaper bag. I'll have Marsha load you up before she takes you to the hospital to get you checked out." He smiled at her. "Congratulations. I'm assuming this means you won't be in to work for a few weeks."

Her eyes grew large. She hadn't thought of that, either. He had every right to be angry. "Yes, sir. Uh, I'm sorry. I didn't know. I certainly didn't mean to."

He waved off her protests. "Of course, you didn't. We'll make do. Just take care of yourself and that little boy."

He left the room, and she spent a minute trying to calm herself by slowing her breathing. Marsha returned with a diaper bag bulging with samples.

She handed Libby the birth certificate worksheet. "Just fill this in. The doctor has already signed it."

Libby's hand shook as she filled it in. Was this really happening? Would she wake up in a moment to find this was just a dream?

"How are you feeling?" Marsha asked, eyeing Libby critically.

Libby lifted her hand from the page. "Good, really. I'm relieved David is okay. I'm fine. He was my only concern. Making sure he's healthy."

Marsha smiled. "You're not going to talk us out of taking you to the emergency room, so you may as well stop trying."

"I know the doctor wanted you to take me to the hospital, but that's silly. You're busy, and I'm more than capable of driving myself. Besides, I'll need my car to get home. Okay?"

Marsha nodded. "As long as you go. That's the main thing."

"I'll go." Yeah, she'd go. Go home, that is.

"All right, then." Marsha handed Libby a list of instructions. "Good luck with that little boy." Marsha took the completed worksheet and left.

Libby hastened to collect their things. Her luck was bound to run out any time now.

Aftermath

Cold, so cold. Wrapped in her quilt, Marissa tossed in bed, sleeping and waking in an irregular pattern. Fleeting images danced before her closed lids.

She walks out of Putnam Hall wearing her backpack, carrying a cloth athletic bag in the crook of her arm. The cold wind bites through her shirt as she crosses the street and stumbles down the embankment toward the river. It is misty by the Chippewa, but tears are what dampens her cheeks. Heart racing, she looks over her shoulder. No one. She looks again, unable to dispel the itchy feeling of being watched. The thorny brush reaches for her, tearing at her clothes and her skin like hundreds of tiny hands that are trying to prevent her passage. Their resistance makes her more determined. She shoves through the undergrowth, ignoring the ache in her heart and the tears that blur her vision.

She drops the athletic bag on a pile of leaves and shrugs out of the backpack. Reluctantly, she opens the backpack revealing a bloody towel wrapped around a warm, meaty glob of afterbirth. Just looking at it makes acid rise up in her throat. Using the towel as a sling, she launches the blob into the weeds close to the river's edge, gagging as it flies through the air. When she has her stomach back under control, she wraps the towel around itself so the clean side is out before shoving it into her backpack. Clean is important.

Beside her, the athletic bag moves. Part of her wants to leave it there. Just walk away. Part of her wants to kick it down the hill. She takes a step away and then stops to look at the bag. She likes the cloth bag; cares for it more than she does its contents. It's the perfect size for a swimsuit and a towel, and it always washes up so nice. So clean. It's never stinky like her vinyl one. She acts quickly, wanting the chore to be over. Bending over to unzip the bag, she dumps the towel-wrapped baby and then snaps the towel free. The newborn tumbles down the hill like a broken doll.

Marissa awoke with a strangled scream. She hadn't done that. Wouldn't do that. Just a dream. A terrible dream.

Drenched in sweat, she struggled to kick off her covers. Her room was dark and unbearably hot, her mouth dry and sticky. Nothing to swallow to ease her throat.

Marissa stumbled from her room down the long hall to the bathroom. She had the room to herself. Leaning heavily on the sink, her hand shook as she turned the handle. Water blasted from the faucet and her hair snaked in the bottom of the sink as she angled her face to drink. Long swallows of cold water made her shiver.

Wet and full, she made her way to a stall and collapsed on the toilet. Each heartbeat was loud in her head. She didn't know how long she sat there face pressed against the cool metal wall, passing clots. Too long. It took forever to stand. Eyes closed, she braced herself against the walls until the stall stopped spinning. The hall seemed to grow longer for her return trip.

Back in her room, she looked at her bed and groaned. It was blood stained and damp to the touch. Somewhere in the past day or two, she had found the presence of mind to place a towel under herself. The towel was soiled, and Marissa realized with disgust that her nightgown was too.

She just wanted to sleep, to lie down and die. Crawling back to the bathroom for a much needed shower seemed impossible. Tears trickled down her face. If only she were home. Her mom would take care of her, clean her up, change the bed, and tuck her in. She sniffed. Her hands seemed to move in slow motion as she stripped off her gown, pulled her robe from its hook and put on a clean pad and panties. She stopped and leaned against the wall for a moment before replacing the towel and shoving the whole soiled mess into her laundry bag. Wrapped in her robe's fluffy pink comfort, she fell back into bed.

The dream began almost as soon as she closed her eyes.

Marissa is in Japan. The Japanese woman minding the cash register is hugely pregnant.

"When is your baby due?" Marissa asks, her Japanese shaky despite the classes she is taking. Normally, she can come up with a sentence to say, but only understands one word in ten when someone speaks to her.

Still, she understands everything as the cashier says in Japanese,

"What baby? There is no baby." The cashier is no longer pregnant. Her belly is as flat as a Barbie doll's.

Marissa's face grows hot. How embarrassing. She apologizes, bowing many times as she flees the store. Outside, she's in the courtyard in front of The Great Buddha. There are babies everywhere—on the ground, in the fountain, everywhere. People don't see them. She runs through the crowd scooping tiny Japanese infants from the pavement, rescuing them from being stepped on. She hands one to the woman who dropped it.

"Here is your baby." Her Japanese is still imperfect.

The woman looks her in the eye. "There is no baby." And indeed, there isn't. The infant in Marissa's arms is a small white dog.

Stiff with embarrassment, Marissa apologizes. She pets the dog and sets it on the ground. How could she mistake a dog for a child?

In an instant, she is back in her dorm room.

"Is this your baby?"

Marissa jerks backwards. She'd been alone, and now she isn't. Naked from the waist down, she lies on her back on the dorm room floor with the radio blaring and her knees spread wide. Mortified, she snaps her legs closed.

A girl she doesn't know hovers over her holding a bloody newborn. "Is this your baby?"

Paul appears and leans over her so close his nose nearly touches hers. He yells at her, "I don't want to know. Either way. I don't want to know." His words are insistent and so much louder than necessary. She covers her ears as money begins to rain from the sky. Piles of it collect around her. Her heart is breaking, but Paul is still talking. "Either way, Marissa, either way, there is no baby."

She shakes her head. "There is no baby."

He disappears.

The phone rings.

Inside Marissa's dorm, the phone rang. The sound jerked her free of the nightmare.

"There is no baby." She awoke in her bed with the words on her lips and her face wet with tears. The phone. The baby. She couldn't make herself care about the first and couldn't stop caring about the second. Her eyelids closed as she plunged back into sleep.

Sometime later, when Marissa awoke, sun was streaming through the window. She blinked, blinded and disoriented by memories of the dreams for several long moments. Was there a baby?

Her stomach rumbled insistently. How long had it been since she'd eaten anything?

She felt weak as she pulled herself up and slid to the foot of the bed so she could open the bolster. Inside was her emergency bag of fun size Snickers bars. Shaking, she wrestled with the wrapper and then nearly swallowed the first candy bar whole. They were so tiny, and she was so hungry. She felt better after the third one. Sugar and life-giving chocolate seeped into her blood.

She looked around the room. Her roommate hadn't been home. Everything on that side of the room was exactly the way it had been since before Marissa had gotten sick. The flu, she reminded herself. Jessie thought she had the flu.

Marissa checked her clothes for signs of blood. Holding out the robe, she looked over her shoulder to be sure. Her nose wrinkled as she caught a whiff of herself. Old blood, sour milk, sweat, and plain old stink rose from her body.

She pulled herself to her feet and crossed the room to yank open the window. Worry rushed in along with the cool, fresh air. How many of the dreams had been real? The image of a newborn flashed before her eyes. He'd been warm and solid in her arms. Had she really tossed a meaty blob of afterbirth into the woods below campus, or had that been a dream? Had she tossed the child after it or brought him to Kerm's grocery store and set him on the concrete slab by the door? Had there really been a baby?

It was all too foggy. What was dream? What reality? She refused to examine it further. Grabbing her shower bucket and her last clean towel, Marissa walked to the bathroom.

There were a few other girls at the mirrors, drying and curling their hair. Marissa raised a hand in greeting but didn't break stride. She stopped to use the toilet first.

Her life had been so messy. Was still messy. She could clean up. She would clean it up too. Just wash away the memories and fevered dreams, and she'd be fine.

The shower room was wet and steamy. Never had a shower felt so good. The warm water pounded life into her tired muscles like a million caressing yet nonjudgmental fingers easing the hurt and shame away along with the sweat and blood. Marissa closed her eyes and tilted her face into the spray. Tears mingled unheeded with the water. Too many emotions, too many thoughts. She breathed like she'd learned to do in Japan, acknowledging each thought in turn and letting them go, one by one. She willed all the feelings to pour out of her and down the drain. Clean the body, purify the soul.

Several minutes and a shampoo later, Marissa opened her eyes as she soaped herself. Arms. Stubbly legs that desperately needed a shave. Her belly was flat. Her hands skimmed over it. Well, not flat actually. It was pretty flabby, but the hard mound in the middle was gone. Her breath caught in her throat. The hidden pregnancy had been a nightmare. Was it possible it had really been a dream?

She knew the combination of fever and no food over the past few days had reduced her figure to a reasonable facsimile of her previous form, but she wanted to believe it had all been a dream. Flabby is what happened in college if a person didn't watch the carbs and exercise. But she remembered exercising. A lot. Maybe that had been part of the dream. She looked down at her body. She was pretty thin except for her breasts, which were rock hard, hot and tender.

Paul would love them. She winced when the thought snuck past her guard. Damn you, Paul! The tears began to flow anew.

The letdown of milk accompanied the letdown of tears. The milk began to drip and then spray from engorged nipples. It felt a bit like pins and needles—painful, yet an inexplicably good pain…a release. When the stream decreased, Marissa caressed her heavy breasts, encouraging the flow and its relief of pressure. Soon the pain of breasts and soul ebbed.

She'd dreamed so many things when she'd been sick. Some things seemed so real. Images replayed in her mind—the delivery on the floor of the dorm room, the horrible trek to Kerm's, the Japanese babies… how could she separate reality from the nightmare? Why couldn't it all have been a dream?

§

Libby had David on her shoulder, trying to release the bubble that was obviously in his belly. His wails of discomfort were so loud she almost didn't hear the doorbell. Her belly hurt in sympathy as she looked out the window to make certain it was Cheryl. Libby fumbled with the lock and doorknob with one hand while pressing David to her shoulder with the other.

Cheryl entered, laden with enough food for several meals.

Libby patted David's back and gently jiggled him, but the bubble didn't move. Poor little guy. "This is so nice of you, Cheryl, but like I told you on the phone, it isn't necessary. It's just me."

"Just you?" Cheryl repeated as she put the lasagna on the counter. "Libby, you just had a baby. My mom came for at least a week with each of my kids, and Jack got up in the night to bring the baby to me. Dinner is the least I can do."

David continued to scream himself red.

"Try lifting him up under his arms," Cheryl suggested.

"Under his arms?" Libby repeated.

Cheryl nodded, pulling a zippered bag of oatmeal raisin cookies and a loaf of French bread out of her bag.

Libby tried. Nothing. David's little face was wet with tears.

"Do it again."

Holding David under his arms and still carefully supporting his head with her fingertips, Libby lowered him to her waist and then lifted him to just above her head.

Somehow, the rising motion of David's body stimulated the bubble to do the same. He belched. The silence that followed was as abrupt as if she'd flipped a switch. David sighed and closed his eyes, clearly exhausted.

"Wow." The tension in Libby's shoulders eased. "Does it always work?"

"No, but it's one of the things I always tried when Devon had a bubble. That and laying him belly down over my legs. Sometimes it worked. Sometimes I had to try something else."

"Jenny's kids were all shoulder burpers," Libby said. "I didn't even know there were other ways."

She'd told Cheryl about Jenny that morning during their hour-long phone call. They'd talked about everything except work and the truth about David.

It had been forever, Libby realized, since anyone had really asked about her, what she thought, what she felt…Thanks to David, she and Cheryl were now friends. It was such a gift to share everyday thoughts and feelings with someone that she didn't want to spoil it with thoughts of trouble. She wanted to savor the feeling of being liked for herself, of being connected by shared experiences and more. With Cheryl, Libby felt herself opening up for the first time since Jenny. Cheryl cared. She listened.

Cheryl was telling her of her mother-in-law. It startled Libby to realize she hadn't been listening. She felt her face warm as she tuned in.

"She's a gem. I wish my mom were as helpful. If Jack and I ever broke up, I'd still keep his mom. I'll have to introduce you sometime. You'll love her."

"I'm sure I will. You are lucky to have a good relationship with your mother-in-law. I have a feeling they are rare."

Cheryl folded the paper bag and looked at the kitchen. "Your house is so clean. I'm not this neat, but you'll see that next Wednesday. You *are* coming to coffee, aren't you?"

Libby smiled. "Wouldn't miss it."

"Good." Cheryl gave her a hug. "I'm so glad you had David. It might have taken us another year to get to know each other at work. And that would have been a huge waste, because we're going to be great friends. I just know it."

Libby nodded as tears clogged her throat. "Me too."

"Oh," Cheryl hugged her again. "I made you cry. I'm so mean, I should know better. I *do* know better. Stupid birth hormones. I think I cried for two weeks straight with each kid."

"I'm happy, really," Libby croaked.

Cheryl smiled. "I know, honey. So was I. Think nothing of it. It's just hormones."

But it wasn't hormones. It was profound gratitude. Thanks to David, she had a purpose. Thanks to David, she had a friend.

Cheryl buzzed around her kitchen, pulling out a table setting for one and sliding a gigantic piece of lasagna onto the plate. She put the plate, glass of water, bowl of salad, and two thick slices of French bread on the kitchen table. "There, all set now. Let me kiss that baby quick and get out of here. Jack will feed the kids cookies if I don't get home on time."

Libby handed David over.

"I forget how little they start out." Cheryl looked at Libby. "He's gorgeous." She kissed his forehead. "Can I get you anything? Diapers, formula, feminine supplies?"

"Actually," Libby said, stalling for time while she mentally inventoried David's supplies. What she really wanted was to keep Cheryl a bit longer, but that was pathetic. "Could you take a roll of film in for me?"

"Baby pictures?"

Libby nodded, reaching for her purse, which held the roll of film.

"What a good mother!" Cheryl remarked approvingly. "K-Mart okay?"

"Perfect."

Cheryl tucked David in his seat. "Now eat before it gets cold. I'm leaving."

Libby saw her friend to the door. "Thanks again. For everything."

Back in the kitchen, just as Libby lifted a forkful of food, David began to fuss.

She picked him up and held him close, not minding the growl of her stomach. "Thank *you*," she whispered against his warm, tender cheek. Gratitude didn't cover it. She was living again because of him. From here on out, her life was going to be good.

She looked out the window, and an icy finger ran down her spine as a patrol car cruised slowly by the front of her house.

No News is Good News

In Marketing 265, Marissa took notes in short hand, recording every word the professor said in an effort to keep her mind from wandering. As much as she'd prayed the whole thing had just been a fevered dream, her tender, leaky breasts said it wasn't. So where were the police?

Outside the window, a police siren blared as if in answer to her thoughts. Her hand jerked and the pen gouged the page. This was it. She took a deep breath. It was about time they found her. After all, it had been a week. She closed her notebook and reached beneath her desk for her backpack. Should she meet the cops in the hall or sit here and wait for them?

The sound of the siren receded. What? It was leaving? Somehow, she managed not to jump up and race to the window. Why would it leave? She was right here.

The guy across the aisle leaned over. "No, it's not the bell, but I wish it were. Man, this guy is boring."

It took a moment for Marissa to figure out what he meant. Oh, yes. The class was boring. She forced a smile and nodded her agreement. Getting arrested would definitely have added a spark to this class for the rest of them.

§

It had gone on too long. Marissa stepped off the dirt path and plunged into the woods along the riverbank. The ground was frozen solid. Surely, there would be some evidence somewhere. She walked to where she remembered tossing out the afterbirth. Where had it landed? It seemed to have flown farther in one memory than in the other, and she couldn't be certain which had been the dream and which reality.

The forest was loud beneath her hiking boots. The snap and crackle of leaves and twigs seemed overly loud. She'd heard Native Americans could travel silently in the woods, and she wished she knew their secret. There was ice on the shore at the river's edge, but no bloody leaves or any other sign that something meaty and dead had been there.

She walked back and forth, pushing at leaves with the toe of her boot. Shouldn't there be signs of disturbance? A frozen chunk?

It grew colder as the sun dipped low and the shadows grew long. She wouldn't be able to see to find her way up the hill to campus if she didn't leave soon. Still, she made one last search of the woods at the edge of the river bank. How could there be no sign?

§

"You wanna go to supper?" her friend Alyssa asked as Marissa trudged into the dorm.

"No thanks. I'm not hungry." She wasn't. And she wasn't in the mood for the small talk that dinner with a friend would entail.

Why hadn't she been caught? Why hadn't there been a buzz around the university? Had she slept through it? That hardly seemed possible. An abandoned baby in the Kerm's parking lot would cause more than a day's or two worth of speculation. Kerm's was too close to the university not to suspect a UW student. Where were the police investigators?

The ride in the elevator to the library's third floor had to be the longest in recorded history. She should have taken the stairs. Then, at least, she'd have been moving while she worried about what she'd find in the *Eau Claire Leader-Telegram*.

Her hands shook as she collected the papers, starting with November 3rd. She needed proof it hadn't been a dream. Proof she wasn't crazy.

Marissa started looking before her rump hit the seat of the chair. She read the headlines on the first page of the paper dated November 3rd. Nothing.

Nothing? She read them again, more slowly. Her heart stood still as she turned the page. It should have been front-page news. But it wasn't. It wasn't second-page news, either.

Her lungs burned, reminding her to breathe.

Okay. Maybe it hadn't been reported by press time. That didn't seem right, either. She'd left him at dawn. Certainly, the newspaper would have learned about it by press time. Obviously not. She reached for the next paper.

November 4: "Elk Mound Barn Fire Roasts 40 Head," "Nursing Home Reform Ordered," "Area Teen Wins Writing Contest," and "Large Voter Turnout Reported." No "Baby Found in Kerm's Parking Lot."

How could that be? She shivered as the cold finger of worry ran down her spine. She flipped through each page of the paper, reading headlines.

November 5: "Reagan wins in Landslide Vote." Oh, yeah, that's right—the presidential election. It sickened her that she'd forgotten all about the election November 4th. She'd voted by absentee ballot, so it wasn't like she'd missed voting. It was just that who became president was important. She was supposed to keep up with news like that. She'd missed it. And she hardly cared. She turned back to the newspaper. Everything was about the election, voter turn-out, local races, the local referendum….

November 6: "Jury Panel Asked about Death Penalty," "Organ Donation Up," and "Entries Needed for Holiday Parade."

November 7: nothing.

November 8: nothing.

She stared at the scattered pile of papers before her. How could this be?

A tiny part of her wanted to rejoice that it had all been a dream, but she couldn't. It had happened. Hadn't it? She touched her left breast and winced. It was hard and tender. If it hadn't happened, why were her breasts so different?

But wouldn't it be nice if it had all been a dream? If she could move past it without regret? If she could be thankful she'd dodged this bullet? She hid her face in her hands. She wanted to. God knows, she wanted to. But her body knew the truth. She uncovered her face and stared at the pile of newspapers in front of her. *Oh, my God. He'd died.*

Her belly cramped. She tore through the papers again, this time looking at the obituaries. No newborns.

Where was he?

It didn't make sense. If he wasn't a dream, and he hadn't died, why wasn't anything in the newspaper?

The woman hadn't turned the baby in. Marissa's body jerked as the thought hit her.

Was it possible?

Marissa remained frozen before the clutter of newspapers. Her mind looped the thought over and over in countless variations of: *Was it possible the woman hadn't turned him in?*

She'd gotten away with it.

She wasn't supposed to get away with it. She was supposed to get caught, be given counseling. She was supposed to get her hands slapped and a scolding. She was supposed to get help.

She was supposed to get her baby back.

Marissa hadn't realized she had counted on that, until now.

Who is the lady who picked him up? Why hadn't she turned him in? Was he okay? It hadn't been *that* cold the day she left him. He couldn't have died in the short time he was outside. And the athletic bag was cloth, so she knew he hadn't suffocated.

No dead babies in the headlines. No babies at all except in the birth announcement column in the paper. Other people's babies.

Marissa blinked several times, staring into space. Where was her baby? Her son.

§

Avoiding Kerm's, Libby drove halfway across town to shop at Cub Supermarket. She took David from his car seat and slid him in a chest pack inside her coat. He was comfortably nestled out of sight against her heart. She told herself she did it because she loved him, the car seat took up too much room in the cart, and he slept better and was more content held close. She told herself she wanted him to be extra comfortable, because she'd put off shopping until the last minute, and the size of the list and the unfamiliar store would slow her down. All those things were true, but none were the real reason.

Libby turned her head left and right, and then twisted in her seat to complete scanning the parking lot before leaving the car. She knew she was being silly. She had no idea what David's birth mother looked like. There was no reason, other than her own paranoia, to believe someone was looking for him. No news of baby abductions or the like had been in the newspaper, radio or television. But it didn't matter; her palms were still slick and her stomach still touchy.

Someone had to be looking. How could they not? Unless they truly didn't want him. Please, God, let that be the case. She couldn't fathom it. How could someone have left him without a backward glance? Libby knew she couldn't have. If she were the birth mother, she'd be searching everywhere. Of course, she wouldn't have abandoned him in the first place. Who knew what the birth mother would or would not do?

Libby covered David's head with a blanket, held her coat as closed as she could, and walked into the store. He was too little to leave at home even if she did know of a baby sitter to watch him. Too little to leave home with a sitter, too big to hide.

Part of the problem was that newborns always attracted attention. Mothers of all ages notice the tiniest of babies, even before older infants. Children, especially, are attracted to babies and often comment, "Mommy, look…." Having cared for Laura, Timmy and Michael, Libby knew this. Hidden in her coat, David wouldn't get the looks that frightened her so. Hidden next to her heart, he would be safe.

Inside, she pulled her list from her purse.

The produce section was the worst because it was the first department nearest the entrance, and people hadn't settled into the shopping zone yet. Most conversations seemed to take place there. She grabbed a bag of mixed fruit and hurried to the next aisle. Empty. She slowed and decided between brands.

Concern followed her like a shadow into the baby aisle. It made no sense. It should have been the securest row. No one without a baby of their own would be in it.

"This will be easier when I have your birth certificate," she silently told David as they waited in line at the checkout. Once she had a copy of that certificate in his baby book and another locked tight in her safe deposit box, they'd be safe—and legal, sort of.

§

Libby pulled the car full of groceries next to the mailbox at the end of the driveway, rolled down the passenger side window, and climbed over the seat to get the mail. Two bills and an envelope decorated with crayon rubbing leaves. She smiled at the sight.

"Look, David, your cousins sent a letter."

Her smile froze.

Cousins.

She hadn't told her brother-in-law Mark, his wife Carrie, and the kids about David.

Her stomach clenched. How was she supposed to tell them? "I had a baby. Forget that I don't have a boyfriend and haven't dated in forever." She groaned. That was going to be the world's most awkward conversation. She shifted the car back in gear and drove into the garage. Of course, it didn't matter how uncomfortable she was, she would tell them. She had to. Soon. There was really no sense in delaying it. It wouldn't get any easier.

She turned off the car and pressed the automatic garage door opener, waiting until the overhead door was completely closed before getting out of the car. Telling them meant, of course, that she had gotten pregnant in Marshfield after Jenny's death while she'd been taking care of the kids. It meant she had met someone somewhere and kept him and it a secret.

Having David was a confession to all sorts of sins. Sins Libby hadn't committed, but they couldn't know that. Her face grew hot at the mere thought. The problem wasn't her virginity or apparent lack of. It was that she hadn't dated in Marshfield. She had rarely gone out at all unaccompanied by one kid or another.

Carrie and Mark knew that and were bound to suspect something.

"It's amazing how a lie multiplies," she told David as she lifted his seat from the car and carried him into the kitchen. "Be certain you don't tell lies. They're traps. They might look like the easy way out, but they end up requiring a lot of imagination and a very good memory."

David stared trustingly at her with his big blue-black eyes. He didn't know he was the cause of all her lies. She winced at the thought. "But sometimes," she whispered, kissing the bridge of his nose, "it's worth it."

Maybe she could send a birth announcement, complete with picture, and save the lying for later. It was a cop-out, to be sure, but a cop-out she could live with.

Possibilities

Marissa rocked gently in the La-Z-boy recliner, holding twelve-month-old Devon McCann's head in the crook of her right arm while his sleeper-clad body curled in her lap. He'd gotten huge. It had been six months since she'd seen him last, but that didn't seem to account for the change. Maybe it was just that her most recent physical memory was of a much smaller child. She shoved that thought and the accompanying tears aside. She'd promised herself she wouldn't think about motherhood. It had nothing to do with her. She was babysitting to get some money and to see if, by applying the developmental stages from her psychology class to the kids, she could actually remember which stage was which. Think clinically, not emotionally. She blew her nose.

She reached out and flipped her textbook closed. The theorists were full of crap. No one, not even a child, fell neatly into one category. Different characteristics reflected different stages. So, as a study tool, baby sitting was a bust. The heck with applying the different theories, she'd just have to memorize them. She rocked Devon and watched the movie of the week.

On top of the television sat the dried, brown remnant of a dead spider plant. Marissa stared, the sight of the dead plant brought tears to her eyes. What kind of abuse and neglect did it take to kill a spider plant? She dashed the tears with the back of her hand. What was wrong with her? It was a stupid plant, for heaven's sake. She turned her attention to the television.

A soda commercial came on and reminded Marissa of the can of Diet Coke in the fridge that awaited her once she got the kids to bed. Looking down at her charge, she observed his closed eyes. Devon had stopped sucking. A dribble of formula had escaped from his slack mouth and clung to his soft, round cheek. She pulled the nipple from his mouth and set the bottle down on the magazine-strewn coffee table before rising to tiptoe up the stairs.

Having tucked the baby into his crib, Marissa poked her head into the next bedroom to check on the girls before heading back downstairs. She picked up the few toys left in the living room and the hall while she made her way to the fridge for the soda. It was 9:30, but the children's parents were at a wedding reception and wouldn't be back for several hours yet.

Marissa collapsed into the recliner and opened her diet soda. A huge yawn stretched her mouth. She had been baby-sitting since noon. The middle child, a two-and-a-half-year-old girl, wasn't quite potty trained. She had hidden behind a chair twice to fill her pants.

"No more applesauce for you," Marissa had told the stinky child the last time she had caught and pinned her in order to change her clothes.

The oldest child had helped find a new outfit for her little sister in an over-flowing drawer. At six, Becky-the-bossy was angelic one moment and a total know-it-all-tyrant the next. She was the one who exhibited the most developmental stages.

Marissa looked at the television screen. A commercial for scrubbing bubbles played. She needed to get sucked in to the movie's plot, now. A diaper commercial was up next. Shit. Just what she needed. Where was that movie? She closed her eyes and her son's face flitted through her brain. It had only been a couple of weeks. Where was he? How was he? Tears trickled down her face. Stupid, stupid commercial!

It was best he was gone. She could hardly stand to babysit for one day. No way she could do it all day, every day. She didn't know how Mrs. McCann stood her kids day in and day out? Heck, how had *her* mother stood it? But it was different for her mother. Her mother loved being a mom. She'd been married and ready for kids. But Mrs. McCann probably had been too, married and ready.

Marissa thought of her psychology class and developmental stages. Her parents were "enlightened adults." The McCann's appeared to be, as well; except the messy house spoke of denial of responsibility or something, didn't it? That's what made the developmental stages so useless, in her opinion. They didn't really say anything useful. For example, they didn't tell if the difference between her parents and the McCann's was social or economic or had something to do with their environment as children. The parenting styles and living environment could be attributed to something other than developmental stages. Dedication? Personal standards of cleanliness?

Her parents' house was beautiful and clean, tucked in the midst of upper-middle-class suburbia. Unlike these kids' mother, her mom didn't work outside the home.

Marissa's memories were a mental collage of bedtime stories, baking cookies, camping trips and holidays, yet sometimes she had vague recollections she wasn't even sure were her own of loud voices, a hungry belly and hard hands. Since her parents' home didn't jive with the random flashes she had of something less wholesome, she discounted the latter as probably something she'd read. Or dreamed about. She'd always dreamed too frequently and too vividly.

The soda fizzed in her mouth as she took a sip. There hadn't been a totally quiet moment all day. She deserved more than just a soda. Hadn't she seen a bag of chips somewhere? She got up and went to the kitchen.

She'd put the dishes they'd used during the day in the dishwasher as they'd dirtied them, but there were still dirty dishes piled in the sink. She sighed seeing the mess, knowing she should take the ten minutes to fill the dishwasher even if she didn't want to. It wasn't her house. She shouldn't have to clean it. If only she hadn't noticed the mess. If only she'd just grabbed the chips and ducked back into the living room. But she'd noticed them, and now she had to do something.

Help out whenever you can.

Why did her conscience sound like her mother?

"Next time I'm in this house, I'll wear blinders," she grumbled as she pulled open the dishwasher and reached for the first dish in the pile. There was always some chore that needed doing here. She could clean up after others now and again, but not like a mom. Not like her mom. She wasn't that good.

After one day of work or one day of chasing after the little stinkers, she could muster the energy to help out. But every day? No. She wouldn't have energy to keep up on the laundry and the dishes every day. She also wouldn't have the motivation of the grateful look on the mother's face or a few extra dollars. There'd be no words of praise for doing what she was obligated to do.

She understood why most times when she arrived to sit at the McCann's the house was littered with toys and smelled of dirty diapers, sour formula and peanut butter sandwiches. Kids were labor intensive. Not enough return on the investment.

She finished the dishes, swept the floor and returned to the living room where she settled into the recliner and picked up the remote.

Yawning, she flipped through the stations looking for something decent to watch. A smile curved her lips as she stumbled on Johnny Carson's monologue.

Marissa opened the bag of chips and was about to pop the first one into her mouth when Devon's cry interrupted. Damn. She set the chips next to her soda. Never failed. Damn kids had a sensor. Just when you were about to enjoy yourself or rest for a few seconds, they needed attention. She hurried up the stairs to calm Devon before his cries woke his sisters. Sometimes, her favorite part of babysitting wasn't the money, it was the knowledge that the kids weren't hers. That eventually the parents would return home and set her free. No, she definitely wasn't mother material.

§

She'd changed Devon's pants and warmed up another eight ounces of milk. Time to relax. Johnny was seated behind his desk chatting with some actor Marissa didn't recognize, so she changed stations.

Devon's eyes were closed as he sipped his bottle. Again, her son's face flitted through her mind's eye. Did he look the same? What did a couple of weeks amount to in baby development? Was he less scrawny, more rounded like a Gerber baby? Every time she thought of the baby, she tried to convince herself it hadn't happened. Consciously decided it hadn't. Why, then, did she keep having to remind herself again and again? Did some whacked out part of her brain need convincing? Of course, it did. Who was she trying to fool? She knew the truth. Her throat tightened as tears filled her eyes.

"I wasn't ready," she whispered to the sleeping child in her arms. "I'm still not ready."

Tears splashed on Devon's sleeper making dark blue polka dots on the pale blue fleecing. She was tired. That's all. The grandfather clock told the hour. She dashed the tears with the back of her hand.

Devon was asleep again. It was time to get him to bed and herself back under control. His parents would be home soon.

She was too young to be a mom. Had too many dreams and aspirations to do the job justice. Babysitting on occasion was more than enough. The baby was a bad dream. Giving him up had been the right thing to do. He was better off wherever he was. She'd have just ended up resenting the kid.

After Devon was back in bed, she gave herself fifteen minutes. Ten minutes to cry and five to get herself back under control. Despite everything, she was still sniffling forty-five minutes later when the parents arrived home.

"Marissa, what's wrong?" Mrs. McCann's eyes were wide with concern. Her purse slipped from her hands and hit the floor with a thud. "Are the kids all right? Did something happen?"

Marissa held up a hand. "Everything's fine," she managed to squeak out, angry with herself. She was supposed to be done now. She swabbed her face with a damp handful of tissue. "It's nothing. I just…"

She struggled for an excuse for her tears. Her eye lit upon the television where Barbara Streisand, as Esther Howard, sang the reprise of "Watch Closely Now" in the last few minutes of the 1976 remake of *A Star Is Born*.

"…the movie." That was it. She always cried when Desmond Howard died.

The McCann's turned in unison to look at the TV.

"*A Star Is Born,*" Cheryl McCann laughed. Her brittle tension was replaced with an understanding smile. "I always cry at the end of that one, too."

Her husband shook his head in disgust. "Women and sappy movies," he muttered as he picked his wife's purse from the floor.

Carrie's Call

The following Wednesday, while Libby packed the diaper bag in preparation for coffee at Cheryl's, the phone rang. Libby grabbed it, afraid it would be Cheryl canceling. Devon hadn't been sleeping well for the past few nights, and Cheryl thought he might be coming down with something. If he woke up sick, Cheryl was going to call so David wouldn't be exposed.

"Libby?" The voice was not Cheryl's.

Libby smiled. "Yes?" She didn't recognize the caller.

"It's me. Carrie."

"Carrie?" Carrie who? Her body tensed as she realized it was Mark's wife.

Oh, no! They must have gotten the birth announcement already. She only mailed it Monday and had counted on it taking a couple of days to reach North Carolina. She hadn't expected to hear from them until tonight, at the earliest. And then, she had expected Mark to call, not Carrie.

"Hi, Carrie. It didn't sound like you at first," Libby said, covering her shock. "How is everyone?"

"We're fine," Carrie answered, carefully. "Mark's at work." Her voice betrayed her agitation. "I got your card." She paused, as if uncertain how to proceed.

Libby found herself frozen. She knew she should say something, but she couldn't. Her mind was blank. Silence hung awkwardly on the line.

"Libby," Carrie began again, "you had a baby?"

"Yes." *Oh, God, help me,* Libby prayed, biting her lip. She felt hot as she sank into a kitchen chair. *Here we go.*

"I didn't know you were expecting." Carrie's voice sounded cold, uncomfortable.

"I know," Libby began, eyes darting around the room as if the answers were written there somewhere. "I didn't know how to tell you." She still didn't. Would they suspect the truth or would they think she was a slut?

"Does..." Carried hesitated, cleared her throat and continued. "Does Mark know?"

"No." Libby paused uncertainly. "Not unless you told him or he saw the card."

"You didn't tell him?" Carrie's voice sounded surprised.

"No...well, not before now, anyway." Libby wiped her sweaty palms against the legs of her stretch pants, but it didn't help.

The silence lasted so long Libby began to wonder if they had been disconnected.

"Libby, who is the baby's father?"

Carrie's words stunned Libby. "David's father?" Libby repeated, stalling while she mentally scrambled for an answer. She'd never gone that far in the make-believe process. "Well..."

"Is it Mark?" Carrie asked.

Icy sweat ran down Libby's back as she felt her heart contract. "Mark?" she repeated stupidly. "No! No, Carrie, it wasn't Mark." Libby's stomach felt knotted and queasy. This was why Carrie sounded so cold. "Mark is like a brother to me. He could never...we would never ...we didn't...No. It definitely wasn't Mark."

"Then who?" Carrie's voice was cold, her tone disbelieving. "You never went anywhere." Her words implied it had to be Mark.

"It's true I didn't go out *much*, but I *did* go out." Libby was frantically trying to think of a plausible lie. She hadn't prepared herself for this conversation; she'd hoped inspiration would hit her when the time came. Well, the time was here now. "I went to visit Jenny's grave a couple of times alone," she said, remembering.

Carrie remained silent.

The silence begged to be filled.

Suddenly hungry, Libby scanned the kitchen counter for leftovers. The cupboard that usually held the Oreos was filled with bottles and formula.

"Well, one of those times, I met a guy. He was there visiting his girlfriend's grave. She had been killed in a car accident." It was getting easier now. Once started, the lie seemed to grow and develop a life of its own. "They were supposed to get married."

She ran her hand through her hair, hoping the story sounded plausible.

"I told him about Jenny, and he told me about his fiancée. We cried in each other's arms. You know, to comfort each other. And then, somehow we were in his car and…well…neither one of us had planned to take it quite that far, but…" Once again, Libby wiped her hands on her now damp pants.

"I was so embarrassed. We both were. He apologized and apologized." Libby paused, shaking her head. This was easier than she had thought it would be. She could almost see it happening. "I left as soon as I could. I got back home and remembered I didn't even know his name. I don't think he ever told me."

"You're sure?" Carrie asked, sounding young and in need of reassurance.

"What? You think I'm lying?" Defensive anger rose to mask the rising fear of discovery.

"No. I—"

Libby hardly paused for a breath. "I was so embarrassed I didn't say a thing about it when I got home. It's not like it's something you tell people. Can you imagine *that* conversation?"

"No, I—"

"I haven't told anyone until now," Libby rushed on. Well, at least *that* was true. "And then…well, I could never figure out how to tell you. I guess I was in denial about the pregnancy. I somehow thought if I didn't say anything about it, it would go away. That it wasn't a baby, just gas and more fat."

Libby wondered if that was how it was for the real mother. No. She stopped herself mid-thought. She *was* David's real mother, and this was the way it happened!

"As stupid as it sounds, I didn't really know I was expecting a baby until he arrived."

"Oh, Libby, I'm so sorry," Carrie burst out, relief and guilt evident in her voice. She didn't sound like the poised woman Libby knew. "I was so afraid. I thought…."

"I know." The thought of Carrie worrying, picturing her with Mark turned Libby's stomach. "But that wasn't the way it happened. It was that guy at the cemetery."

She was telling the truth about Mark. Could Carrie hear the truth of it in Libby's voice or was it overshadowed by the lies?

"Mark was Jenny's husband. He's my brother."

If Libby ever hoped to see Jenny's kids again, she had to make certain Carrie understood and believed her.

"Mark is my brother," Libby repeated. Carrie had to be nearly as desperate to believe as Libby was to make her believe.

"I know he is. Oh, Libby, I'm sorry. If Mark ever finds out I accused you, he'd kill me. After all you've done for the kids." Carrie sounded as rattled as Libby felt. "Do you think you can forgive me?"

"Absolutely. Better yet, let's just forget this entire conversation. Pretend it never happened."

"Could we? Do you think? Oh, Libby, thank you."

David's cries from the other room, spurred Libby to end the uncomfortable conversation.

"I'm sorry, Carrie, David just woke up. I need to go."

"But we're okay?"

Libby's entire body shook with adrenalin.

"We're okay." She wasn't sure this was a lie so much as wishful thinking. Her hands quaked as she placed the receiver in its cradle.

David's cries grew louder.

She took several shaky breaths before going to get David from his crib.

Caring for her son, Libby realized that despite the lies, she felt confident, like the one in charge. There was something about being David's mother that made her strong. Strong and clever. Clever enough to make all her lies real. Clever enough to keep him.

§

Somehow, Libby managed to get to Cheryl's without eating anything. It was a major milestone Libby overlooked. Normally when something bothered Libby, food helped her swallow the pain or discomfort. This time, however, thanks to David's timely call, Libby had been so busy seeing to his needs and getting to Cheryl's she had somehow forgotten to eat. Now at Cheryl's, she wasn't hungry—wasn't even tempted by the bakery-fresh caramel rolls Cheryl and the kids were devouring.

"Sure you won't have one?" Cheryl asked. "This might be your last chance."

Both two-and-a-half-year-old Lindsay and twelve-month-old Devon were crying for the last roll.

"I'm sure," Libby assured her, patting her belly. "I want to lose this baby fat." She had often jokingly referred to her excess weight as baby fat in the past—as if she were so young as to still have baby fat. Now, the term took on a different meaning.

"Your loss," Cheryl commented, cutting the last roll in two and distributing it to her children, thus ending the whining.

"I know, but I'm still full from the other night. You sure make good lasagna."

"Thanks." Cheryl smiled at the compliment. "But I think it's your sister-in-law's call that has you rattled."

"I shouldn't have said anything. I promised her we'd forget it ever happened."

"And you will. You'll never mention it to her or your brother-in-law, and I certainly won't, but you needed to vent it first. Besides, I knew something was off, and I wasn't about to let it go. How could you not say something? If it happened to me, I know it would knock me for a loop. I'd have to tell you about it. I mean, Jack's brother Jeff is nice, but if someone suggested we'd had sex, it would turn me off food for weeks." She smiled. "Or at least hours. We're talking me, after all." She shook her head. "Seriously though, it's not even so much that I love Jack too much to ever cheat on him, which I do. Love him so much, that is. It's that Jeff is like a brother."

Libby nodded. "You understand then. Carrie's asking about Mark was horrible." She was guilty of not turning David over to the authorities and lying, but not… she couldn't even think the word. "It makes me ill." She swallowed hard, trying to alleviate the sick feeling in her stomach. "I cared for that family for years, and this is what they think of me."

"I know it seems that way, but I doubt she really thinks it. And you know your brother-in-law didn't have any idea she called."

It felt like one of the bricks in Libby's belly dissolved. "That's right. He didn't. He hadn't seen the card yet, and she said he'd kill her if he knew she'd called."

Cheryl wiped Lindsay's and Devon's faces and shooed them into the playroom. "That's it, then. You've cared for the family for so long that your new sister-in-law feels like an interloper. I'll bet it's why they moved so far away, so she didn't have to compete with you for those kids' love."

"I wouldn't—"

"Of course not," Cheryl interrupted. "You'd never stand between a mother and her child. Even a stepmother. You'd have supported her at every turn. The thing is; I think this morning's conversation was all about her insecurities." She held up a hand. "Don't get me wrong. It was still a crappy thing to suggest, but at least it makes sense."

"I guess." Libby drank the last of her coffee. "I'll have to think about that." Carrie's insecurities or not, the phone call had left her rattled. And Cheryl's reassurances had, as well. Had taking David meant she'd gotten between a mother and her child? The woman had abandoned David. Maybe standing between them, if that's what she was doing, was what needed to be done. She didn't want to talk about it anymore, much less think about it.

"Say, speaking of thinking," Cheryl began, kindly changing the subject as she filled Libby's cup, "have you given any thought to having Jack's mom watch David when you go back to work?" Cheryl picked up her cup, cradling it between her hands. "I told Ann about you and David. She wants to meet you both. She meant to stop in today, but she had a dental appointment, and you know how tough those are to change."

"Yes." Libby looked at David sleeping in his car seat. His rosebud mouth curved into a brief smile as if he could feel her loving gaze. He looked so small—far too small to consider leaving him. "I hadn't thought of day care yet."

"You really should consider Ann," Cheryl insisted. "She's *so* good with the kids—a real treasure."

"I don't know," Libby hedged. "It seems so early."

"I know, but you'll be amazed by how fast time goes when you have kids. You think you have all the time in the world and then *poof!* Your six weeks are almost up, and you have to scramble to find someone. It's much better to think of these things in advance."

"I suppose you're right," Libby said, bowing to Cheryl's experience. She would eventually have to leave him to go to work. She needed to work to keep him.

"Great!" Cheryl said, picking up her caramel roll as she continued nonchalantly. "I thought next Wednesday, if you don't have plans, you could come for coffee again and meet her. I know she's free. No more dental appointments."

Libby laughed. "You had this planned all along, didn't you?"

Cheryl smiled, chewing.

"What if I'd said 'no?'"

Cheryl took a quick sip of coffee. "You'd have been nuts. Ann may be Jack's mother, but she really is good. We didn't always used to live here. I know how hard good daycare is to find. And you'll thank me, just you wait."

Libby smiled. Cheryl was such a good friend. "I already do."

Photographs and Memories

The room was dark and stuffy, the sultry air rank with the stench of old cigarette butts, stale beer, dirty dishes, and other things even less savory. Somewhere, a tiny baby cried. At first, it wailed and screamed, but as the hours passed, its little voice grew hoarse. Marissa couldn't reach it and wouldn't have known what to do to calm it if she had. There was nothing to feed it.

The floor was littered with clothes, papers, cans and other discarded things. The sink was piled high with dishes while the counter was lined with glass bottles, some empty, some nearly empty. A stained mattress sat in the corner as its occupant snored, oblivious to a telephone that rang and rang.

The incessant ringing urged her to struggle to the surface. Marissa jerked free from the nightmare to find she was in her dorm room. She stumbled out of bed and grabbed the receiver.

The dial tone buzzed in her ear. It had probably been her mom. The woman was nearly psychic when it came to nightmares. She always knew just when to step in and wake her, and just what to say to make the dream disappear. Besides, Marissa had been expecting a call from home ever since she'd sent the letter explaining she wasn't coming home for Thanksgiving.

Returning to her bed, she wished the images of the dream would fade. She rubbed her face, surprised to find it wet with tears. She'd been crying in her sleep again.

She didn't understand the dream. If the lady had indeed taken the baby and kept it, she wouldn't let it cry like that. She wouldn't keep it in a filthy apartment. If she'd taken it at all. She must have, though. And not turned it in. There had been no news. No outcry.

Marissa blew her nose and lay back down. Her eyes were wet, but that was okay. She was still in bed.

She didn't cry during the day. Well, her breasts occasionally wept, and that worried her. It also made it impossible to pretend the birth had been a dream. Shouldn't she have stopped lactating by now? It had been three weeks. She pushed aside the thought. She didn't cry. Why would she? She was happy. Relieved.

The shrill sound of the phone startled her, and she leapt across the room to silence it.

"I want to say up front that I understand about the job and the homework and everything, but I'm going to miss you."

Just the sound of her mother's voice made Marissa's eyes brim with moisture, spill over. "I know, Mom. I'll miss you too." She wanted to go home. Needed to, but couldn't. It was too soon. There was just no way she would be able to handle the welcoming hug she'd get as greeting without bawling and confessing all. Just the thought of her and Mitch's baby pictures on the living room wall was enough to send her to the tissue box.

"I wish I could send you some pumpkin pie."

Marissa's mother was all about nurturing. She always made certain Marissa had her favorite foods. She was the type of mother everyone should have, the type of mother Marissa knew she could never be. The type of mother her baby deserved. It made Marissa feel worthless. She'd made the right decision, leaving the baby, staying in Eau Claire.

"I'm sure there will be pumpkin pie here. I understand the dining hall is doing turkey with all the trimmings." She knew downplaying the importance of the meal would bother her mom, but she did it anyway.

"Couldn't we come get you, just for the day? Your dad wouldn't mind the drive."

"Who are you kidding, Mom? He and Mitch will be so focused on the television they won't even notice I'm not there." Marissa mopped her face with a tissue.

"Now, Marissa," her mother laughed. "That's not true. They'll know you aren't here."

"We're talking about Allen and Mitchell Fleming, right?" Marissa tried to sound joyful and amused, but she was uncertain of her success.

"All right, then. Maybe they won't, but that will just make me miss you more."

Her throat felt thick, as if she were being smothered by her mother's attention. "Say, Mom, I've gotta go. I need to get ready and grab some breakfast before work starts." Her eyes flashed to the red numbers on the clock radio. She really *should* get moving.

"Okay, but are you all right? You sound congested."

Her mother loved her, but Marissa couldn't help wondering how unconditional the love would be if her mom knew the truth. Marissa caught her sob in time to turn it into a cough. "Allergies," she lied. "The leaf mold must be really bad this year."

"Sounds more like a cold to me. You need to get something from the drugstore. Do you have enough in your checkbook? I'll deposit some money into your account this afternoon."

"Thanks, Mom."

Marissa hung up the phone and blew her nose. The pregnancy had been easier to conceal than this sadness. She hadn't seen her son for long, but his image was burned into her memory with laser accuracy. She closed her eyes, and there was his face. His tiny toes. His perfect little fingernails.

Each morning and afternoon she filled her left pocket with fresh tissues and emptied her right pocket of the used ones. When her eyes got too full, she faked sneezing attacks. Allergies, not tears.

If it would only snow, she told everyone. Her allergies always got better once the snow covered the ground.

§

That afternoon, Marissa sat hunched on her bed as Jessie packed her duffle for the weekend. "Have a great Thanksgiving. When do you expect your parents?"

"In a couple of hours. I'm going to try to get some studying in before I go. This morning was so busy I didn't have time to record everything from lab. You've got to hear this one." Jessie tucked her curly blonde hair behind her ear, zipped her backpack and plopped her skinny butt on her bed. "There was this new mom on the floor today that delivered last night. And Carol—you know, that nurse I was telling you about—said they brought her up from the emergency room fully dilated and insisting she wasn't pregnant. Can you believe that?"

Marissa's heart skipped a beat, but she held her face still and said nothing. Jessie had begun her O.B. rotation and was eager to share her experiences. Open textbooks with photos of neonatal development and labor stages were constantly on her desk.

Jessie continued, heedless of Marissa's lack of reaction. "She lives with her folks, and no one so much as suspected she was expecting. Can you imagine?"

Marissa's stomach cramped and sweat dotted her brow. The student nurse might be unable to imagine it, but she'd lived with it every day since they'd started the fall semester.

"She was a bit on the chunky side, so I guess they couldn't tell," Jessie offered by way of justification. "Still… I think you'd have to be blind not to recognize a pregnant person."

You didn't. Recovering from her initial shock, Marissa tried not to show the fear and pain that scantily covered the gaping hole in her heart. "I guess," she said aloud.

"Cute baby, though," Jessie continued, oblivious to Marissa's agony.

"Is she going to keep it?" Marissa asked despite herself, half of her hoped this girl would give the baby up to justify her own desperate decision, and the other half hoped she would keep it and avoid what Marissa now considered to be the biggest mistake of her life.

Jessie shrugged, reaching for her hairbrush. "Beats me." She attended to her hair in silence for several seconds. "If it were me, though," she continued, "I'd give it up." She put aside the brush and began untying her white clinic shoes. "It's not like she wanted the baby or anything. She didn't even know she was pregnant."

Marissa sat on her bed, fidgeting with her comforter, not looking at Jessie.

"She *should* give it up," Jessie insisted. "There are plenty of people out there that'd give anything for a baby. Some people would probably give her money for it, even."

Marissa nodded, not looking up. She used to think that way too, that it would be better to give him up. But now? Now, all she could think about was her son. How he looked. How he smelled. What he sounded like. How he had felt in her arms. Marissa had to force herself to concentrate on her schoolwork and to do things with friends just to forget. Concentrate on things she could control. Act normal. Close the door. Fake it until you make it. Keep busy. The trouble was, she didn't like to go out so much anymore. Alcohol made things worse—made her maudlin.

Jessie continued to change out of her white clinical uniform. She shook out the smock and pants and sniffed them in the classic test to determine if they were good for another day before arranging them neatly on a hanger and putting on jeans and a sweater.

"What about you?" she asked, looking at Marissa.

Startled out of her recriminations, Marissa looked up, the edge of the comforter still in her hand. "Me?"

"Yeah," Jessie asked. "What would you do?"

"I'd keep it," Marissa answered without hesitating to think.

"Really?" Jessie's eyes widened. "I thought you didn't want kids."

Marissa blushed crimson. "Well," she stammered. "I didn't. I don't."

Jessie smiled. "Who's the guy?"

"No one," Marissa lied, as images of her son flitted across her mind's eye.

"Liar," Jessie accused. "Who is he? There's got to be some reason you're softening your stand on kids." She pulled her hair into a ponytail. "Can't be Paul. He was as bad as you were. Worse. What was that story he liked to tell about growing a strong spider plant? Don't let it have babies and it gets big and strong. Let it have them and it gets so scraggly you may as well throw it away?" She shook her head. "He was a real prince. I don't know what you saw in him."

Marissa didn't answer. She'd thought she'd loved him at one time.

"It would serve him right to marry a woman who wants ten kids and a dog." Jessie laughed at her own joke. "So, who is this new guy? Have I met him?"

Realizing she was not going to get away without confessing something, Marissa decided to tell the truth. To an extent.

"You don't know him."

"Does he go to school here?" Jessie watched Marissa.

"No. In fact, he's younger." Marissa stared off into space, the image of her baby's face hovering before her eyes.

Jessie laughed. "Younger, huh? Not still in high school, though, is he?"

Marissa shook her head. "Nope. Not in high school."

"You've really got it bad, haven't you?" Jessie's eyes sparkled.

Marissa returned Jessie's look with a slight blush. "I guess I do."

"Bring him by sometime. I'd like to meet the guy that's changed your mind about children."

The smile faded from Marissa's face. "If I can." It was an empty promise. She'd probably never see her baby again. Marissa swallowed hard but couldn't move the lump in her throat.

Thanksgiving

Cuddled together in the corner of the couch, Libby gave David his bottle. The Macy's Thanksgiving Day parade was on television. David watched her in that cross-eyed way newborns have as she described each float and balloon in elaborate detail. He always watched her closely when she talked to him, as if he were trying to understand. Libby grinned. He was such a smart baby. Such a good baby. He hadn't made a peep all during Thanksgiving Day Mass.

"That's Snoopy," she said, as the huge beagle filled the screen. "When the Christmas shows come on, we'll watch *Charlie Brown's Christmas Special*. Snoopy is in that." She knew David didn't understand a word she said and that he wouldn't appreciate the show for another year or two, but it was never too early to start family traditions.

"When Jenny and I were kids we used to talk about maybe going to see the Macy's parade in person someday. We never did. It was always too far away. But we always watched. Even when she was sick. I'd gather your cousins into the living room so we could all be together and watch it." There was comfort knowing that in North Carolina Laura, Timmy and Michael were watching too. They'd been about to sit down when she'd called to wish them a *Happy Thanksgiving*. A month ago, a phone call was as close as she'd thought she'd get to family on the holiday.

Tears filled Libby's eyes as she shifted her son a little closer. He'd saved her from being alone.

David yawned, his precious little mouth still around the nipple, and then he resumed drinking.

She remembered when she and Jenny would stuff the turkey while the kids watched. Or one of them would hold one of the kids while the other worked on the bird.

Libby wasn't having turkey today. Thanksgiving had never been about the food for her. She liked the stuffing, but didn't particularly care for turkey. She just liked Thanksgiving. It was tradition and family. No tree, no presents, no wild expectations that never came true. Even more than Christmas, Thanksgiving meant family.

For the Love of *David*

David stopped drinking without finishing his bottle. Her heart filled just looking at him. A tear ran down her cheek as she smiled. "You are what I'm thankful for this year."

§

With nothing else to do, Marissa sat watching football on television in the dorm lounge. There were only a couple of guys there. Most of the students that had stayed on campus for Thanksgiving were foreign exchange students who didn't really appreciate the game. Not that she did. Her dad and Mitch always watched it while she helped her mother in the kitchen, either ladling up food or cleaning up.

She hadn't thought she'd miss it.

Her stomach hurt. The turkey had been dry and the cranberries all wrong. Thick cranberry gelatin out of a can. Yuck! Hadn't anyone in this place heard of real cranberries?

The game wasn't bad. If you liked football, which Marissa didn't. Or if you were a Chicago Bears or Detroit Lions fan, which, being raised in Minnesota with rabid Vikings fans, she wasn't. Thanksgiving was always the most boring holiday. No good television. Her friends always had people over. As far as Marissa was concerned, it wasn't even a holiday. It was just a big, messy meal that took half the day to make and the other half to clean up. She wasn't missing anything. So why was her chest so tight? Why did her eyes burn with the need to cry? Why did she miss her mom more than she had that first week freshman year?

Damn Paul. Damn baby. If it weren't for them she'd be home.

§

Marissa shivered in her thinsulate and flannel-lined jean jacket as she walked through the Kerm's parking lot. She'd left the lounge when the Chicago/Detroit game went into overtime. When everyone came back on Monday, classes would head into the last frantic stretch before finals week. She should be studying instead of looking for the blue Ford with the LDY plates. She wasn't even positive the heavy-set woman had kept her baby. She wasn't sure, but it stood to reason. What else could have happened? She hadn't imagined the whole thing, after all.

Her feet carried her past familiar college hangouts into less familiar residential areas. The car was nowhere. Despite her desire to embrace the delusion, she knew the pregnancy hadn't really been a dream. She really had abandoned her son. But why hadn't he been turned in? That's what she wanted to know. Why wasn't the newspaper full of speculation? Why wasn't the campus over-run with detectives looking for the mother?

It almost made more sense if she'd imagined the whole thing. Stunned by her idiotic breakup with Paul last winter, she'd let her mind run through the possibilities, imagining what she would do if she found herself pregnant. That explanation made sense, as far as it went. But even without the changes in her body she knew it hadn't happened that way.

Not looking where she was going, she stubbed her toe on uneven ground and stumbled onto the train tracks. It had been a long time since she'd seen a train. Marissa stood in the middle of the quiet street and looked down the tracks. To the left, they went over a trestle that bridged the river. It took her back to summer camping trips with Paul's family. A train passed behind their families' favorite campground, and the kids often placed pennies on the tracks in anticipation. The thin copper discs they peeled from the rails never lost their appeal. She had a jar of them in her bedroom at home.

The summers were always hot in her memory. Cicadas screeched in the trees, and grasshoppers whirred in the tall grass. Dandelions held under the chin proclaimed a preference for butter. The same flowers were beheaded in singsong chants of "Mama had a baby and her head popped off" or gathered and brought by the armload to their mothers.

The last time she'd walked the tracks was the summer before senior year with Paul and Mitch. One last camping trip before school started. They'd left their parents by the river and walked the tracks for miles. There was a trestle bridge that crossed the river just outside of town and the three of them would lie with their ears pressed to the sun-hot rails, listening. Supposedly, they'd hear the train through the rails long before they'd see it. The theory was unproven, as far as Marissa was concerned, since the trains only came past the campground in midmorning or the dead of night, never in the afternoon. Still, they listened to the rails before crossing the bridge. And speculated, all the way across, what they'd do if a train did come.

She walked the tracks toward the bridge. It was as easy as she remembered, step, step, step. Somehow, it was always easy on the ground. The railroad ties were light against the black cinder bed or dark against the gravel, but for some reason it was easy to walk them. She didn't even have to look down. Crossing the bridge was different. The water below the bridge was dark in comparison to the ties. They were less regular on the bridge. Single ties and then random double ones as the track passed over a support beam. Fear that a misplaced foot would result in more than a small stumble had her watching her step on the bridge, carefully reminding herself to step on the light ties.

She stood in the middle of the bridge and looked at the water of the Chippewa. It was steel gray like the sky, cold and mildly threatening—nothing unusual for the typical, if unpleasant, Thanksgiving day. She should go back, call her folks and say hi or study for psychology. Five different theories on developmental stages. All the same and yet slightly different. She'd thought she had them memorized, but they blurred in her mind like the river before her eyes.

A gust of wind made Marissa wobble. One cold foot slipped off the wood. Hands whipped from her pockets, arms windmilled for a panicked second before her hands met an angled beam. Grabbing hold, she righted herself. Her heart pounded.

She could have fallen.

Momma had a baby and her head fell off.

She shook. Her arms, wrapped around the thick timber, quivered.

What had she been thinking, walking the bridge? The wind was strong. The ties were slick. She hated railroad bridges. Was she nuts? A train could come, and she hadn't even listened to the tracks. Sweat trickled down her back.

She could have fallen in the river and drowned. Floated away like trash. Enough of this insanity. She was done. No more searching for a baby that wasn't meant to be found. It was past time to leave off delusions and get her life back. She had school, for heaven's sakes. Tests and papers to do. And a future. She inched her way off the bridge one shaky footstep at a time.

Starting this afternoon, she would be installed in a library cubical studying. No more walks foolishly searching for something she didn't really want found.

Her left foot found solid ground first, then her right. She laughed, tears streaming down her face as she ran toward campus.

Six Weeks

There was mail in her box. A surge of excited anticipation warmed her as she dug in her pocket for the key.

Marissa looked at the two letters as she crossed the lobby. One was from her brother Mitchell, who was a senior in high school, and the other was in her mother's tight script. She opened Mitchell's first as she headed up the institutional-green concrete stairs.

> *Rissa,*
>
> *You are coming home for Christmas, aren't you? Thanksgiving stank. All Mom did was ask me why I thought you hadn't been home. Like I knew or something. I don't know why she just didn't call you.*
>
> *Anyway, she and Dad miss you. I wouldn't mind seeing my big sis, either.*
>
> *You'll never guess who I bumped into last weekend—Paul. He asked about you. It was weird. I hadn't seen him since you guys broke up.*
>
> *Hey, is that why you haven't been home? Are you avoiding him or trying to get out of re-explaining to Mom why she can't have him for a son-in-law?*
>
> *Come home. She'll get over it, eventually.*
>
> *Hope to see you across the table in a week or so.*
>
> *Your bro (like you didn't know),*
> *Mitch*

Marissa reached her door and punched in the combination while she read the last few lines.

How had she forgotten all about her mother's love of Paul and hopes for their future? Maybe because she'd only had that one short conversation with her mom in ages?

She shrugged off her jacket, tossing it to the bed. The shrill jangle of the phone jarred her from her thoughts and postponed the unappealing prospect of reading her mother's letter. She tossed it onto the bed as well and picked up the phone.

"Marissa, I'm so glad I caught you." Marissa recognized Mrs. McCann's voice. "I know finals are about to start, and your schedule is probably too heavy, but the kids are asking for you. I was wondering if you could possibly sit for a few hours tonight."

"Tonight?" Marissa stalled while she considered her schedule and the need to study for her psych test. She had all of tomorrow for that. This was a chance to kill several birds with one stone. She could reaffirm the rightness of her decision to give up her baby, make that crucial first step in getting on with her life, and earn a few unexpected dollars before Christmas. "Sure, as long as it's not too late. What time?"

Having hammered out the details, Marissa grabbed her books and money for a soda before heading for the library. She would hit the books and make flash cards so she could study while rocking the baby to sleep. Then she wouldn't feel guilty about not accomplishing anything. She snatched her coat from the bed and left her mother's letter lying there unread.

§

On the television in the McCann living room, the Abominable Snow Monster of the north bared its teeth and growled just before the station went to commercial.

"He can't eat Rudolph," Becky announced, turning to Marissa for reassurance. "Santa needs him to pull the sleigh."

"Rudolph will be fine." Marissa hugged the little girl close enjoying the freshly shampooed smell. All three kids had been freshly bathed when she arrived. "Remember, this is the story of how he got to be famous. He'll be okay. It already happened." Devon yawned on her lap. He'd probably fall asleep before the show ended.

Lindsey rested one hand on Marissa's arm and pointed at the doll on the commercial with the other. "I want that."

She'd repeated "I want that" during every commercial. Mrs. McCann had mentioned that she might, and to let her write it down if she got too adamant. A densely scribbled piece of paper sat on the end table.

The entire night had been a scene from Marissa's childhood. The scent of Johnson's Baby Shampoo. Cuddling while watching Rudolph. Shivering when the monster roared. Even the commercials seemed as if they'd been dredged out of the past. Norelco razors. Dolly Madison pastries.

Mrs. McCann was so lucky.

The show came back on. Marissa's eyes followed the action, but her mind skipped elsewhere. Had the kids changed that much in a few weeks or had she? She felt better. More stable. She could do the motherhood thing and the studying thing. Tonight proved it.

If she'd had the baby now, she would have kept it. Thinking of it made her sad, but she didn't cry. It had only been six weeks, but she felt so much older and wiser. She regretted her decision to leave him behind, but knew there was no undoing it. What was done was done.

She'd made the best decision she could at the time. That she'd make a different one now wasn't cause for recrimination. The new, mature Marissa acknowledged mistakes, did what she could to rectify them and then moved on. The important thing was to learn from your mistakes. Like some wise philosopher said, "It's not how many times you fall that matters; it's how many times you get up." Marissa congratulated herself on having gotten back up.

§

Libby stood in the nursery and looked at her son. Cheryl had been right: the first six weeks had flown by. Thanksgiving and Christmas preparations were secondary to Libby. She reveled in each new day with her son, but she didn't pay attention to the days. Thus, she was caught off guard when Ann McCann called to confirm David's drop-off time.

Her first morning back to work was the perfect time for the crispy, chocolaty goodness of Oreos. Dressed for work, she left David's room and walked to the kitchen. She stood in front of the cookie cupboard staring at baby bottles and tins of formula trying to remember the last time she's seen an Oreo in her kitchen. It seemed unfathomable that she didn't have any, hadn't bought any, and couldn't even recall the last time she'd eaten one. Promising herself she'd get some during her lunch break, Libby left the kitchen to get David.

He was sound asleep, his round little butt sticking up in the air. She hated to wake him to get him changed and ready to go. He grunted softly as she scooped him from his crib, his little body so warm and cuddly. She wanted to crawl back into her own bed and take him with her, but she slid him into his car seat instead.

Devon and his sisters were already at Ann's when she arrived. David was asleep when she set his car seat on the floor in Ann's living room.

"I don't think I can do this."

Ann patted her arm reassuringly. "Of course you can. Part of being a working mom is the working part. Now, we've talked about his schedule. I have it all written down in the kitchen. I know just where to call you if I have any questions. And I have that nice pad of paper you brought in case he does anything you won't want to miss."

"I know, I'm being silly."

Ann shook her head. "Nonsense. You wouldn't be a good mother if you didn't agonize a little. He'll be fine. You'll be fine. Now, kiss that baby good-bye and get going. You don't want to be late your first day back."

David was so soft and warm beneath her lips. Libby had to force herself to leave his car seat where it was instead of hoisting it and running back to the car.

She could hardly see to drive. She'd meant to be strong, but she wasn't. Maybe she didn't really need to work. She could stay home with David and go on welfare.

No way.

The thought of living on welfare was enough to keep her driving.

She rushed into the employee entrance as the clock flipped to 7:30.

"You made it." Cheryl smiled at her.

"It was close," Libby admitted. "I almost turned around three times."

"I know how you feel," Cheryl commiserated. "I couldn't do it with Becky when we lived in Boston and ended up quitting. But it gets easier, and Jack's mom is really good with the kids."

"I know David will be fine," Libby sniffled. "It's me I'm worried about." Her attempt at levity was choked by a new bout of tears.

Cheryl smiled sympathetically and handed Libby a box of tissue.

"I'll be all right in a minute," Libby croaked, taking several tissues from the box and handing it back to Cheryl. "I'd better hit the ladies' room first, though. I look a mess."

Dr. Westland spotted Libby when she left the bathroom, make-up newly reapplied and composure at least temporarily restored.

Knowing that the clinic's last receptionist had succumbed to couldn't-leave-the-baby-with-a-sitter syndrome, Libby knew he and the other doctors were concerned that she would be able to make the transition back to work.

"Welcome back, Libby. How is that little guy of yours?" he asked.

Libby wondered what he thought as he looked into her puffy, tear-reddened eyes, but she smiled and managed to keep down the lump in her throat. "David's fine. Thank you for asking."

He put a fatherly hand on her arm. "The first day back is always tough, Libby. I've never had a new mom tell me otherwise, but you'll do fine. And Christmas is just a couple of days away, so maybe that break will help you ease back into the swing of things."

She smiled and blinked several times to keep back the tears. Why did he have to be so nice to her? She could handle it a lot better if people weren't so nice. She tried to combat the wave of sadness that threatened to engulf her.

"Thank you, Dr. Westland," she managed without crying.

He patted her arm reassuringly and then stepped aside.

Libby walked down the corridor, grateful that she hadn't broken down again. She felt Dr. Westland's eyes on her as she walked away. She stopped before she entered her workstation to see if her shirt was tucked in funny or something. Her clothing, though loose, was fine. She wondered what he had been looking at.

She shrugged and turned the corner.

Libby met Marsha as she came into the reception area where someone had strung garland and lights and set up a small Christmas tree.

"Libby, is that you?" Marsha asked, her voice echoing the surprised look on her face.

Libby stopped and turned, wondering at the tone of Marsha's voice.

"You look fabulous," Marsha continued, eyes raking Libby from head to toe. "How much weight have you lost?"

Libby looked down at her body. The stirrup pants she wore were a bit baggy despite the fact that they were freshly laundered. She hadn't really noticed.

"I don't know," she said honestly. She had been so focused on David that her weight and her body hadn't crossed her mind in weeks. "A couple of pounds, maybe."

"More than 'a couple,'" Marsha insisted, eyes wide in disbelief. "You look wonderful. I wish my baby weight had come off like that."

"Uh, thanks," Libby said, stunned. Had she really lost weight? She tried to remember the last time she had weighed herself. It wasn't something she liked to do. Too depressing.

Marsha called to another nurse. "Sally, come look at Libby. Doesn't she look great?"

Libby turned crimson. No one commented on how great she looked when she'd gotten a new outfit before, and now here she was wearing this old thing. It didn't feel honest. Were they trying to make certain she didn't quit?

Sally crossed the receptionist's area to get a better look. "Wow, girl!" she exclaimed, upon inspection. "You've certainly gotten skinny!"

Libby squirmed under the scrutiny.

"What'd you use?" Sally asked, patting her own hips. "I tried that Slim Fast stuff, but it didn't work for me. I'd drink one of them shakes and then have lunch, too. Ended up gaining weight. What's your secret?"

Libby didn't know what to say. She fidgeted under their scrutiny. She was saved from having to answer by the ringing of the telephone.

Later, she asked Cheryl, "Does it look like I've lost any weight to you?"

"Geez, Libby, yes. I told you the other day how good you look."

"I thought you were just being nice," Libby admitted.

"No. You really do look good. You need to get some clothes that fit, though. Those stirrups are about to fall off you."

Libby blushed again. "Are not."

"I bet I could pants you with half a tug."

"You wouldn't!" Libby gasped, mortified.

Cheryl laughed. "Really, though, you should get something that fits better. You could dash to the mall during lunch. I could even loan you a couple of bucks until payday, if you need it."

Libby looked at her pants skeptically and then raised her head. "They look that baggy?"

Cheryl eyed them critically and nodded.

§

Libby made a quick trip to the mall instead of the grocery store during her lunch hour. Everyone seemed to think she needed new clothes. They could be right. The pants she had on *were* saggy. The elastic had probably gone. It happened. She'd get a new pair of pants, something durable. Maybe she'd get two pair, if they weren't too expensive.

She pawed through the racks to find a style she liked. She'd always wanted to try some fitted slacks, but pants in her size had elastic waistbands, not tailored ones. But if she had dropped a size, maybe those would have button closures. She found her size and held it up to herself. The material extended several inches beyond on either side of her hips.

Libby raised the slacks closer to her face and checked the tag again. It said what she thought it had. They must be running large. She grabbed the next two smaller sizes and took them to the fitting room.

She undressed with her back to the mirror, as she usually did. Checking the tags again, she put on the larger of the two. It was loose.

She took it off and stepped into the smaller size. This one fit. She slid it partially off and rechecked the tag. It was two sizes smaller than normal. Two sizes? Was the fashion industry trying to gain customers by changing their sizing standards?

She pulled the slacks back on and turned to face the mirror.

She'd meant to look at her body as a whole, but her own flushed, smiling face filled her view. She hardly recognized the woman she saw. Pretty. Still chunky, but not nearly as fat as she remembered. Her face was slim with easily seen jawbones and cheekbones and a single chin. Libby would have thought she was in a hallway looking at someone else if she hadn't known she was in a dressing room alone.

Her gaze lowered taking in her newly reduced form. Her hands ran down her sides. She could still stand to lose twenty, maybe thirty pounds, but she had to have lost nearly that much already. She turned to examine her reflection from every angle the three-way mirror offered. It was something she normally didn't do. A quick glance straight on was all that was required to see if something fit before. But now…she stared at herself in excited disbelief.

A good portion of the extra flesh she had carried was gone. Hips slimmer, tummy flatter. She pulled her shirt tight in back and then spun around and looked over her shoulder. Her back was even slimmer. Really? She pulled off her shirt and looked again. Her bra was hooked as tight as it would go. Only a little bit of extra flesh bulged around her bra. Amazing. How had she not noticed its departure? She turned to face the mirror. Was this really her? Libby pinched herself—hard. She was awake. She looked closely at herself in the mirror. She desperately needed new bras.

She sank to the little bench. How had this happened? Was she sick? Diets never worked on her. The moment she thought of starting a diet, she got hungry. The same was true of exercise programs. She'd exercise, and she'd get hungry. The only other time she could remember losing

For the Love of *David*

weight was when she helped Jenny after the birth of each child. When she'd stay with Jenny and Mark for a week helping out, she always went home with a bit more play under her waistband. Well, it was true of Timmy and Michael's births, but not Laura's. Jenny's cancer had been discovered during Laura's birth. The diagnosis had changed everything.

Libby looked at herself in the mirror. Her smile faded. Sudden, unexplained weight loss was often a sign of illness. Cancer. Couldn't be. She felt wonderful. For the first time in forever she could truly say she was happy. Motherhood made her calm. Holding David brought peace and joy. Sure, she was a little tired, but that was because David didn't sleep through the night. All in all, she had more energy.

She looked at the person in the mirror. Her reflection wasn't that of a sick person. Her reflection showed a healthy, attractive woman who was going to be late for work if she didn't quit staring at herself.

The navy blue pants looked great on her. She glanced at the tag. They were marked down. She'd get them and another pair if they had one in black—and maybe a sweater, if she could find one she liked in three minutes for fifteen dollars or less.

She stripped and slid on her baggy clothes. She looked normal and healthy. Not skinny, but definitely slimmer than she had. It was all thanks to David. The thought of her son brought a slew of tender feelings. His first day in daycare.

She wanted to drive to Ann's and pick him up instead of returning to work, but she couldn't. She needed to work to provide for him. Her love for him wasn't enough. He needed food, shelter and clothing. Apparently, she needed clothing as well. He'd brought so many blessings into her life. Her mind tripped on the thought of his birth mother. Had leaving him behind been as big a blessing to her?

Libby couldn't dwell on it. She needed to hurry up. She glanced at her watch. Forget the sweater. She grabbed the second pair of pants and hurried to the checkout counter.

I'll be Home for Christmas

Marissa was shoving clothes into her bag in preparation for Christmas break when her mother's envelope fell on the floor.

That's right. She hadn't read it. How had she forgotten she had mail? She finally opened it.

> *Dear Marissa,*
>
> *I met Beth Swenson in Lund's the other day. She's seen about as much of Paul this past year as we have of you.*
>
> *You are back together with him by now, aren't you? I never understood what caused the breakup this time. But I know you love him and your fights never last for long, so I'm assuming your absence from home means you've been spending all of your weekends with him again. His mom assumes the same thing, by the way. We are both happy for you. You and Paul make such a nice couple.*
>
> *Anyway, we thought it would be fun to get together, so I invited them for Christmas Eve.*

"No." The letter shook in Marissa's hand. She never thought of Paul. Couldn't think of Paul. He was the cause of everything. His mistake. His son. She groped blindly for the bed as she sank to the floor.

> *I need you to come home as soon as your finals are over to help. I'm going to make the pecan pie you like so well, and I need you to make your special cranberry salad. Mitchell and your father have promised to have the tree in the stand waiting for your arrival. We are all so excited. Call if you need a ride home. Your father will come get you if you have trouble finding one.*
>
> *See you soon.*
> *Much love,*
> *Mom*

Marissa's stomach churned wildly. She sank to the bed.

This wasn't happening. Her mother wouldn't do this. She picked up the letter and read it again, searching in vain for the "ha ha" or "just kidding" that should be written somewhere, but wasn't.

It was too late to do anything. Her ride would be there soon. The dorm closed in an hour. She'd be home in three. If only she'd opened her mother's letter earlier.

She was overreacting. Imagining the worst. She'd tell her mom how impossible it was. Heck, it probably wouldn't even be necessary to tell her anything. Paul would have told his parents. He'd returned her letters unopened. He didn't want to know about what had or hadn't happened. Obviously, he wouldn't come for Christmas Eve. Her mother and his would be disappointed, but on this Christmas Eve, Paul and his entire family would be at their own house, not seated around her family table.

§

Marissa sat in the back seat of a beat-up Gremlin, squashed like a sardine between the door and the nearest of the three co-riders. Like the other passengers, she had her backpack and a present-laden grocery bag on her lap and her suitcase crammed between her feet. The sun streamed in the back window, adding to the blistering air that poured out of the little car's vents.

"Sorry about the heat," the driver called over his shoulder. "With this car, it's all or nothing. If you jiggle the handle, maybe you can get the windows down a bit."

It wasn't the worst car she had ridden in, but it was close. The physical discomfort almost made her forget the torture that possibly awaited her at home. Almost.

How could she forget about Paul and Christmas Eve? Her only hope was that Paul had confronted his mother and gotten the whole thing canceled.

Yeah right. Who was she kidding? Slim hope that Paul would actually face a problem and solve it instead of running away. She would have to deal with it herself. Her mother wouldn't like it, but once she knew that Marissa and Paul were still broken up, she would cancel her invitation. She had to.

All too soon, Marissa was home. She squeezed out the car door and tugged her luggage after her before turning to look at the house. It was decorated with red and white lights that outlined the entire roofline. A large wreath adorned the front door that was flanked by snow-covered bushes trimmed in red lights.

Marissa took a deep breath and squared her shoulders as she stared at the blue split-level. She could do this. She sighed, picked up her suitcase, and forced her feet to start walking. The snow-framed driveway, whose length had never concerned her before, seemed too short.

Any hope Marissa may have held of arriving unnoticed was dashed when the front door sprang open, and the solid, apron-clad figure of her mother appeared framed by the brightly lit doorway.

"Marissa, honey!" Marissa's mother wiped her damp hands on the dishtowel she held. "You're home."

"Hi, Mom." Marissa kissed her mother's cheek before crossing the threshold. The air was thick with the moist, yeasty scent of bread. "You've been baking. It smells great." Upstairs on the kitchen radio Bing Crosby was singing "White Christmas." The scene was so familiar Marissa's breath caught in her throat.

"Thank you, dear." Her mother brushed a damp, brown curl from her forehead with the back of her hand. "I've been baking up a storm, and I could use your help. I made the pecan pie this morning and just put the rolls in the oven, but we still have to make the little quiches, some cranberry bread, and start the chicken wings."

Marissa grimaced as she kicked off her boots and shrugged out of her coat. She wasn't going to get to relax like she'd hoped. It was probably for the best.

While Marissa hung her coat in the closet, her mother straightened the boots, setting them neatly next to another pair on the rubber tray where they would dry without messing up the hallway. She stood and smiled at her daughter, carefully looking her over as if taking inventory of all changes.

"You've gained a little weight."

Marissa gave her mother a dirty look. "Thanks, Mom." She was back into the smallest of her clothes, but this particular pair of jeans was a bit snug. Trust her mother to notice.

"I didn't mean it like that." Only her mother could make a compliment sound like an insult. "You know I've always thought you were too thin. You look perfect now, more shapely, not so anemic."

"Thanks." Marissa was tempted to pick on the word "anemic," just to be a pain, but she knew what her mother meant to say and decided to drop it. Her continued break-up with Paul would be more than enough pain for her mother.

"Let me help you with that." Her mother picked up her suitcase and backpack. "I'll just drop these in your room, and then we'll have a nice cup of hot chocolate in the kitchen."

She followed her mother up the stairs.

Pausing at the top of the first flight of stairs, Marissa looked into the living room. The house looked the way it did every Christmas. The living room was tidy yet crowded with furniture. The dried flower arrangement on the coffee table was temporarily replaced by the nativity scene, and the candy dish that usually contained lemon drops now offered chocolate kisses in red, green and silver foil, though she was still only allowed one a day. The framed photo of her and Mitch picking daisies, however, still hung between the enlarged snapshot of her as a chubby-cheeked baby and the professional photo of Mitch half hidden by a blanket. Some things never changed, regardless of the season.

The mantle was festooned with garland and lights. Two over-sized knit stockings, complete with names and fuzzy-bearded Santas, dangled from cast-iron stocking hangers. A photo of her and Paul at senior prom still sat in a cluster of framed photos on the coffee table. Marissa frowned. She'd thought her mom had gotten rid of that. The room was a shrine to the past, filled with memorabilia from *before* when Marissa needed to deal with life *after*.

She turned to walk up the second flight of stairs and met her mother coming down. "Why don't you leave that bag of presents here, and we'll go have that cup of hot chocolate."

"Okay." Marissa shrugged, setting the bag on the landing. As she turned into the kitchen, she saw Paul sitting at the table with a mug of cocoa in his hands as he had a hundred times before. Just sitting, sipping chocolate as if nothing had happened.

"Oh, sh—" Marissa bit her tongue to keep from swearing in front of her mother. She turned to her mother. "What the… he…ck is *he* doing here?"

Her mother frowned. "Marissa, that isn't very nice. He's right here."

"I see that." Marissa wanted him gone. "What I want to know is why." One look at him was all it took to bring back the Saturday after she'd missed her period. He'd taken her to the Camaraderie, bought her cheese curds, and broke her heart. She still couldn't eat cheese curds. Just the thought of deep-fried chunks of battered cheddar made her want to vomit. And she used to love them.

"Oh, sit down, Marissa." Paul directed from the table as if he had the right to tell her what to do.

She glared at him as her mother guided her to the table and pressed her into a chair. Her mother was saying something in soothing tones about them needing to work things out so tomorrow night wouldn't be uncomfortable.

Marissa could have told her mother reconciliation was impossible, nothing he could say or do would make things better. Except, she couldn't. She couldn't tell her mother she'd been sleeping with Paul, much less that he'd broken up with her because a condom ripped, her period had been late, and he was too much of a chicken shit to face up to the possibility that they might be pregnant.

"I missed you, Rissa." Paul reached across the table and covered Marissa's hand with his. He acted as if there was nothing wrong, as if he hadn't pushed her into hell all alone.

She snatched her hand back and stared at him. Her hand itched to slap his face. "Liar."

"I've prayed about it a lot, and I can see now that our breakup was my fault…"

No-shit. Marissa wanted to say, but her mother was waiting for her response. She couldn't bring herself to speak. Paul broke the silence.

"…I want us back together again."

"No." Marissa stood, clutching the table for support. Her stomach churned. Sweat sprang to her brow. "I can't do this. You…" Marissa turned away from him and looked at her mother. "He has to go."

Paul stood as well. "Give me a chance to explain."

Her mother stood next to Marissa with a cup of cocoa in her hand and her mouth agape. "Oh, honey, I'm sorry." Her hands shook around the mug. She set it down on the table, sloshing cocoa on the Santa placemat. "I thought the two of you were…I thought…He said…" She looked from Paul to her daughter and back again. "He told me about wanting to get back together with you. About you seeing him with that girl in Japan. That she was the reason—"

"Is that what you think this is about?" Marissa shouted. "Some blonde slut in Japan?"

"Marissa!" Her mother scolded.

"Well, it isn't. We broke up in February. The girl was this summer."

"Which is why I thought she shouldn't matter," her mother continued. "Not if you still love each other."

Marissa's breath came in irregular pants. She remembered

that day at the Camaraderie. When he'd turned to leave, she'd grabbed her frosty mug of Pepsi and whipped it at his head. It had whizzed by his ear, spraying diet soda and ice all over his back and side before crashing to the tile some ten feet past him, splintering into a thousand shards. Now, the steaming mug of cocoa called to her, begged her to perfect her aim. Her mother would never understand, and Marissa would never be able to explain it.

"Are you okay?" Her mother's familiar, warm hands felt her forehead. "Marissa, I'm sorry. I misunderstood."

Marissa slapped her mother's hands away and stomped out of the kitchen. It felt good to be the one leaving this time. She wanted Paul gone. Or dead. Didn't much matter which as long as she never had to see him again.

She heard her mother's voice. "Paul, this was a mistake. I think you should go. Marissa…"

Marissa marched downstairs. How dare he come back? How dare he win over her mother with his insincere smiles, his shallow charm, and false morality?

In the entryway, she yanked her coat out of the closet so hard the metal hanger clattered to the floor. Standing on one foot and then the next, she tugged on her boots. A moment later, the door slammed behind her and she was outside.

She was halfway down the driveway when Paul came out of the house.

"Go away," she stated firmly and clearly, proud that she had not screamed it or sworn.

She could hear the squeak and crunch of the snow beneath his feet as he hurried down the drive.

"I told you to go away," she yelled, picking up her pace.

"Wait!" he called after her. "I don't have my boots tied."

"Good. Maybe you'll fall and hurt yourself."

The next thing Marissa knew he was right behind her. "You don't mean that."

She spun to face him. "Yes. I do."

Ignoring her protest, he wrapped his arms around her.

Marissa shoved at his chest and swore in his face. "Let me go." What made him think he could touch her?

He held her all the closer in response.

She remembered when she'd felt safe in his arms. Safe and loved.

"Damn you." Her booted foot battered his shin.

He let go, and she stumbled back.

"Shit, Rissa, that hurt."

"Good." She wanted to haul out and kick him again, but turned her back on him and walked away instead.

"I'm sorry."

His voice sounded so sincere, she stopped walking. "For what?"

"For everything."

She snorted and began walking. He was clueless. Her boots made a satisfying crunch with each step she took. She looked straight ahead, blocking out Paul and breathing in the cold, crisp December air flavored with a hint of wood smoke from a neighboring chimney.

Paul walked beside her. His un-laced boots clumped loudly, and his breath came out in frosty puffs. She wished he would leave.

"You're even more beautiful than I remembered."

She glared at him. "Liar."

"How did I ever let you go?"

"Easy. You're a consummate asshole."

He was an idiot if he thought his canned lines were going to work. Marissa turned away from him.

"Please, Riss. We need to talk."

He was wrong. She didn't need to talk, but she knew from experience he wouldn't go away until he'd had his say. "So talk," she commanded without sparing a glance in Paul's direction. She began walking rapidly down the street, leaving Paul to catch up as he would. She wanted this over with.

"I missed you," he began, his long, athletic strides easily keeping pace with her despite the clunky boots.

She shrugged and remained silent.

"Did you miss me?" Paul grabbed Marissa's arm, causing her to turn and face him.

She wanted to tell him "no," but made the mistake of looking him in his familiar eyes.

"At first." She pulled from his grasp and resumed walking. She didn't want to tell him that it hadn't really ended, that she still missed him. Hated him. Wanted him gone, but missed the closeness they'd once shared. The security he offered. The peace of mind. The love.

Marissa looked at her boots.

"Well, I missed you."

"Why?" She stopped and turned to search his face. If he was going to make her participate in this talk, she was going to ask the hard questions. And maybe be a little snide and hateful too. "Couldn't find anyone else willing to spread her thighs in your bed, huh?"

"No. That isn't it." He blushed. "It's because nothing was the same without you. Nothing was as fun."

She glared at him. "It was your choice."

"Well, I changed my mind." He reached out to grab her arm again. This time she eluded his grasp and took several quick steps to get out of his reach.

He stopped, standing in the snow-packed street. "I want you back."

"Go to hell." She kept on walking. The words didn't make her feel as good as she'd hoped.

Paul raced to catch up with her. Touched her. Like old times.

She wanted the old times. She turned to face him, hated tears pouring down her face. "I hate you." That wasn't as satisfying as she'd hoped, either. Maybe it wasn't loud enough. "I hate you!" she screamed.

He shook his head. "I don't believe you."

"Believe it."

He shook his head more vehemently. "I can't."

"Why not?" The words came out as sobs. She stumbled away from him.

"Marissa. I love you."

"Bull shit." This time she stopped and turned to face him, impatiently dashing the tears from her eyes with the back of her hand. "You love me so much that the mere thought that I might have been pregnant with your baby sent you high-tailing it." She yelled it at him, heedless of whether or not anyone was near enough to hear. "'Don't call me,' you said. 'Don't write me. I don't want to know,' you said. 'Here's some money for an abortion,' you said. 'Murder the baby, but don't tell me about it,' you said." A sob escaped her throat. "And then you left."

Paul reached for Marissa, but she slapped away his hands.

"I didn't say 'murder the baby.'"

"It's what you meant. You told me abortion was murder and then told me to get one."

"I know. I'm sorry. I shouldn't have. But you didn't, did you?"

"Go away," she managed between sobs.

"But you didn't have an abortion, did you?"

Marissa could see that Paul believed he knew the answer or he would never have asked the question. He'd have expected her to tell her mother, who would have told his mother. And since the shit hadn't hit the fan, he would be reasonably certain that she hadn't had an abortion. Unless she'd kept it all a secret. She knew he had to have wondered that, because that was the iffy thing. They both knew she could keep a secret.

Tears still streamed down her cheeks. She wasn't sure if she was crying over her abandonment or her baby's. It was all too raw. Her feelings were so close to the surface that it took everything she had not to blurt out the truth.

She wanted to tell him everything, but she couldn't. He believed nothing had happened. And, despite knowing the truth, she wanted to believe it too. She wanted them to be how they'd been before. She wanted her hopes and dreams intact. If she told him about the baby, it would end all chance of her ever having that, of ever having Paul again. And for some illogical, self-destructive, insane, revisionist-history reason, having Paul again was important. Marissa shook her head.

"I knew you didn't." His relieved smile said it all. "I knew that if push came to shove, you wouldn't be able to. But I'm so glad that it didn't come to that." He looked at the night sky as if in thanks.

Marissa blew her nose and watched Paul revel in ignorance.

"I was so scared that day. I thought you'd be pregnant, and my life would be ruined. I freaked." He put his hand on her arm in apology. "I was an ass. But I've done a lot of thinking since then, and I've grown up a lot. That wouldn't happen now."

Marissa looked at him in disbelief, knowing full well that he'd do it again in a heartbeat.

He caught her look. "No, really. I've learned to accept my mistakes and work through them. That's why I needed to talk to you. Breaking up with you was a mistake. We were so good together and will be again if you'll just give me the chance."

"How do I know it won't happen again?" Marissa eyed him skeptically. "Other than by never letting you near me?"

She tried to summon their baby's face, to make it superimpose on Paul, but she couldn't. Maybe the baby's features had been too generic. Maybe it was Paul's ignorance. Maybe it was his fervent belief in the future she'd once hoped they would share. She didn't know, but somehow looking at Paul made her forget their son. Could Paul make her forget it for good? If there was even a chance, she'd take it.

She had been happy with Paul before. She could be happy again if…if she could somehow forget the nightmare memories of what she'd been through and what she'd done.

"I'm asking for another chance. A chance to prove to you how good I am for you. How good we are together."

"I don't know, Paul." She frowned and shook her head. This was insane. How could she even contemplate going back to him? "I loved you so much before. But now, I don't know if I can trust you again."

He grabbed her gloved hands and held them in his own as he faced her and pledged, "I won't ever leave you. Not unless you send me away," he amended. He looked her in the eye. "I can make you forget."

It was the only thing she wanted.

And They Meet, Not Merely By Chance

David was awake and not crying when Libby went into his room to get him up. He smiled, and her heart melted.

"Good morning, pumpkin. What a beautiful smile." She plucked him from his bed and nuzzled his warm cheek breathing in his baby smell. "Did you wake up happy just for my birthday? You are such a sweetie, yes you are."

It was the first morning since she'd gone back to work a little over a month ago that she hadn't had to scoop his sleeping form from the crib and listen to his cry of protest.

By the time she'd finished changing his pants, he had his wrinkled brow, hungry look. She grinned at him. "Let's go get that bottle." His expression cleared when she picked him up.

She retrieved the bottle from the pan on the stove, tested it on her wrist, and settled into the recliner. Mother and son gazed into each other's eyes. "I love you, sweetie." And she felt that love reflected back. Her heart was as warm and soft as a freshly baked cookie.

His eyelashes were so long and black; his sweet cheeks rounded and gently pulsing as he drank; his warm body molded into hers like a puzzle piece. This was all she wanted for her birthday.

Soft, classical music came on in the kitchen. Libby didn't have to glance at the clock to know they had five minutes to get out the door. Just because it was her birthday didn't mean she had the day off.

§

Libby was seated at the reception desk listening to the messages on the machine when Cheryl came in with a bouquet of balloons.

"Happy Birthday!"

Libby smiled, taking the balloons from Cheryl and setting them on the floor beside her desk where they gently bobbed and swayed. David would love the bright colors and motion. "Thanks."

"I know you didn't really want to have plans, but you can't stay at home on your birthday. Let's grab a bite after work. Nothing fancy."

Libby shook her head. "I really can't, I have to get David."

"I talked to Ann. It's all set. Jack will meet us for a drink, and then we'll go somewhere and eat."

"Well, I guess it's all settled then." Libby smiled in uneasy resignation. Sometimes she felt swept away by Cheryl's take-charge attitude, but she hadn't learned how to tell her friend "no."

§

The bar was dimly lit and fairly empty when Libby and Cheryl walked in. Libby never felt comfortable in bars. What few memories she had of them involved manning the table while her friends or sister danced.

"Happy Hour will start soon. You want to sit by the dance floor?"

"How about here?" Libby chose a table near the bar, catching their reflection as she sat. She recognized Cheryl instantly, but it surprised her to realize the second pretty woman was her. The scale at work said she was down another ten pounds, but she hadn't seen it herself until now.

The cocktail waitress arrived as soon as they were seated. They placed their orders and started a tab.

Cheryl checked her watch. "It's almost 6:00. I wonder what's taking Jack so long?" She glanced around the bar, looking for her husband. "I'm going to go call him." She unhooked her purse from the back of the chair and left.

Libby sat looking idly around the bar, listening to the music over the speakers. She smoothed the leg of the black wool-crepe pants she'd gotten herself at an after-Christmas sale along with the black turtleneck and fitted leopard-print jacket. She'd made good use of the after Christmas sales. She'd had to since nothing from before David fit anymore. She looked at the table tents. One listed the live entertainment for the month. The band for tonight was called Jazz Junction.

The waitress delivered the drinks. Libby smiled and thanked her.

Muskrat Love played on the overhead speakers. *Captain and Tennille.* She never cared for the song. "Sam is so skinny." Implying Muskrat Suzie wasn't. Why was everybody obsessed with weight?

Beautiful people were starting to sift into the bar. Each woman was slimmer and prettier than the next. Alone at the table with a glass of Merlot untasted in front of her, Libby glanced at her watch. What was taking Cheryl so long?

A far-too handsome man stood across the table from her. "Mind if I sit down?"

She blinked at him. There were empty tables, granted not as many as when she and Cheryl had arrived, but there was no need for him to want to sit with her.

"I'm waiting for some friends." Libby mentally winced over how cliché that sounded, but then his line had been clichéd as well. Besides, he looked like a cliché: tall, dark and handsome.

"So am I." He nodded at an empty chair. "Maybe we could wait together."

Libby shrugged to hide her confusion. Cheryl wasn't there. Why would a good-looking guy like this want to sit with her?

"But I really am waiting for someone."

"So am I." His was a full smile that made his eyes sparkle and crinkle at the corners.

Libby knew her own smile was over-broad. She felt it stretch her face uncomfortably. This guy was easily six-one, maybe taller, with wavy hair the color of good chocolate and nearly as irresistible. He was far too handsome to be talking to her, yet his eyes didn't skim off of her to assess the rest of the women in the room. Instead, those warm brown eyes looked at her as if she were the only woman there.

Blood surged to her face in a heated wave. She touched her cheek though there was no way to conceal the blush. Libby's mind went blank, but her mouth opened to say something. She was saved from embarrassing herself by the sound of Cheryl's voice.

"Jeff, you made it! I'm so glad."

He rose out of his seat to kiss her cheek.

Somehow, Libby managed to close her mouth as her gaze darted between the two. They knew each other.

"Is Jack with you?" Cheryl turned her head looking for her missing husband.

"He should be along any minute." Jeff pulled out a chair for Cheryl. "Dad stopped in at the office and wanted to go over some figures, so Jack told me to hurry over to meet you and your friend." He smiled at Libby.

Libby felt a resurgence of heat to her cheeks. She stared at her wine glass. Why hadn't Cheryl warned her it wouldn't just be the three of them tonight?

Cheryl nudged Libby under the table.

Libby looked up into Jeff's warm, brown eyes. He extended his hand. "Jeff McCann."

Libby took his hand, automatically. It all made sense now. He must have recognized Cheryl's coat on the chair. That was why he'd asked if her could sit down. She wished he'd said so to begin with.

His warm hand engulfed hers, holding it instead of shaking it as she expected him to.

"L-l-l-libby." Ugh. She stammered over her own name. Libby repeated it hoping she sounded more confident the second time. "Libby Armstrong."

His eyes captivated her. Her heart froze for a moment. Could someone like him really be attracted to someone like her? Not that there was anything wrong with her. It's just that guys tended to look at other girls this way, not her.

"Oh, I'm sorry. I thought you'd already met. Libby, this is Jack's brother, Jeff." Cheryl's words allowed Libby to reclaim her hand, if not her dignity. She'd been staring like this guy was an open packet of Oreos or something.

Jeff grinned at his sister-in-law as he sat down.

He turned a good-humored grin on Libby. "My official title is actually either 'Dan and Ann's youngest son, Jeff' or 'Jack's brother, Jeff.'"

A familiar disappointment pricked her. She'd misread his interest. He was just a nice guy. That was all. Libby felt herself relax. This she knew.

Cheryl hit Jeff's arm. "Watch it or I'll introduce you as my brother-in-law."

"Anything but that," Jeff moaned in false horror.

"Jeff and Jack are partners at McCann Construction, but Jeff runs the building and supply store, and Jack is head of construction," Cheryl explained. "You knew Jack was in business with his brother, didn't you?"

"Uh, yeah. I think so." She made the mistake of looking at him. He was so handsome he looked like he should be on a magazine cover instead of across the table from her. "I just didn't know his brother was so…" She bit her tongue. Had she really been about to say it aloud? "Uh…I mean, that he was… that they were… in business together." Good, Libby, very good. Sound like an idiot, why don't you?

If Jeff had laughed, Libby would have crawled under the table and died, but he didn't. He smiled as if he had no idea what she'd almost said and had only heard what she'd actually managed to get out.

"I can understand your confusion. I look at the amount of work

I do and the piddly little that he does, and I can't believe we are in business together, either."

"Hey," Jack slid into the empty chair. "I heard that. And I resemble that remark."

Everyone at the table laughed, and the tension in Libby's shoulders eased.

Cheryl sidled up beside Libby as they moved next door to the restaurant. "I think Jeff likes you."

Just the thought of if made Libby warm all over. "You're kidding, right?" This conversation felt like one Libby should have had in junior high. It made her want to laugh.

"Do you like him?"

Libby laughed. This *was* a junior high conversation. She was thirty-two, and she felt as awkward as a thirteen-year-old. Did she like him? Of course, she liked him. Who wouldn't like someone who looked at them with eyes that said, "You're special?" She liked him all right, but she'd probably misread him. He was a hunky, successful businessman. She was a single mother of a newborn. She froze. That was it. He looked interested because he didn't know about David.

The men were deep in a discussion when they sat at the table. "What do you think, Libby?" Jack asked after the waitress left. "Did you watch the inauguration?"

Cheryl groaned. "No politics, Jack. This is Libby's birthday."

At the moment, she preferred politics to thinking about what she felt for Jeff, what he might feel for her, and whether or not he knew about David. "I didn't catch the inauguration itself, but I watched the speech."

Jeff winked at Libby.

Her heart skipped a beat, and she felt her cheeks get warm. Had he really winked at her?

Jack smiled. "Cheryl refused to. She's still a bit testy because she wanted to re-elect Carter."

"I knew I shouldn't have told you." Cheryl glared at her husband, but she ruined the effect by smiling. She turned to Libby. "We always cancel each other out. Every election he tries to convince me that I shouldn't bother voting, but I have to. I know he's going to vote, and I need to neutralize him."

Jeff laughed. "Neutralize him? Cheryl, it will take more than a vote to neutralize him. Maybe you should just neuter him instead. I hear geldings are much less trouble."

Cheryl laughed. "Really? Now, there's a thought." She looked at her husband and winked.

"Say, now," Jack protested.

Jeff leaned toward Libby. "Jack's kind of a wild man when it comes to politics. He's just a mite competitive in everything. It's why we should probably change the subject."

Jack gave his brother a steady look. "Don't listen to him. He's as bad as I am."

Jeff shrugged and sat back in his chair.

"So," Jack continued, "what do you think of our new president?"

Jeff laughed. "That's my brother's not-so-subtle way of asking who you voted for. Don't feel you need to tell him anything."

Libby smiled at Jeff. He'd done that all night, explained inside jokes so that she felt more comfortable. "Happiness or disappointment aside, I think it was telling that the Ayatollah released the hostages right before the inauguration."

"Listen to her, Jeff. Libby's not just another pretty face."

"I know." Jeff's smile warmed Libby.

"But who did she vote for?" Jack insisted. "I don't think I could stand for you to be involved with a Democrat. Cheryl's about all I can stand."

"Jack," Jeff growled at his brother. "That's enough."

"Well, you voted, didn't you?"

Libby's smiled faded. She hadn't.

"You didn't vote?" Jack looked shocked.

"Jack," Cheryl scolded.

Jeff covered Libby's hand with his large, warm one. "Libby's son was born the day before the election. I'd be surprised if it even dawned on her to go out and vote. If he were my son, I'd have forgotten all about the whole election."

Libby stared at Jeff. He knew about David.

"Cheryl told me."

Libby's face felt all aflame. He knew about David and he still seemed to like her.

"You really didn't vote?" Jack repeated.

"I'm sorry, Libby." Cheryl's face was red as she shot out of her chair, grabbed her husband's hand, and spoke through clenched teeth. "Will you excuse us a second?"

Jeff continued to look Libby in the eye. "Do you have a picture of him? Your David?"

Realizing her jaw had dropped, Libby closed her mouth. What did asking to see David's picture mean? Was he truly interested in her or just being polite? His eyes looked warm and sincere, but guys like Jeff weren't interested in women with small children. Who was she kidding? Men hadn't been interested in her even before David.

"Picture of David? Yes, of course, I have one." She reached for her purse. Her heart beat in a strange cadence. Jeff was such a nice guy. All night he'd paid attention to her, listened like her words mattered, and explained family jokes to her so she felt at home. He'd even touched her hand once or twice.

She pulled out a recent snapshot of David.

His hand touched hers as he took the photo. He looked at it, really looked at it, not the brief glance most people would have given it. "He's beautiful, or maybe I should say handsome. He's got a nice head of hair."

"Thank you."

He handed the photo back to her.

She looked at the photo before putting it away. Of course she thought David was beautiful, but she was his mother.

"I have to apologize for Jack. He's normally not so over-the-top like that. It's my fault, really. I asked him to take Cheryl off for a bit, so I could ask you out to dinner, but Cheryl doesn't take subtle hints well. So, he pushed the envelope. He's usually not obnoxious, and he doesn't care that much about politics. Or whether or not someone voted." He paused and smiled at Libby. "I'm babbling.

"He wasn't that ob..." She looked at Jeff. "You really asked Jack to leave so you could ask me to dinner?" That had to be the nicest compliment a man had ever given her.

"Yes. I suppose I could have asked you out with Jack and Cheryl there, but I didn't want you to feel pressured. I would really like to see you again."

For an instant, the world stood still. "I'd like that, too." She smiled into his chocolate, brown eyes and felt like a character in a sappy movie. The one where the gorgeous, perfect man sees past the geeky, unpolished, social misfit exterior of the protagonist to her wonderful inside and falls desperately in love with her while the evil-yet-beautiful girl seethes and plots revenge. The movies Libby never believed were possible but always wanted to come true.

"I'm glad. I heard the new theatre in Putnam Heights is doing dinner theatre every Saturday night. Jack and Cheryl went a couple of weeks ago. I can't remember the name of the play, but they said it was good. Would you like to go?"

Under the table, Libby gave her arm a hard pinch. Jeff was there waiting. "Yes, I'd love to."

§

The phone rang as Libby took off her coat and unstrapped David from his car seat later that evening.

"Hi, Libby, it's Jeff."

Libby's smile faded. He was calling to cancel. She forced a smile. It was okay. She had David. "Hi."

"I know it's against some rule to call you this soon, but I wanted to tell you how much fun I had tonight. And how happy I was to meet you. I'm really looking forward to Saturday night."

"Me too." She laughed. "And if there is a rule about calling, I'm glad you broke it."

Forty minutes later, Libby hung up the phone. David was asleep in her arms. She floated to his room and tucked him into his crib. The refrain from a South Pacific show tune played in her head, something about being in love with a wonderful guy.

She was smiling so much she had a hard time brushing her teeth. She laughed. Who would have thought a guy like him and a girl like her... Libby looked in the mirror at the trim woman before her and her smile dimmed a few watts. Did he like her or this body? Had she been the heavy Libby, the normal Libby, would he have looked at her twice? If he'd been fat, would she have looked at him?

Of course, she would have.

She closed her eyes.

No matter what the mirror said, she was still heavy in her head. Jeff's good looks had almost had the opposite effect—put off rather than attract. Had he been fat or ugly, she'd have felt more comfortable from the start. It was easier to see inside an imperfect body than a perfect one. She'd given the beautiful Jeff a chance because he was Cheryl's brother-in-law. Was she really as prejudiced against beautiful, skinny people as some were against fat or ugly ones? She finished getting ready for bed. Would she have missed out on the wonderful person Jeff was if she'd been fat or Cheryl hadn't invited him?

Libby crawled between the cold sheets, shivering until she built a pocket of warmth around her. Her heart grew warm. Jeff liked her.

Paul, Again

An insistent, high-pitched beep yanked Marissa from a blissfully dreamless sleep and dropped her into the reality of her dorm room and the naked man snoring beside her. She crawled over Paul's body to silence the alarm. Well, that explained the lack of dreams. When you started making the stupid, nightmarish mistakes in reality, there was no need to dream about them. Next, she'd attend class naked or discover it was time for the final in a class she'd never gone to.

She got out of bed, slipped on her thick terrycloth robe, and tied the belt.

Had she really slept with him?

"You're not going to leave me, are you?"

She turned at the sound of Paul's voice. "I have accounting at 8:00 a.m."

"Couldn't you skip it?"

The old Marissa wouldn't have hesitated. The old Paul wouldn't have asked. As much as their relationship looked the same from the outside, it was different this time.

She shook her head.

"Come on, Rissa. I'm skipping all my classes to be here."

"I know." But she hadn't asked him to.

"You're on The Dean's List. You can afford to skip a class now and again."

She turned on him. "I'm on The Dean's List because I *don't* skip classes now and again. This is my future I'm preparing for."

Paul sat up. "Whoa, Riss, calm down. It's just one class, not that big a deal." His voice quieted to a whisper. "Someone sure got up on the wrong side of the bed."

Marissa bit her tongue. She *was* overreacting. It *was* just one class. Still. She took a deep, cleansing breath. "Sorry. Not enough sleep, I guess."

"So, you coming back to bed?" He held the covers open invitingly. His naked, half-aroused body was showcased between the blue, polka dot sheets.

She shook her head. "I'm up. You go back to sleep, though. I'll be back in an hour-and-a-half, and we'll go to breakfast." She wished he'd get mad and leave in protest. She watched him, silently daring him.

He yawned and pulled the blankets back over his body. "Okay. Rain check." He closed his eyes.

Or almost closed his eyes. Marissa didn't doubt that he watched her dress through his lashes. The thought both angered and excited her. Everything about Paul seemed to anger and excite her. Every request he made seemed like a test of power to her. A question of *did she love him?* Would she do this small thing for him? It felt as if he were testing his level of influence over her. Every "no" made her stronger, harder, angrier. How could he ask anything of her?

Then, he'd back down or she'd back down, and that was even worse, somehow. She felt he backed down out of strength and that she did it out of weakness. It was all about control. Or it was to her. She knew she'd lost it with her first *yes,* and a million *nos* wouldn't get it back.

The Date: Act One

On Saturday night, Libby checked her hair in the hallway mirror and smoothed the sides of her new dress before reaching down to tug at its hem. It was a beautiful crushed velvet dress, one that a few months ago she wouldn't have considered for fear that it would make her look like a sofa cushion. The pearl pendant on her necklace hit in precisely the right spot. No, she didn't look like furniture, but she was showing a bit more cleavage than she normally liked.

"What do you think of Mommy's red dress?"

David was loosely strapped into his car seat watching as she got ready.

"Auntie Cheryl says this red dress is perfect, but don't you think it's a tad short and shows too much of Mommy's legs?" She pointed at her legs as she looked at him.

David grinned. She took one last look at the thinner, sexier woman in the mirror. She still wasn't sure how she had let Cheryl talk her into buying the dress. Or how she'd lost the weight in the first place.

She shrugged her shoulders and turned back to unbuckle David. "Come here, sweetie."

She kissed David and was rewarded with a wide, toothless grin. "Can you believe Mommy has a date?" She spun them both around the room. David squealed in delight. "Me neither." There was no answer to the weight issue. She had never understood why the same hot fudge sundae that stuck to her hips didn't affect her sister's weight at all. Or hadn't. *I sure miss you, Jen. You would have loved David.* Breath caught in her chest as she looked at her little boy. Would she have David if Jenny had lived? If Jenny had been alive, she wouldn't have been in Eau Claire the day he was born. She cradled her son, sickened by the thought. What would have happened to him if she hadn't been there to pick him up?

Libby shook her head. *I had him in the bathroom. I didn't even know I was pregnant.* The sick feeling in her stomach remained.

But Jenny *had* died, and Libby *had* been there. She nuzzled David's neck, making him smile. He was safe. She checked his diaper and carried him to his room to change it.

"Jeff and the new babysitter should be here soon." He didn't understand her, but she talked to him as if he did. He listened attentively as she told him about the things that he'd be doing that day.

"You have a new babysitter who will be watching you tonight. She's sat for Devon, Lindsey and Becky a lot and knows just how to take care of good little boys like you." She taped the clean diaper closed and blew a raspberry on her son's fat little belly, laughing at his squeal.

The doorbell rang as she lifted her son. "Sounds like they're here."

Jeff stayed in the living room while Libby took the babysitter around, showing her where everything was and telling her about David's schedule. She watched the pretty, long-haired brunette, looking for signs of competence.

"He'll want a bottle in another hour or so. Heat the bottle in the pan of water. The microwave gets it too hot."

"Okay."

"I'm sorry if I seem a little protective. Cheryl says you're wonderful. It's just that you're David's first sitter, other than Jeff's mother."

"Don't worry, I understand. I'll heat the bottle in the pan. That's the way I used to do it when Devon was little."

Libby smiled. "I don't know what else to tell you. I left the number of the theatre by the phone."

"Don't worry, Libby. David will be just fine with me. Go and have a good time."

"Thanks." She handed David to the girl and watched as the young woman handled him confidently.

Jeff stood and took the car keys from his pocket. "Shall we?"

As Libby walked to the closet to get her coat, she kept her eyes on her little boy in the sitter's arms. "David loves to look at books and things. There are plenty of books and toys in the basket next to the couch."

"We'll be fine." The babysitter followed the couple to the front door.

Libby watched her take David's little hand and wave it. "Bye, Mommy. See you soon."

Libby took a deep breath and smiled. "Thank you."

Jeff pulled the car onto the street. "She seems competent. I know Cheryl really likes her."

Libby smiled. "Do I seem as nervous as I feel?"

"Well, I'm not sure how nervous you feel, but you looked just fine. Actually, better than fine. You look fabulous in that dress."

Libby felt her face heat. "Thank you."

§

Libby was laughing at a story Jeff told when the waiter stopped at the table. "Miss, was your Beef Wellington not to your liking?"

Libby looked at the plate, surprised to find there was food there. As a charter member of the clean plate club, she couldn't remember not being able to finish a meal before. "It was wonderful, just too much."

"Would you like me to wrap it for you?"

Leftovers. From a restaurant, no less. The thought tickled her. "Please."

"So, did you end up keeping the dog?"

"How could we not? You are what you eat. So, with Dad's shoe, Mom's purse, Jack's mitten and my sock in its belly, that chow hound was already part of the family."

Libby shook her head. "Jenny and I never had a dog, growing up. I'd like to get one for David when he's older." She couldn't quite hide her smirk. "Would you recommend a chow hound?"

Jeff laughed. "Well, my mother never had to tell Jack and me to pick up our stuff. If we left it out, it was gone."

"Would you like something to sip on during the performance? A grasshopper or something?"

Libby considered for a moment, being full had never stopped her from eating or drinking before. "No, I'm good, but you've reminded me of a joke."

"Great, let's hear it."

Libby smiled. "Okay, here goes: A grasshopper hops into a bar. The bartender looks up and says, 'Hey, grasshopper, welcome. You know, we have a drink named after you.' The grasshopper looks up and says, 'Really, you have a drink called Larry?'" She held her breath, waiting for his reaction.

He laughed, seeming genuinely amused, and her spirit lifted even higher.

Then the waiter returned with an elaborately formed tinfoil swan containing Libby's leftovers. "Can I get you anything else? Ten minutes until curtain."

When he left, Libby turned to Jeff. "Would you mind if I called home? It's the first time I've left David with anyone but your mother and…"

"Don't worry about it. I've seen Cheryl when they have a new sitter watching the kids. She always phones home. This sitter is a good one, though. Cheryl and Jack have her a lot." He winked at her. "Besides, I like it that you are so devoted to your son."

Libby hummed a tune as she wound her way to the lobby. The sitter picked up on the third ring.

"Hi, this is Libby. How is everything going?"

"Fine. I just put David in bed."

"I'm calling because I forgot to tell you what you could have to eat. There's a pizza in the freezer and soda in the garage, and there's some popcorn in the cupboard above the microwave. The play is going to start soon, so the earliest I'll be back is eleven-thirty."

"No rush. Everything is great here. Don't worry. I'll treat him like he was my own."

Like he was her own. Libby shivered as if someone had just walked over her grave. Why did the sitter have to say that? She knew it was meant to be comforting. It was the attitude she should want and expect from a good baby-sitter. Yet the words dogged her heels all the way back to the table.

The Date: Act Two

Marissa hung up the phone and walked into the living room. She plopped herself on the couch and reached for the television remote.

She didn't understand herself lately. This was the third babysitting job she'd had in just over a week. Last Saturday she'd watched the McCann kids. Tuesday night she sat for her sociology professor's newborn and now David Armstrong. Paul teased her that it was almost as if she liked kids now. She didn't know what it was, exactly. She felt the same toward kids. They attracted and repulsed her in equal measure. It was as if babysitting was an obsession now. Children, especially infants, were a sore tooth that she couldn't seem to leave alone.

Like an allergic person craving the allergen. This Armstrong boy was the best and the worst. He was the right age and gender to apply the perfect pain. It was so stupid, but she couldn't help herself. Was she looking for absolution? If she was good enough to these other people's kids could it make up for how horrible she'd been to her own?

She didn't know. The need to psychoanalyze herself was probably some remnant of last semester's stupid psychology class. Did normal people think like this?

David's cry reached her as she struggled to figure it out.

She walked down the hall to his bedroom. The baby lay on his back, wailing. He looked so angry.

"What's your problem, David?" She scooped him up, and he quieted. "Bad dream?" *Did babies this age dream?* she wondered as she checked his diaper. Dry. What kind of milky dreams could this little tyke have? Nothing had happened in his life to give him the type of nightmares she had.

She carried him to the kitchen to heat another bottle. If he were her baby, she'd kiss that chubby little cheek. She rubbed her cheek against his, and he turned his face, open mouthed, looking for the nipple. The rooting instinct. Psych 101. Meant to help the baby find the breast.

As if on cue, her breasts ached like they hadn't in nearly a month. If he had been hers and she'd been nursing...

She abandoned that thought.

Paul had noticed the difference in her breasts, but had accepted her claim of exercise and sexual arousal as the reason.

The bottle had to be warm by now. She covered the end of the nipple with her thumb and shook the bottle as she carried David to the rocker recliner.

While he drank, Marissa examined her small charge. She stroked his face and blew on his downy hair to watch it dance. Libby was so lucky. He was the perfect baby. Gerber-esque, if that were a word. Marissa held his little hand and smiled through over-moist eyes as his little fingers wrapped tightly around one of her own. What would it hurt if she pretended that he was her son for a little while?

His mouth grew lax around the nipple, and a little saliva dripped down his cheek.

Marissa nuzzled his head with her nose, breathing in the scent of him, reveling in the warm, clean smell of her son.

Stop it! She scolded herself abruptly. That way lay madness. He's *not* your son. She got out of the chair and carried David to his crib.

David Armstrong was Libby's baby. You abandoned your baby, and some dowdy woman driving a blue Ford four-door with LDY on the plates picked him up. You aren't worthy to touch this baby. Tears raced down her cheeks. If only it had been a dream. She knew it was the lack of consequences that tempted her to believe it had all been nothing but a feverish nightmare. A large part of her wanted to embrace the illusion.

Standing near the door to the baby's room, Marissa looked at Libby's son. He wasn't hers, and she nearly hated him for it. Hated Libby, too for doing what she should have done. Why had Libby embraced her child when Marissa had abandoned hers?

A year ago she'd have declared another woman in her position unfit. People who abandon children don't deserve to see them again. Ever.

You are unfit. An unfit mother.

Marissa fled from David's room, threw herself on the couch and sobbed into the cushion. She'd thrown away her baby.

"I'm sorry," she sobbed as the image of her newborn son played in her head. "I'm so sorry. I didn't mean for you to be gone forever. I was just so scared. I didn't mean to throw you away for good."

The pillow was still damp long after her eyes were dry. He was gone. Why couldn't she just forget it? She hated the heavy feeling she got in her heart every time she did this. She was so damned tired of being sad. When could she be done? When would she be normal again? What did she have to do to make things right?

§

The clock on the microwave read 9:00 when Marissa got the bag of popcorn out of the cabinet. She walked to the garage door and tugged it open. She looked for the promised soda on the floor next to the door. There were several kinds, and she felt the wall for a light switch so she could see to make her choice.

With a flick of the switch, the garage was instantly ablaze with light. Marissa pulled a can of Diet 7-Up out of its cardboard carton and turned back to the kitchen door. She had the door open and her finger on the light switch before the appearance of the car registered: a late model blue Ford four-door.

Could it be?

She turned slowly back to the car to take a closer look. It wasn't possible. She went around back, checked the license plate and her heart did a flip.

This was the car.

The blue Ford four-door with LDY plates.

It all came back to her in a rush—the coolness of the day, the weak, wobbly feeling in her legs, the trash caught in the long grass, her son in a tan cloth duffel bag, and the blue Ford with the LDY plates. She dropped the can of 7-Up, and it went spewing across the garage floor.

Marissa found herself in the kitchen. She didn't remember turning off the garage light or closing the door and walking back to the kitchen, but she must have done so. The refrigerator hummed, and the clock on the wall marked the passage of time with a faint tick. Dazed, Marissa sank into a kitchen chair.

Libby had the car, but the woman at the store wasn't Libby. The woman at the store was heavy and dumpy and middle-aged—maternal looking. Libby was slim and pretty and looked to be in her mid-twenties. Who was that other woman? Who was Libby? She didn't even dare to think about David and who he was, not yet.

Marissa rose to her feet and walked into the living room. There were pictures there, she remembered. Marissa scoured the room, examining each photo she could find. Three young children and a pretty, dark-haired couple. The woman looked like a darker version of Libby. A sister, maybe.

Pictures of David. Snapshots. Professional. With Libby. Alone.

Marissa stopped.

She stared at a picture of the three kids, a little older than they appeared in the first photo, and a heavyset woman with a blue car. Marissa snatched up the photo and studied it. The car was the one in the garage, and the woman was Libby. A heavy Libby, but Libby, nevertheless. Marissa was sure of it.

Marissa stared at the photo without really seeing it. If Libby were the woman that day, then…

David's cry from the other room startled Marissa from her reverie. She dropped the picture.

David?

She raced to the room and scooped him up.

"Baby, my baby," she crooned, holding him firmly to her chest.

Secure and comfortable in Marissa's warm arms, David stopped crying and opened his eyes.

Marissa stared into eyes that had been blue black the last time she had seen them and now were brown. She wanted to see her red-faced, crooked-chinned newborn in this round cheeked peaches-and-cream baby, but she couldn't, not really.

Still, he was hers. Wasn't he?

That picture of Libby? Was she pregnant there or just fat?

Doubt nibbled at the corner of her brain. Doubt that she couldn't allow, not if…

She walked into David's room and grabbed a diaper bag that sat ready near the door. Marissa didn't recognize that she'd made a decision until the strap was in her hand. She was taking David.

Dinner

On stage, the play progressed like a series of Kodak Her life was better than fantasy commercials where Paul Anka sang, "Celebrate the moments of your life." Libby's eyes brimmed. Jeff reached over and held her hand.

She glanced his way, and their eyes met. The tenderness in his eyes was more romantic than anything happening on the stage. She melted against him.

This didn't feel like a first date. After a week's worth of phone conversations, being with Jeff was as comfortable as a pajama Saturday.

His thumb gently stroked the back of her hand. Her eyes were on the play, but her mind focused on his thumb. Round and round. Could there be a happily-ever-after for Jeff and her? Was happily-ever-after real or just something she wanted to believe in, like love at first sight? But love at first sight was real. She'd loved David at first sight and Jenny's kids. And Jeff.

She knew of no happily-ever-after stories. Her parents hadn't had one and neither had Jenny. But that didn't mean she couldn't, did it? Miracles happened. David was proof. Why couldn't Jeff be, as well?

The applause startled her. She'd missed the end of the play. *That's okay,* she thought as Jeff helped her on with her coat.

§

They drove home slowly through the snowbank-lined streets.

"I had a wonderful time tonight."

He smiled. "I'm glad. I did, too."

"Do you ever wish a night didn't have to end?"

His chuckle warmed her. "Like tonight? Yes, but I thought I was taking the sitter home."

"You could come back." She winced. "That sounded bad."

He chuckled. "I thought it sounded wonderful." He pulled into her driveway and turned off the car.

"You'll think I'm easy."

He pulled her into his arms.

"No. I think we are on the same page. That we've been on the same page from the start." His kiss took her breath away. "You invited me back for coffee. I'll come back for coffee."

The heck with coffee. She'd take his kiss. And maybe something more. His tongue caressed hers. Someone moaned softly. Libby was afraid it was her. Afraid she was too needy. But he made her want things and remember dreams she'd all but forgotten.

Libby broke the embrace. Looking into his eyes, she saw mirrored there the love and desire she felt. Love? Maybe not yet. She might feel as if they'd known each other forever, but it had only been one date. Still, the feelings she had and those she saw were not simply desire. There was something more, something deeper. There had to be.

"Jeff." Libby was a little short of breath. She pulled her hands out of his suit coat. How had they gotten there? She looked into his eyes. She had no idea what she wanted to say. "I..." *I what? I want you. I think I love you? I wish I didn't seem as desperate as I'm afraid I do?*

He kissed her nose. "I'll drop off the sitter and come back for coffee."

They held hands as they walked to Libby's door. The perfect gentleman, Jeff took the keys from her hand and unlocked the door. He helped Libby off with her coat, and she smiled into his eyes.

They walked into the empty living room together. Jeff sat down.

Libby expected the baby sitter to be in the living room watching TV or something. The television was on, but the house seemed unnaturally quiet. The heat she'd felt with Jeff evaporated. Libby shivered.

"Marissa is probably changing his diaper or something." She hurried out of the living room.

David's bedroom door was open, so Libby saw before she reached it that Marissa wasn't at the changing table. Ice filled Libby's stomach. Oh please, God, please. She quickened her step to peer into the crib.

Empty.

No baby. No blanket.

"David." His name caught in her throat; ripped at her heart.

Tears filled her eyes as she spun toward the door. She ran to her own room across the way and the spare one down the hall. Both were empty, just as she'd feared.

Every inch of her was cold when she stumbled back into the living room.

Jeff looked up from the magazine he'd been looking at.

"Libby?" He rushed to her. "Libby, what's wrong? Where's Marissa?"
No words could break free of the cold. She shook her head. Ice shards sliced her eyes before sliding down her cheeks.

Jeff gathered her in his arms and held her close for a moment.

"Something must have happened," he reasoned aloud. "There must be a note."

Libby looked up at Jeff. She would have given anything to have made a note appear. Anything.

They searched everywhere, the kitchen, the bedrooms, the bathroom and the living room—to no avail. Sick with fear, Libby went to the garage.

She opened the door and flung on the light. A crushed can of 7-Up lay in a puddle on the floor of the otherwise empty garage.

The car was gone.

David was gone.

Libby's world blackened and crumbled.

§

She came to on her couch, wrapped in an afghan. It seemed horribly unfair that she woke up knowing that David was gone. *Please, God, keep him safe.* She didn't even have the grace of a second of disoriented peace before the memory returned. No, the crushing weight of knowledge was there the instant she awoke. Tears blurred her eyes. It was odd that the house looked the same. Shouldn't it be gray or something?

Jeff was in the kitchen, talking on the phone. She watched him through the arch that separated the two rooms. She could tell he was talking to the police by the answers he was giving, the times, their names, her address.

He glanced her way, noticed that she was watching him. "She's awake now. I've gotta go." He hung up the phone and was at Libby's side in an instant.

"Libby, honey. How are you?"

He looked so worried that Libby wanted to tell him that she would be okay, but she couldn't get around the numbness that filled her. She stared at him. His image was blurred by her tears.

He took her in his arms and held her tightly. In his arms, her frozen numbness thawed a little, and pain slammed into her heart. She preferred being numb and gently disentangled herself.

Please, God, please. "David? Where's David?" Her voice sounded small and pathetic to her ear.

"The police'll find him." His brown eyes looked at her with tender concern, but she felt nothing but shock and pain.

"I called the hospitals to see if Marissa might have brought him there. But neither Sacred Heart not Luther had anyone that matched their description."

Libby nodded as tears streamed unheeded down her face.

Jeff fumbled for a handkerchief, which he pressed into Libby's hand.

She stared at it. "She took his blanket."

"Yes." Jeff's voice cracked with emotion. "She'll keep him warm."

Shortly after midnight, the police arrived. Jeff let them in.

It was an episode of *The Twilight Zone*. It only lacked Rod Serling's voice-over. Libby moved as if in a dream, answering questions, showing the detectives around the house which somehow no longer seemed like home.

The crib had grown in emptiness until it gobbled every inch of space in David's bedroom. Where was he? Her arms ached. There wasn't even his blanket for her to hold.

The police asked her if she knew why Marissa might have taken him. She knew, but didn't say. He was gone because he wasn't really hers to keep. She shook her head. No, he was hers. She loved him. She cared for him. She'd rescued him.

"When I called to check on David, she said everything was going fine. She said she'd treat him like he was her own." She wanted to vomit. Was this her fault?

The detective finished writing on his pad and looked up. "Does she have children of her own?"

Libby shrugged, unable to answer for a moment, struggling not to think about whether or not Marissa had had a baby.

"It's the first time she's sat here." Tears choked her. She wiped them away with the back of her hand. "David's never had a sitter except…" Her look at Jeff was a plea.

He nodded and finished for her. "My mother watches David while Libby works."

Any other day, Libby would have smiled her gratitude to Jeff for his help, but now she couldn't make the attempt. She should have researched Marissa. She knew nothing of her except that she babysat for Cheryl's kids. Sure, Cheryl had never steered her wrong before, but that wasn't an excuse. A good mother researched her child's caregivers herself. And she hadn't. She was a bad mother.

Jack led Libby back to the living room as he talked to the detective. Another officer stayed in the nursery. "Marissa sits a lot for my brother, Jack and his wife's kids. My sister-in-law, Cheryl highly recommended her to Libby."

Libby sank to the couch and wrapped the afghan around herself. Fatigue and sadness took a firm hold. Jeff's voice faded into the background. She was a bad mother. A horrible person. She'd taken David in the first place. Never mind that he'd been abandoned out in the cold. Never mind the welfare system that shifted kids from one foster home to the next so they never felt wanted, never felt loved. Never mind her motives. It was wrong.

She'd die if anything happened to David. She'd kill anyone who hurt him.

Libby looked at Jeff's face. When Jeff learned the truth, he was going to hate her. Where was David?

The detective asked Jeff something about Marissa and if he had had any contact with her before.

Libby felt Jeff's eyes on her as he answered.

"I've picked her up for Cheryl and Jack before, so I picked her up at the dorm for Libby tonight."

She was having a nightmare. She was in bed asleep. Any minute now, David's cries would wake her and she'd stumble to his room, grateful it had only been a dream.

A policeman crouched in front of her. His mouth moved, but the words bounced off her unheard. She didn't want to think or speak. She wanted to wake up.

A continuous movie looped through her mind. Marissa and David…Marissa and David…Marissa and David.

Marissa took David. Why would she take Libby's baby?

Jeff and the detective stepped away, leaving her to her silence and doubt.

Was David Marissa's baby?

No, David was hers. The labor came so quickly that she didn't have time to phone anyone. She had him on the bathroom floor. She had the birth certificate to prove it. SHE HAD THE BIRTH CERTIFICATE TO PROVE IT!

Images of the tan duffel bag on the sidewalk outside Kerm's and David's small, red body wrapped in a blood-stained towel kept coming back to her.

David is mine. Please, God, please. Whoever abandoned him gave up all rights to him. That made David hers. *Marissa stole my baby.*

But would the courts agree? And what would it matter what a judge ruled if she couldn't find David?

The pain was like a physical blow. Despair clung like a coat of molasses.

She listened to the voices of the officers and Jeff while they talked about her as if she weren't even there.

Jeff's voice: "You've seen this before. Will Libby be all right?"

A man: "She's had a shock. People handle these things differently. Some people scream and go crazy, some become emotionally detached, some try to lead the search themselves and some, like Miss Armstrong here, just cry."

She felt the weight of their gazes, knew on some level that their eyes would be filled with concern and questions, but she couldn't make herself care enough to look up. *Where was her baby?*

"I know this is a bit much for a first date, but she shouldn't be left alone just now. Do you know someone to call who would stay with her? A family member?"

"It's okay," Jeff answered. "I'll stay with her."

The police disappeared to search the basement and the yard.

Jeff sat next to her on the couch and pulled her close. She didn't resist. Again, the warmth of his embrace penetrated the cold shield she had erected around herself. The pain rushed in again, but this time she let it.

Tonight should have been so different. It hadn't felt like a first date at all.

She wanted to lose herself. Could she hide in his arms? Could she drown in his kisses? Would passion sweep her away for even a little while? She tilted her face and pressed her lips to his. Jeff gave her a peck, but he wouldn't cooperate when she tried to deepen the kiss. He shifted her in his arms so that his chin rested on the top of her head. She pressed herself against him wantonly, but he refused to take advantage of her offer.

"I know what you're doing, Libby, but sex isn't going to stop the pain. It's not what you need now." He pulled her close, like a child. "There will be a time, God willing, but this isn't it."

His hands stayed on her back, caressing and soothing. She was safe with him. David would have been safe too. But there was never the chance. *Oh, God, please.* She wrapped her arms around Jeff and clung to him as if he were the one thing that could save her. If she could have crawled inside him, she would have.

The detectives made calls. More people came. Fingerprints were lifted. More questions asked and answered. Libby let Jeff's arms keep away the cold numbness that threatened to swamp her.

Cheryl and Jack were suddenly standing in front of them.

"Who's got the kids?" Jeff asked Jack.

"Mom. I called her, and she came over."

Libby looked at her friend. Cheryl's hair was crushed on one side. Her open coat revealed a sweater that was on inside out. No make-up was there to be marred by the tears that streamed down her face. Cheryl looked as broken as Libby felt.

"Oh, Libby." The look on Cheryl's face said it all. She believed Libby had taken the bullet meant for her. Libby wondered how many times Marissa had watched Cheryl's kids. She left the safety of Jeff's arms and stood, opening her arms to Cheryl.

Her friend fell into them, crying.

"I'm so sorry. I don't know what could have happened. Marissa was always such a good baby sitter. I never would have recommended her if…" Her face crumpled.

"I know." She petted Cheryl's hot, damp hair. Comforting someone else was a balm to her soul. "I know. It's not your fault." Her throat grew tight. "You love David, too."

Cheryl tightened her arms around Libby and sobbed into her shoulder. Jack gently loosened Cheryl's grip and led her to where the detective was waiting to talk.

Libby sank back into the couch where Jeff still sat. She felt awkward now, next to him. Now that she wasn't in his arms, she was ashamed of her behavior. She'd thrown herself at him. This was their first and probably their last date. It was embarrassing enough that she'd clung to him and cried. She had to find David. She couldn't think of dating. Couldn't make anyone else have to go through this. He'd already done so much. Saved her from drowning. This was not what he had bargained for. She needed to thank him. For everything.

He was a wonderful guy, but no doubt he would thank God when she told him to go. She needed to find David. Make sure he was okay. Now was not the time to try to start a new relationship.

She dropped her face into her palms with a sigh. It was maybe an hour ago that she was fantasizing about a future with Jeff. An hour ago that she'd asked him to come back for coffee, that she'd fantasized of them as a family—her, David and Jeff. Now, there was nothing. No David. No family to join. Nothing. She had nothing to offer.

She needed Oreos. Their chocolaty goodness would carry her through this. Except, she didn't have any. The cabinet they used to rule was now filled with David's baby bottles and cans of formula.

Oh, God. Please don't have her life go back to Oreos and lonely nights.

She rose from the couch. David needed her. She had to find him, but had no idea where to look or what to do. The two policemen turned toward her. Their attention pinned her in place. Her heart pounded as she looked at their unreadable faces. Did they know David had been left in a bag on the cold sidewalk? Did they know she'd rescued him?

Had Marissa done that? How could she? How could anyone? It had been cold. Libby wrapped her arms around herself, but it didn't help. She was still cold. David was probably cold.

Why take David now? What if motherhood proved to be too much again? Where would Marissa leave him this time?

Libby sank back to the couch.

Jeff pulled her close again reminding her he was with her in this nightmare. Her nightmare. He didn't have to be there. No matter how much she needed someone, needed him, this was her mess. He probably wanted to go but felt obligated to stay. Too nice to hurt her.

Libby closed her eyes. She needed to do the right thing, whatever that was. Tears leaked from eyes tired of crying. She didn't know the right thing; had thought keeping David was the right thing.

She opened her eyes and sat forward, pulling out of his embrace. Cold filled the space between them. She wanted to reach for him, but wedged her hands between her knees. This wasn't Jeff's problem.

"You've been so good…" She stumbled over her words, knowing what needed to be said, but not wanting to say it. She needed someone, but it wasn't fair to him. She had nothing to offer. She needed everything she had left to find David.

"Don't." Jeff stopped her, placing his large, warm hand on her arm. "Don't thank me and send me away." He turned her by the shoulders until he could easily look into her eyes. "I need to be here as much as you need me to be. We've only just begun together…"

She could see he was struggling for the words. His eyes searched hers, gently pleading.

"But I think I want what we've started. I know I don't want to let you go until I know for sure. And, if I'm right, then I won't ever let go." He firmly held her upper arms as if fighting to resist the temptation to pull her to him. "So, please, don't tell me to go."

The warmth in Jeff's eyes offered safe haven. She wanted to grab him and hold tight. Had she been right before? Was he as ready as she'd been? Had he shared her fantasies? She knew it wasn't fair to him to let him stay, but she couldn't muster the strength to offer a second time. She nodded slightly.

"Stay."

"Thank you." He pulled her to his chest, held her tightly, almost crushing her against him.

For a moment, her heart felt the warmth it had earlier. Hope.

His embrace was too tight, as desperate as she felt. She didn't mind, didn't squirm. It was a glimpse of Heaven from her place in Hell. She felt as safe as she imagined David did when swaddled tightly.

"David." Heart-wrenching, soul-burning pain.

"We'll find him," Jeff promised, speaking into her hair. His voice sounded determined, as if by saying it, he could make it so.

Dawn came slowly; its faint fingers of light reached into the darkness, gradually pushing away the cruel night.

The police left with the night. Jeff and Jack saw them to the door while she and Cheryl huddled on the couch, clutching each other's hands. Sleep tugged at Libby's eyelids, closing them despite her efforts to the contrary.

She heard footsteps and voices from the kitchen. "Take her home," Jeff said to his brother. "She looks done in."

"She wants to be here for Libby."

"Libby needs to go to bed, too." They were talking low, but Libby heard every word. Even with her eyes closed, she had no trouble distinguishing Jeff's deep, melodic tones from his brother's.

"Do you think it's wise to leave her alone?"

"I wasn't planning on leaving her alone."

She could almost see his face. Was he looking through the arched entry at her? Her lids were too heavy to lift.

"I know you're attracted to her, Jeff, but I don't think this is the time for romance."

"Geez, Jack. Give me some credit, will you?" His voice was filled with disgust and disbelief. "Libby's son is missing. I care about her, and I want to help. I'm not about to hop into bed with her."

"I'm sorry, Jeff. I was out of line. I don't know why I said it. I know how attracted to Libby you are, and, well... I planned on taking Cheryl home and loving her until she sleeps in my arms."

"It's been a long night. Go on. Take your wife home to bed, and I'll see that Libby is safe, but not alone."

"I really am sorry, Jeff."

"Forget about it."

Libby was grateful for Jeff's restraint. Really, she was. But was it wrong to want to sleep in his arms? Was it wrong to want a future with him when she needed to be working on getting David back? But how could she get David back? What could she do?

The next thing she knew, Jeff was picking her up. She fought to open her eyes. "Cheryl and Jack?"

"They went home a few minutes ago. I thought you'd sleep better in your bed."

She pushed on his chest. "I can walk."

He held her close. "I know. This is for me."

Jeff tucked her in, kissed her forehead and left for the guest bedroom.

Sleep left her lying alone in her bed to stare at the ceiling. She tried to pray for David, but she couldn't seem to think of words.

"Hail Mary, full of Grace, the Lord is with you, blessed art... blessed art what?" She choked. She knew the words by heart. "Blessed art..." The harder she tried to grab at them the more they slid from her grasp. Oh, please. Was this a sign of God's condemnation? Had she been wrong to keep David? Had Marissa suffered as she was now?

She curled into a ball and wrapped her arms around herself to keep from splintering beneath the covers. Hot tears wound their way down her cheeks.

Her mother had left her. Jenny had left her. Now, David.

She'd thought she'd been justified in keeping him. But now, she could see that she'd convinced herself that keeping David was best for him, for her, for everyone. She'd deluded herself into believing his birth mother, if it even *had* been Marissa, hadn't wanted him. Had left him. Endangered him. She'd told herself she hadn't denied Marissa, or whomever, the child. The mother's actions had. If Libby had turned him in, he would have gone to foster care, not Marissa. But it was a lie. She'd been selfish. Sure, with her David was well loved, well cared for, and very wanted. But it hadn't been her right.

Still, hadn't keeping him been best for Marissa, as well? She wasn't ready for motherhood. She was unemployed, a student, unprepared for that kind of responsibility. Unfit. She'd declared that she was unfit when she left him on the concrete.

But Marissa seemed so normal, so nice. How could an average, bright, popular co-ed, give birth and abandon her child? Had she? What would make a sane person wrap a baby in a duffle bag and leave it? And once done, why would she take him back? Was she more prepared now or had this been a spur-of-the-moment decision? Had she plotted it out? Had she considered the consequences?

What kind of a monster kidnapped a child?

Libby got out of bed and walked to the dresser. She looked tired, heart-sick and over-dressed in the beautiful, wrinkled velvet. Unzipping the dress, she peeled it off and shook it out before hanging it on a hanger and pulling on her pajamas. Her reflection looked softer now and sadder. Had she stolen David? Was not returning him the same as taking? Did Marissa see *her* as the monster?

She crawled back into her cold bed. She'd thought he was kittens when she'd first reached the bag. Poor, unloved kittens left to die, trapped in a bag. She got out of bed. He hadn't been kittens.

She tried to imagine the scene differently. Calling the police. Handing David—no, not David, the baby. Handing the baby to social services. They'd have put him in emergency foster care and started the search for his mother. The mother who'd left him in the cold. And if they found her, they'd have given him back. Blood was the key. Blood was more important than love, in the eyes of the law.

She couldn't imagine making the call.

Even now, knowing that Marissa had taken David, she couldn't give him to a well-meaning, yet impersonal system.

She stood in the hall. David's room emanated emptiness and loss.

No, given the chance to do it all over again, she'd have done everything the same except for one thing. She'd have found a different sitter for tonight.

Maybe that made her a monster.

She looked down the hall to the open door of the spare bedroom.

If she told him the truth, would he see her as a monster?

Kidnapping

Marissa lowered David into his seat on the floor of the bedroom. He cried and squirmed as she buckled him in and tucked his blanket around him. She slid a pacifier between his trembling lips. He watched her for a moment as he began to suck.

"Go back to sleep. Mommy's got you." The words brought another wave of tears to her eyes. Mommy. She was David's mommy. Her arms ached to hold him.

Unaware of the tenderness of her feelings, his eyelids drifted shut.

She let her son sleep.

If David was her little boy, was his name really David? The thought stopped her as she lifted the seat. She hadn't named him before. Couldn't. Not then.

Could she now?

Maybe later. She hoisted the car seat, surprised by its weight, and walked to the kitchen.

Libby's spare set of keys hung on a hook beside the garage door just asking to be taken. Marissa looked at the Oreo key chain. Everything was falling in place so neatly it had to be destiny.

She moved forward as if taking David and leaving weren't something she'd decided to do, but something scripted—a role she was playing. One moment she was in the kitchen, and the next she was backing out of the garage with David buckled in the back seat.

Through a haze of unreality, the lights of the gas station were giant stars as she pulled into the driveway and parked beside the building. She still wasn't certain she was committed to leaving or if she'd decided anything, for that matter. She wasn't certain she even felt like herself. It all felt like a dream.

David was so quiet in the backseat, she had to look to make certain he was there, that she hadn't left him behind. Satisfied he was okay, she walked into the Mobilmart, flirted a little with the pimply-faced clerk and wrote a check to empty out her account plus a bit more. Wanting a beer, she poured herself a large cup of over-heated coffee instead. The burned smell made her add several shakes of non-dairy creamer in a futile effort to make the brew drinkable.

A guy waiting in line behind her looked her over as the clerk counted out her money. He gave her the willies. Her smile froze.

The clerk slid the money across the counter to her. "Have a nice night."

"Thanks." Was that fake, perky-sounding voice really hers?

She was nearly back to Libby's car when the station attendant rushed from the building. "Miss."

Marissa froze. Her heart slammed against her ribs. Busted. The coffee slid from her hand and exploded on the pavement spewing the acrid brew everywhere.

"Sorry." The guy apologized holding aloft the Oreo with its three keys dangling. "You forgot your keys on the counter."

"Thanks." Her hand shook as she took it from him.

"You want a new cup for free?"

She shook her head. "I'm wide awake now."

He laughed and apologized again before returning to the building.

She took a shaky breath.

Her left shoe and the bottom six inches of her pant leg were wet and cold now that the heat of the coffee had dissipated.

She walked the last few feet to Libby's car. If she brought David back now, no one would know she'd taken him.

It took several attempts to get the key in the lock.

Inside, she locked the door again and then looked over the seat at the sleeping child. David was hers, wasn't he?

She turned forward again and jabbed the key into the ignition. The car roared to life.

Where to now?

She needed to think. If she went back to Libby's, Libby would come home, pay her and that would be that. David would stay with Libby. In effect, Marissa would be abandoning David all over again. Could she do that? Now that she'd finally found him, could she leave him behind again?

She didn't know. She dropped her head to her hands. She just didn't know. Tonight was almost like a dream where she was the star of the play, but for the life of her, she couldn't remember having ever seen the script. She raised her head, wishing someone would whisper her lines from off stage.

Think.

If she didn't go to Libby's, where would she go?

Her dorm was out. If she was taking David, the dorm was too close and just plain stupid. She needed to go farther. Leave Eau Claire. She shifted the car into gear.

She'd take the highway. She could think while she drove. She pulled out of the station and headed toward I-94. The signs came quickly—east or west.

Darn. She wasn't ready for another decision. West. She hit the blinker to turn left.

No. She flicked off the blinker. Not west. West took her to Minnesota and her parents' house. The mere thought of the disappointment on her mother's face was enough for Marissa to pick a different destination.

So, east.

She drove past the first exit and under the bridge before flicking the turn signal on again.

Crap. Once again, she flicked it off again almost immediately. Going east to Madison and Paul was out. Their relationship now was moody, sexual and as dishonest as they came. She knew it was her fault, but it didn't matter. Even at its best, their relationship hadn't been able to handle a child. It certainly couldn't handle this now. Double crap.

She pulled into another gas station and stopped the car. When had she become so darned indecisive? She used to have it all plotted out—school, career, life...everything. Now, it took her half a day to decide whether or not to take a babysitting job.

The choice was simple—east or west. She needed a destination where she could think. Somewhere where she would be safe and cared for while she figured out what she wanted. Somewhere where she wouldn't be judged. Aunt Bess. She smiled as she thought of her mother's less-than-conventional aunt. Bess was a hippy before the term hippy was invented. If ever there was a woman who embodied the live-and-let-live attitude, it was Aunt Bess. Why hadn't she thought of Bess earlier?

Like nine months earlier? Bess would have welcomed the pregnant Marissa with open arms. She wouldn't have frowned, wouldn't have judged. She would've just loved Marissa and given her the time to think and decide.

Marissa shrugged. Better late than never. She stepped on the gas. East and Milwaukee it was.

For the Love of David

A police car sat at the stoplight on a cross street. Marissa's eyes shot to the speedometer and the clock. She was fine on both accounts. Libby and Jeff were still at the play. That didn't make her safe for long, though. Marissa's damp palms slid against the wheel. In another two hours or so, police would be looking for Libby's car. She couldn't be in it.

She glanced over her shoulder. They couldn't be in it.

Again, she drove past the exit to I-94 East. If she went west, away from Milwaukee, then abandoned the car, it might fool the police into thinking she had gone west. She took the exit for I-94 West. West to... to where? She merged with traffic trying to remember what towns the bus went through on the way home. Baldwin. Baldwin was one of the little towns without a bus station, but the Greyhound bus from Minneapolis to Chicago stopped there at ten thirty-something. At a gas station, as she recalled. She'd seen others board there and buy tickets from the driver.

Baldwin was perfect, small enough and rural enough that one, extra old car parked in a field of slowly rusting vehicles wouldn't draw any attention.

A blue sedan came up behind her and hovered to her right. Marissa held her breath and concentrated on driving. Unmarked cops drove navy sedans. As the other car accelerated past, she shot it a quick glance. A plastic Garfield the cat waved from the back window.

She willed her hands to loosen their grip on the steering wheel. You're safe. She said the play wouldn't be over until after eleven. If Marissa drove the correct direction, she could be halfway to Milwaukee before the car was reported stolen. She wiped one damp palm against her jean-clad thigh and then the other. It didn't matter. She was sticking with Baldwin. Her nerves couldn't handle much longer in this car.

Fifty minutes later, she took the Baldwin exit. Behind her, David was beginning to fuss.

"You're okay, sweetie. Mommy will stop in a minute."

She pulled the car off the road and into a moonlit field. He was crying in earnest as she climbed over the seat. "Come here, David." She unstrapped his little body and held him for a moment. "Let's check that diaper." He was so wet the edges of his undershirt were damp. She changed his diaper, but left the one-piece, footed pajamas on. The car was warm, but not warm enough to strip him naked if she didn't have to.

"We are going to take a bus ride to our new home." It felt good to explain it to him, as if that somehow made them a team. "We'll go to Milwaukee to your Great Auntie's house and then—" She stopped.

And then what? She didn't have a job. Staying with Aunt Bess and thinking was all fine and good, but she couldn't stay there forever. Did she think Libby wouldn't send the police out looking for David? Did she think they wouldn't eventually get around to checking Aunt Bess?

So she'd leave Bess and do what?

Diapers and formula weren't free. She was going to need a job. Perhaps she should finish school before reclaiming her son. It's not as if Libby was going to suddenly take him and run away.

Marissa checked her watch. It wasn't too late. If she hurried, she could beat Libby home or follow her by a couple of minutes. She could tell Libby she borrowed the car trying to lull David to sleep. Worst case scenario, Libby would think she was nuts and never hire her to sit for David again. But would that be so bad?

The minutes ticked by. She was no more ready for a child now than she had been when she was pregnant. Not that that mattered anymore. David was a wonderful, warm weight in her arms. He was hers. Wasn't he? His dark eyes looked at her so lovingly. Why was she considering taking him back to Libby?

She glanced at her watch again. Oh, my gosh. It was ten o'clock. Think. Make a decision. Should she give him back to the woman who'd rescued him, loved him, could take care of him, and provide a home for him, or…? No! She corrected herself. He hadn't been rescued. He'd been…stolen. Well, maybe not stolen exactly, but found and kept like a bangle bracelet on the floor of the mall's food-court. *Her* bangle, which should have been turned in to the lost and found, not kept.

Her bracelet, her baby.

Marissa returned David to his car seat and buckled him in before getting out of the car. She tugged on her mittens and went to the back of the car. Someone would be looking for it. She packed the license plate with snow and rounded the car to do the front, as well. She turned off the car, checking to see if she'd left anything important behind before closing the front door and opening the back. She covered his car seat with a blanket and walked the half a mile to the gas station that served as a bus stop. The car seat bumped against her leg repeatedly, bruising her.

Beneath his blanket, David cried loudly. For most of the walk, his voice filled the frigid darkness like a nightmare. Like in her dreams, her gentle shushing didn't work. The poor little guy was probably cold and hungry, but there wasn't anything she could do about it. She couldn't stop and take him out of the car seat. It was hard enough just lugging the seat and the diaper bag. With every step, it seemed that one or the other slapped her in the thigh. Her left foot, with its coffee-wet sock and shoe, was frozen. The bottoms of both pant legs were coated with dirty road slush.

By the time she reached the gas station, David had cried himself to sleep. He was quiet when the bus pulled up belching a cloud of noxious diesel exhaust.

Marissa lugged the car seat and diaper bag up the narrow stairs and onto the bus. Sweat dribbled down her back. The exhaust made her stomach hurt. The driver scowled at her. She almost forgot to purchase a ticket to Chicago rather than her true destination.

The jostling involved in pushing the car seat through the narrow aisle to the open seat in the middle of the bus reawakened David.

"Shut that goddamn brat up." The stale stench of cigarettes, alcohol and sweat that emanated from the gaunt, greasy man reached Marissa at the same time as his words. She shoved her way past him another two rows and plopped into the empty seat. The bus rumbled away from the stop as Marissa slid toward the window, tugging the car seat after her.

She unzipped her coat and breathed in. She'd made it. The air around her smelled of the deodorant sprayed in busses in the vain attempt to cover the stench of cigarettes and perspiration left behind by previous passengers.

David bellowed his neglect. His red and sweat-dampened face contorted in infantile rage.

Marissa stared at him in annoyance. She wanted to tell him that he should have finished the bottle she'd given him back at the house because he couldn't now, but she knew how futile that would be. Already she regretted abandoning the car. The seven hours it would take the bus to reach Milwaukee spread out before her like days of torture.

"Shut that damn kid up, or I'll do it for you." The drunken man was hanging in the aisle, half out of his seat.

A short, large-breasted woman with a quilted coat and neatly combed gray hair rose from the seat behind the drunk and made her way to Marissa's seat.

"I've just been visiting my daughter and her new baby in Minneapolis, and I miss them already." She spoke loudly to be heard over the caterwauling. She reached for David, looking down at Marissa for permission.

"May I?"

Marissa nodded, grateful to abdicate responsibility for her angry son, if only for a moment. She watched while the older woman gently and efficiently loosened the straps and removed the baby.

David stopped crying the moment he was free of the car seat and started looking for the expected bottle. When none was forthcoming, he loudly expressed his disappointment.

The woman eyed the diaper bag wedged in the seat next to Marissa. "Might there be a bottle in there?"

Marissa started to say she hadn't packed any, but she caught sight of several small, sealed bottles of formula. She pulled one out and then dug for a nipple. There were four nipples, each in its own sealed container. She opened the bottle and attached the nipple before handing it to the woman.

The woman put the nipple in David's mouth and gently lowered herself into the seat across the aisle.

The effect was instantaneous. David clamped down and gulped vigorously, sniffling through his runny nose.

While Marissa watched, the woman held and fed David with one hand and reached into her coat pocket with the other. She pulled out a neatly pressed handkerchief and wiped David's face and nose with it.

"Poor tyke was hungry, that's all." She smiled reassuringly at Marissa, but Marissa didn't feel reassured. She should have made an inventory of the bag's contents before she'd left the house. What would she have done had Libby not thought to stock it with formula?

They both watched him eat. The first half of the bottle of formula disappeared rapidly and then the cadence of his noisy gulping decreased. He closed his eyes and drank more leisurely. Marissa watched the woman smile at the baby in her arms. Some people were naturals when it came to babies. Too bad she couldn't count herself in that category.

"What's his name?"

"David." Marissa felt her face grow warm. She had meant to rename him to make it harder for the police to follow them. She had also meant to be inconspicuous. She looked at the woman holding David. How likely was this lady to forget the frazzled, inept mother and child she'd seen on the bus?

"Some mother I'm turning out to be," she mumbled to herself.

David finished the bottle and stopped sucking.

The growl of the bus engine was oddly soporific. Marissa's eyelids were heavy. She didn't know why she was so tired. Usually, she could study late into the night without difficulty.

The grandmother put the empty bottle on the seat.

Marissa forced her eyes wide and watched as the woman shifted David to her shoulder and expertly extracted a burp from her now sleepy charge.

Marissa's eyes drifted closed for a moment. When she opened them again, the grandmother had David in the crook of her arm. She smiled at the little sigh of pleasure that escaped his lips as he settled in to sleep.

She yawned and reclined the seat the full inch it would go. Sleep sang a siren song.

"I'd be glad to hold him here if you'd like to rest a bit."

It took Marissa a moment to figure out who the woman was referring to. Oh, yes. David. She was babysitting David. She meant to nod and smile her thanks, but wasn't sure she actually did it.

Sometime later, she awoke briefly as the bus pulled out of a tiny town. Disoriented, she sat up. Her hand rested on a baby's chest. A baby? She pulled her hand away and watched the rise and fall of its small chest. For a moment she couldn't remember his name or where he'd come from. Fear jolted her as it all came back. She looked at the baby. David. At some point the woman, the stranger she'd handed him to before falling asleep, must have returned him to his car seat and strapped him in before leaving.

Once again, she'd let a woman she didn't know take her son. She was turning out to be a horrible mother.

Sunday Morning

Libby opened one eye a slit, mildly annoyed that she'd left the shades open and allowed the sun to wake her before David. Why hadn't David wakened her? Both eyes opened wide.

Pale yellow striped wallpaper hung where blue paint should have been. Her heart raced. Where was she?

It took a moment for her to recognize her spare bedroom. What was she doing there? Her stomach rolled as memory returned. "David." She whimpered and clamped her eyes closed tight. Make it a dream. Make it a dream. The next time she opened her eyes, it would be morning. She'd be in her own bed. David would be calling for breakfast. Please. Please.

Warm, bare arms pulled her close. Jeff. .

"No!" Libby struggled her way free. Last night was a dream. It had to be. She didn't want Jeff there.

Jeff instantly released her. "Libby?"

She sat on the bed and hugged her knees to her chest. Her cream nightgown with its pale pink flowers covered everything but hands and face. Tears filled her eyes to over-flowing.

"It wasn't a dream, was it?" She stared pleadingly into Jeff's sympathetic eyes. "I want it to have been a dream."

He shook his head sadly. "No, Libby. David's gone. Marissa took him."

"No." She shook her head. "It has to be a dream." She stumbled from the bed. David would be asleep in his crib. He had to be.

His drapes glowed a baby blue. His crib was empty, the diaper bag missing from the door knob and the car seat absent from the floor. Tears dripped from her chin onto the rug. "David." Was he all right? He still woke up hungry in the middle of the night. Had Marissa been prepared for that? How many bottles had there been in the diaper bag? One? Two? Libby usually restocked it before they went out. Where had Marissa taken him? Was she taking good care of him?

Jeff came up behind her.

"Libby?"

She turned to face him. He was so handsome it stunned her. He'd put his dress shirt back on, but hadn't buttoned it. A thick thatch of dark brown hair decorated his broad, firm chest. She closed her eyes. Under other circumstances, she would have appreciated the view. Now, thoughts that didn't revolve around David shamed her. What did it matter if Jeff's shoulders were broad and muscular when David was gone?

What did anything matter?

Memories of last night crowded her mind. Had she really crawled into his bed instead of sending him home? Had insanity permeated every aspect of her life?

She smoothed her hand over David's mattress. David was gone. She picked up a teddy bear Mark and Carrie had sent, a bear David had been too young to play with, and hugged it tight. Soft and squishy, it was a lousy replacement. Libby wanted to sink to the floor, to curl in a ball and die.

Instead, she wiped the tears off her cheeks. This was her life. This had always been her life. She couldn't hide from sorrow. Growing up, being passed from one foster home to the next, had taught her that. Taking care of Jenny and her family for so long had reinforced it. Life went on. Moping didn't help. Crying wasn't going to get David back. Progress required action. She needed to make coffee, take a shower, and find out if the police had found Marissa yet. She should research the girl's family. Check women's shelters. What else?

"Libby?"

Her eyes turned to Jeff. Why couldn't she have had him? There was a spark there. Maybe more than a spark. Why couldn't Marissa have left them alone, left her and David with a chance at the dream of a normal family? Maybe she wasn't meant for normal. Maybe the happily ever after of a loving husband and kids was beyond her reach, but it shouldn't be beyond David's. He deserved loving parents.

"Come here." Jeff pulled her into his arms, unwittingly gathering her fragmented self into one being. She was victim and perpetrator, virgin and slut. And she was all alone. Even in his arms, she recognized that she was alone. He had a life. Soon, he would leave.

"I don't think I can do this." She hadn't meant to say the words aloud. They heaped obligation where there should be none.

"Do what?"

She shook her head. No matter how horrible alone felt, captivity was worse. She would hold no one captive, not her brother-in-law, not Jeff, not anyone.

"Libby, do what?" He shook her gently. "Tell me."

"Survive alone." She was pathetic, claiming in one breath that she wouldn't do something and doing it in the very next breath.

"You aren't alone. I'm here."

What remained of her heart broke. She wanted his words to be true, but promised herself she wouldn't hate him when they proved not to be. He was a nice man. He meant well. He'd never been alone; didn't know what he was saying.

If he knew the truth of how she got David, he'd run. She should tell him. Cut him loose.

Instead, she said, "Thank you. I won't hold you to it, but thank you."

He didn't know what to say. She could feel it in the sudden stiffness of his arms. She side-stepped the issue and extracted herself from the comfort of his embrace.

There were things she could do. There were always things to be done. Find Marissa's family. Contact the women's shelters. But first, coffee.

"Uh…you take your coffee black, right?"

Jeff nodded. "Black is good."

She felt his eyes on her as she left. Was he watching her with pity? Or with longing, with friendship, with confused feelings of obligation? She felt guilty wondering. How could she think about any kind of relationship with Jeff when David was missing?

§

"Look, Tyler, a baby." A young woman's voice nudged Marissa from sleep. She opened her eyes and blinked several times to clear the sleepy blurriness that filled them.

Awareness came abruptly, followed by panic. She had fallen asleep on the bus and now had no idea where she was.

"Excuse me," she addressed a good-looking couple across the aisle from her. "Could you tell me what stop this is?"

"M'waukee." The man eyed her questioningly, as his girlfriend craned around him to admire the baby.

"Milwaukee? Darn, I almost overslept." Marissa struggled to her feet, pulled the blanket over David's head and, snatching up the diaper bag, pushed her way down the walkway and off the bus.

She stepped off the bus just before the driver climbed on. The door closed, and the bus roared to life, spewing thick diesel exhaust as it rolled away from the station.

She'd just made it. Shifting her grip on the car seat, Marissa walked through the greasy slush to the large, glass doors of the bus station.

There was something about riding the bus that always made her feel dirty and poor, and something about sleeping on a bus that added to that feeling. She made her way to the phones.

"Bess?" she inquired of the sleepy voice that answered the phone on the fifth ring.

"Tammy? Is that you?" The voice was awake now and concerned.

"No, Aunt Bess. This is Marissa."

"Marissa?" There was a pause. "Calling from Eau Claire?"

"No, actually I'm here in Milwaukee at the bus station. I was wondering if you could come get me?"

"Here? At the Milwaukee bus station? Why? What's wrong?" She stopped abruptly, interrupting herself. "Never mind, you can tell me if you want later. What time is it?"

Marissa consulted the clock high on the wall above the ticket counter.

"4:55."

They'd made pretty good time, considering all the stops.

"4:55, almost 5:00." Another pause while Bess calculated. "I can be there in a half hour. Do you feel safe enough waiting for me, or do you want to take a cab? I'll pay."

Marissa quickly looked around. Bus stations were generally scary places where derelicts came to get out of the weather under the guise of waiting for a bus. Milwaukee's bus depot was pretty standard, rows of molded plastic chairs in a variety of colors where a dozen or so people slouched. A man with a scraggly beard and a knit black cap pulled over greasy locks smoked a cigarette. An elderly couple talked quietly over steaming Styrofoam cups while they kept a sharp eye on the pile of luggage that sat at their feet. A thin girl with dreadlocks slept next to the curved form of a toddler.

A small section of empty chairs had television sets bolted in front of them where a traveler with a pocketful of change could kill time while waiting for the bus.

A heavy-set man in a biker jacket plugged coins in one of the vending machines that lined a section of two walls near the bathrooms. Two uniformed clerks manned the ticket booth.

It wasn't bad, considering the size of the city. Still, it wasn't a place anyone would choose to spend a lot of time in.

"Marissa?" her aunt's voice called her back to the question. "Do you want to take a cab?"

"I'll wait for you."

"Okay. I'll be there as soon as I can. I'll probably have to park in a loading zone, so keep a watch for me. I'll be a half hour, thirty-five minutes."

"Thanks, Aunt Bess."

"Thank me later, love." Bess's voice sounded wide-awake and cheerful as if she viewed the trip to get Marissa as the start of an adventure. If that were the case, her great-aunt wouldn't be disappointed.

Marissa grimaced as she hung up the phone. She hadn't felt comfortable since she'd left Libby's house. She looked forward to getting somewhere safe. Her eyes focused on the covered car seat at her feet. The blanket moved when David shifted in his sleep.

She took David with her to use the rest room. She put the car seat on the floor of the handicapped stall, the only one large enough to accommodate them both. She made certain to tuck the corners of his blanket firmly into the seat to avoid getting them soiled by the puddle of questionable origin that covered the floor in front of the stool. Marissa had no idea how or what she was going to tell Bess about David. The truth, she realized, might not be the best choice in this case.

When they left the restroom, Marissa caught sight of the hot cocoa vending machine. As a child, she had loved vending machine hot chocolate. It arrived all hot and foamy. On ski outings, she invariably had one or two cups of the sweet, brown liquid. The memory made her feel safe and warm. She stopped in front of the machine and rummaged through her purse for the correct change.

Carrying baby seat, diaper bag, and cocoa ended up being more of a hassle than she had anticipated. She ended up leaving the chocolate in the machine while she deposited David and his accessories in front of a nearby chair and then returned for her drink. The frothiness had dissipated by the time she got to take the first sip. The chocolate was hot, but watery. Disappointed, she set it in the cup-holder molded between her chair and the next.

As it turned out, she had nearly forty minutes to wait for her aunt, but no more than a few seconds to think about how to handle the meeting.

At a few minutes past 5:00, David decided it was morning. Another trip to the rest room for a change of diaper and clothes was in order. Marissa ended up lining his car seat with course brown paper towels in a vain attempt to absorb the wetness that had leaked into the padding. She piled them thick and hoped that they would protect him until they could get to Bess's house.

Holding David in the crook of one arm and the carrier laden with the diaper bag in the other, she returned to the waiting area to open a bottle for her hungry son. She blessed the thoroughly stocked bag while being careful not to think of the stocker herself.

Libby had to be frantic. She remembered how she'd felt when the fever passed and she realized no one had turned in her baby. She'd worried. Was he all right? Was someone feeding him and caring for him? Libby would undoubtedly be feeling the same. As well she should. After all, Libby was no saint. She was a liar, wasn't she? A kidnapper herself, she tried to pass David off as her own when he didn't really belong to her. It was only fair that she knew exactly what she'd put Marissa through.

Except, it wasn't quite the same.

Marissa shoved that thought aside and looked at her son. "Don't eat too fast, sweetie, Mommy doesn't have another bottle right now."

David ate contentedly and then proceeded to fill his pants. Again.

Damn it. Now they'd be down to the last diaper.

It's a Boy

"Ick. You got the last of the clean stuff." Marissa stripped her son bare. "Now what am I going to dress you in?" Exposed to the cold, he shot a stream of urine, hitting Marissa's coat and making a puddle on the plastic changing shelf. "Damn it, David."

She grabbed a handful of the non-absorbent, coarse paper towels and tried to wipe up the mess, but only succeeded in smearing it around. His poop stuck to everything. The kid needed a bath, and so did she.

She got him as clean as she could using every last wet wipe from the diaper bag. He was okay, but not a powder fresh baby, by any stretch of the imagination. She wrapped him in his blanket—the only thing he hadn't managed to soak or soil.

Why were babies so messy? She wiped the spit-up off her shoulder with a cloth diaper before using it to replace the soggy paper towels in the car seat.

Damp and smelly clothing now filled the diaper bag. Marissa looked at the clock with panicked disbelief. Was it that late already? Where had the time gone?

She crammed David back into his seat. Wrapped as he was, he didn't fit beneath the straps very well. Marissa tugged on the buckles to create some slack as the seconds ticked off. The stupid straps wouldn't loosen. "Sorry, kid." She partially unwrapped him in order to snap him in. The strap lay next to his tender skin. She jammed a corner of the blanket under the strap so it wouldn't chafe and then covered him with the rest of it.

Awake and squirming, David kicked off his covers.

"You're gonna get cold." Marissa tucked the blanket back in, none too gently.

David protested the rough handling and squawked. His little arms came free of their covering and thrashed in the air.

"Fine! Be cold then." She looked at the clock. Bess was probably double-parked outside. She left him uncovered.

A cold blast of air hit them as they neared the door. "Crap." She couldn't expose his skin to that kind of cold. She set the car seat on the floor, and then she tugged and tucked feverishly. "Will you stay still for a second?"

"Marissa?"

Squatting in front of the car seat, Marissa raised her head. She spotted Bess just inside the street door, and her eyes filled with tears.

Her aunt was dressed in her normal, gypsy-like garb. A flowing, multicolored skirt peeked out under her long appliqué-cluttered, turquoise pea coat. Her frizzy, red halo of hair was partially tucked beneath a button-bedecked, purple beret.

Marissa brushed aside her tears, stood and waved her hand. "Over here, Bess."

Bess rushed forward and enveloped her in a quick, perfume-scented hug.

"Welcome to Milwaukee, kiddo." She bent down to take the luggage. "We'd better go, I'm…" Her hand met Marissa's at the car seat handle. "Well, now who do we have here?"

She crouched down next to the seat and caressed David's cheek. The little boy had kicked free of his blanket again. Bess turned to Marissa with raised brows.

Marissa's mind went blank. She couldn't remember the baby's name. "Ah…" She stalled for time. "Uh… Aunty Bess." Marissa hadn't called her aunt by that name in years and then, only when she wanted something or wanted to get out of something. David's name came to her just in time. She really needed to name him something else. "This is David."

"David, huh?"

Marissa felt the weight of Bess's question-filled eyes. But thankfully, Bess Frost did not give voice to those questions. Marissa followed her aunt's eyes as they turned to the poorly wrapped, semi-naked infant and cringed. She wasn't giving a stellar first impression of her capabilities as a mother, that was for sure. As she watched, Bess tucked in a corner of David's blanket.

"Well, Marissa. And David." She stood. "We'd better go. I'm parked in a red zone."

Marissa grabbed the handle of the seat and followed Bess to the car. Her mother would have launched a barrage of questions, but Bess said nothing. Her mother, had she managed to hold her tongue, would have radiated disapproval. Bess radiated nothing but unconditional acceptance and love.

Bess started the car as Marissa buckled David into the back seat. "I need to stop for milk on the way home, if there's anything you need." Her tone was light and casual, as if she hadn't noticed how desperately the baby needed things—like clothes—and was offering the way she'd call an ailing neighbor to ask if they needed anything from the store because she was going there anyway.

"That would be good."

Her mother would not have been able to restrain herself from a litany of questions, moral judgments, and advice. Bess merely looked at Marissa out of the corner of her eye and said, "Tell."

Marissa looked at her hands. "I had David, and I need somewhere to be while I figure some things out. Can we stay with you?" She looked up and met Bess's eyes.

"Your mother never mentioned him when she wrote at Christmas." Bess scanned Marissa's face, but Marissa doubted there was anything to read besides exhaustion and worry.

With no time to come up with a plausible story, Marissa didn't make one up. "That's because she doesn't know about him."

David squirmed and burbled in the back seat.

The heater blasted out enough hot air for the nearly naked baby to ride in comfort.

Bess drove in silence.

Marissa struggled to come up with something that didn't make her sound like a monster that had abandoned her baby and only now reclaimed him, but there was nothing.

"I can't help if I don't know the problem."

A part of Marissa wanted to yell. *Can't you see the problem? It's right there in the back seat, half naked and stinky.* But Marissa knew, and clearly Bess did as well, the baby was just the visible part of the problem. "I know."

"Can I ask where David was at Christmas?"

Marissa closed her eyes. "A woman watched him for me for a while." It was strange how the way something was worded made all the difference. That hadn't sounded so bad. She opened her eyes and looked at her aunt.

"Why?" Bess divided her attention between the road and her niece. "Why didn't you tell your mother?"

Tears formed in Marissa's eyes, and she savagely brushed them away.

Why, indeed? Sure, her mother would have been disappointed at first, but after the initial shock had worn off, she'd have been supportive and maybe even excited over the prospect of having a baby around. Maybe things would have ended up differently with Paul, as well.

Marissa swallowed heavily. But that wasn't the decision she'd made at the time.

"I didn't want to disappoint her…them."

A liquid rumbling sound came from the back seat.

Marissa grimaced. Stinky, slimy baby. Why couldn't he have stayed the cute Gerber child he'd been at Libby's? She sighed. At least his constant needs provided a distraction.

"Aunt Bess, if you don't mind, I think we should stop sooner instead of later. David used more supplies than I thought possible on the trip."

Bess chuckled. "Babies have a way of doing that. Your mother was a veritable fountain of baby slime when she was that age." She shook her head. "And then, there was you." Her smile tightened visibly. "Of course, that was different."

Marissa didn't ask why it had been different with her or why she'd mentioned Marissa's mother rather than her own daughter, Mora. Maybe that was why Bess never seemed to press or judge. She had secrets of her own. She never talked about her daughter or her ex-husband.

As a child, Marissa had overheard things and asked questions, but her mother had put a stop to that. All Marissa knew was that her mom and Mora had been best friends once. As kids, they'd been more like twins than cousins. Then, Mora went away and Bess's husband left, and Bess had no one. So, Aunt Bess was like a third grandma to her and Mitch.

Bess was better than Marissa's real grandmothers. Somehow, she'd always felt as if Bess loved her more than they did. Maybe it was because her real grandmas seemed to like Mitch better. They didn't, really. They never skimped on gifts, treats or hugs. It was just that they never hugged her as long as Bess did, never made her feel as special. It was probably because as a child, she had looked so much like her mother. She probably reminded Bess of her missing daughter.

Marissa watched as Bess turned to take a quick look into the back seat. Her aunt's wrinkled face softened again. "It's been a while since I've had the carpet cleaned and the upholstery shampooed, so do your worst, little boy."

§

Marissa snuggled into the soft comfort of the blue bedroom. The door to the living room was ajar, and she could hear her great aunt playing with David's toes. "This little piggy…"

She stared at the ceiling. She should be out there, lying next to him on the thick blue blanket playing with his feet while rainbows from the sun-catchers danced on the wall. She should want to. But she didn't. She should be thinking, deciding what to do next, but she didn't want to do that, either. Her eyes burned and her shoulders were tight. A weight she didn't remember having pressed against her chest. Life used to be about her, about what she wanted, but now it was complicated. No decision was simple. It felt as if everything she did or would do was being scrutinized. Judged. Not by Bess, necessarily, but by everyone.

She felt like a test subject in a psychology experiment. Thousands of eyes watching her, dissecting everything she did and finding her unworthy.

Tears trickled out of the corners of her eyes. There were too many decisions to make. Too many thoughts to think. But not now. She closed her eyes. She couldn't deal with anything right now.

Bess must think she was the worst mother. Sure, David was chubby and healthy, but she was so awkward with him. Bess had to know he wasn't hers. Heck, she was more confident with the children she babysat than with her own son.

It wasn't her fault. She was over-tired, that was all. She'd been up half the night and then slept in a bus. If she'd been rested and less stressed, giving him a bath wouldn't have been so hard.

How was she to know that the temperature she preferred for a bath was too hot for a baby? How could she have guessed how slippery kids got when wet? The memory of David's frightened eyes looking up at her from under water stuck with her. He'd coughed and coughed for so long she'd thought he'd never stop.

Naturally, the more mistakes she made, the more ill at ease she felt and the more mistakes she made. She held him too tight, and he cried. When she didn't rinse the wash cloth well enough and got soap in his eyes, they both cried.

There was no way that Bess or anyone else would believe that she'd been caring for David since his birth.

She did well at school. She was bright and personable. She was never this incompetent. Tears soaked the pillow. She was…

For the Love of *David*

The trilling of the portable phone interrupted Marissa's thoughts. She rolled onto her side, pulled the covers higher and strained her ears to listen. There was nothing like murmured conversation in another room to lull a person to sleep. She'd drifted off countless times listening to her parents' conversation drift up from the kitchen.

"Tammy, what's wrong?" Bess's voice sounded worried.

Marissa winced. Mom.

"Calm down, honey. It can't be as bad as all that."

Marissa closed her eyes and listened harder. She knew Bess was wrong. The situation was impossible. She should have told Bess the truth. She should have left David where he'd been. She should have had the abortion. She should have never had sex in the first place.

Bess was silent for quite a while. "What?" Her great aunt's voice shook. "The police said she did what?"

Marissa trembled. The police were involved. Of course, the police were involved. She had David. Had she thought that Libby would do nothing?

"Oh, Tammy." Sympathy, pain and confusion were all evident in Bess's choked voice. "Why?" It sounded as if Bess were crying.

Marissa's heart fell. She'd managed to disappoint the one person she could count on to be on her side.

"Did they say why? Did they give a motive?"

Marissa left the bed's warm haven and picked up her shoes. Any moment now, Bess would tell her mother that she and David were there. Any moment, a police car would pull up to the door and haul her away. Would she get the help then, or would she get a prison sentence?

"They tapped your phone?" Bess's voice shook.

Acid rose in Marissa's throat. She swallowed it down. It wouldn't do to vomit on the plush-pile carpet. She needed to leave. She quickly tied her shoes.

She hid behind the door, peering through the crack into the living room. Bess was huddled on the straight back chair next to the phone stand. She cradled the phone, crooning words of comfort and reassurance. "Marissa is a good girl. I can't believe she would do a thing like that. There must be some mistake."

Marissa strained her ears to catch some sound of the voice on the other end of the line, but there was only silence as Bess listened. "I'm sure she's fine." More silence. "No, honey, you're a good mother. It's not your fault." A short silence. "No, I don't think it's genetic." Bess's voice had an irritated edge it hadn't had before. Another longer silence. "It's okay, Tammy. I know you didn't mean it that way." A pause. "Hello, Allen."

Marissa winced and ducked out of the crack. Daddy.

"Yes, I know. Tell her I know."

Marissa wished she could hear both sides of the conversation.

"Tell Tammy I'll pray."

Marissa froze. Bess didn't believe in God. Mother Earth maybe, but not God. She could almost hear her dad snort. Bess's spirituality was a running joke between the two of them.

"For you, I'll stoop and pray to that Jesus fellow you're so taken with." Marissa could almost see Bess's amused smirk. It was like Bess to try to lighten things, to put even the worst of situations into a better light. Not that there'd ever been anything half this bad to try to shine a better light on.

"I know, Allen. I don't blame you in the least."

Her parents felt guilty. That realization made her feel even worse. It was her fault. Well, hers and Paul's. Her parents hadn't done any of it. Except to encourage her ill-fated relationship. How could they possibly feel guilty?

"We probably should have told her."

Told who what? Marissa wondered.

"I don't know, Allen. I really don't. You'll have to do what you think is best."

Marissa opened the bedroom door wider. Bess had been staring at it as she talked.

"Take care of Tammy and yourself."

Bess's eyes were bloodshot and streaming. "Thank you for calling. It would have killed me to see it on television."

Marissa looked at David, lying on the blanket watching the light from the prisms dance.

"I'll call you if I hear anything."

One final pause. "Good-bye."

The silence was thick and tense. Marissa was tempted to ask, "Who was that?" as if she hadn't heard every word.

They locked stares.

"I'm sorry." Marissa's voice was that of a much younger girl.

Bess shook her head.

Sorry wasn't enough.

"What really happened, Marissa? What's going on?"

Marissa wrapped her arms around herself. She wasn't sure she knew. "You didn't tell them I was here." It boggled her mind that she hadn't, given the state David had arrived in, the debacle of a bath, and everything she'd heard on the phone.

"No, I didn't, but I'm not sure that was the best decision."

Marissa looked away first. She wasn't sure it had been, either. David lay on the blanket. He was back to being a Gerber baby.

"Why don't you tell me why the police are looking for you and a stolen baby?"

"I didn't steal David." Marissa crossed the room and sat on the couch with the blanket at her feet. "Not really. He's mine." She looked down at the wriggling child, but she didn't smile. This wasn't all her fault. Part of it was his. If he hadn't been born…

David found his fist and mouthed it.

Well, she really couldn't blame him for that. Still, it wasn't all her fault. Part was Libby's. If she hadn't kept him, if she'd turned him in, like she should have…

"Then why are the police looking for you?" Bess left her chair to perch on the one opposite the couch.

Marissa wanted to lie. A fabricated story, or a partially fabricated one, might have been easier to swallow than the truth, but she was too tired to lie. Too tired and too honest. At least that's what she wanted to think.

She started with Paul's defection.

It was strange how short the story was to tell, and how long it had been to live. Somewhere around the story of David's birth, the real David let out a hungry squawk and was wordlessly lifted into Bess's lap and provided with a bottle.

When Marissa had exhausted her story and fell silent, Bess finally spoke.

"So you aren't positive that David is yours?"

"Well…" Marissa ran the fingers of one hand through her hair. They caught in the tangles, and she wiggled them free, stalling for time. She was certain, wasn't she?

"I…"

Wasn't she?

"I wouldn't have taken David if I hadn't been sure, would I?" Her voice was a plea. Bess was supposed to chime in and tell her she'd done the right thing; that she'd done what anyone else in that situation would have done.

"I don't know, Marissa."

Her words slapped Marissa. Bess couldn't be judging her. Bess didn't judge. She raised questions designed to help Marissa see all sides of an issue, but she never made a decision for her or passed judgment on that decision no matter what it was.

When Marissa's Uncle Phil had come out of the closet and been disowned by the rest of the family, Bess hadn't judged. When he got sick and lost his job, she opened her home to him.

When she found out that a much younger Marissa and Mitch had stolen candy from the bookstore she worked at, she helped them to see it from the owner's point of view. She asked a few key questions that helped the children decide what to do. Never once did she suggest that they "make it right" or lecture them on the evils of stealing. She wasn't that way. She allowed them to make the decisions they were most comfortable with while being true to the type of people they wanted to be. She was big on that: being true to one's self and letting everyone be the type of person they wanted and needed to be. So, she couldn't be judging. Not now.

"I didn't take David because I wanted him to be mine," Marissa insisted, watching Bess's face for some sign of opinion. Sometimes, Bess held her own counsel too closely.

Marissa glanced at David who sucked slowly, his eyelids getting heavy as the bottle emptied. Shouldn't she be the one holding him? If she were his real mother, wouldn't the maternal instinct make her grab him first?

"The picture in Libby's living room. The one where she was fat. I'm sure that was the woman at Kerm's."

"I thought you said you didn't see if she picked up the baby or not."

David was her baby. It wasn't so much that she wanted him to be. She simply knew he was.

"The car was the same. I wasn't sure about the shade of blue, but the license is the same. I remember looking at the license that day and thinking that the baby was gone and that the lady probably had my baby. I phrased it like that, 'the lady has my baby,' so that I would remember the license was LDY something."

It was so quiet in the room. Marissa focused her attention on David. His eyes were closing. Soon, he would be sleeping again. Marissa's eyes burned. She needed a nap.

"But you didn't actually see her pick him up. And you didn't catch the entire license number." Bess raised the questions Marissa refused to. "And you said Libby wasn't fat when you babysat for David."

"How many blue Fords have a LDY plate?"

Bess shrugged. "I don't know. How many?"

Marissa growled. "And have a baby boy my child's age." There couldn't be another dowdy-looking woman with a blue car and those plates who had her son. Could there? Libby had been fat in the picture, not pregnant—hadn't she?

Marissa looked at her hands and wished her mind would shut up. "David is mine."

Bess rocked the baby to sleep. "You said you didn't tell anyone you were pregnant? Not even Paul?"

"Especially not Paul. Not after the way he'd abandoned me." From the corner of her eye Marissa caught sight of something moving outside Bess's window and jerked her head to look. The naked trees in Bess's backyard swayed in a gust of wind.

"Paul told me to get an abortion if I needed to, but not to tell him whether I had needed one or not because abortion was murder. No, Mr. Morality didn't mind it I killed his child. Heck, he gave me money to do it. But he couldn't know about it. Couldn't be party to murder." She shook her head again, hating him all over again. "He'd be the last person I'd tell." Had she really gotten back together with him? Was she nuts? She should have left the baby with Libby just to avoid Paul finding out about him.

"And you kept the pregnancy to yourself?"

Marissa narrowed her eyes at Bess. "I didn't imagine I was pregnant, Bess. I know what pregnancy is."

"Of course you do. It's just that you've always had such a cute little figure. It surprises me that people didn't know, couldn't see that you were pregnant?"

Bess didn't believe her. "People only see what they want to. Take me, for instance. I wanted you to understand. I came here because I thought you would, but you don't. You're just like everyone else. You think I stole David because I want a baby."

"It's not that, dear." Bess smiled reassuringly, her voice soothing. "I'm trying to sort things out in my mind."

"Sort what out?" Marissa wanted to rip the sleeping child from

Bess's arms. "Everything I told you is a fact. There's no need to sort through anything."

Bess seemed to ignore the outburst. "It sounds as if you've needed to talk for a long time."

Marissa took a deep breath and tried to calm herself.

"You're probably right, but…" Marissa fell silent again. Bess didn't believe her. Would she, Marissa, believe the story if someone else told her? Probably not. No, not even probably not. Definitely not. Had it really happened? She'd spent so much time training her mind into thinking it hadn't that she wasn't certain any more. Was it possible that she imagined the entire pregnancy? Could a slim girl like her hide a pregnancy? Could someone in a dorm really hide a birth?

"You're sure about all this: being pregnant, hiding the birth, abandoning the baby, everything?"

Marissa's calm evaporated. "You think I made it all up or that I'm lying, don't you?" She shouted, and David jerked in Bess's arms. It was all right if she doubted, but it wasn't all right if Bess did.

Her eyes filled with tears. Aunt Bess never judged. If Bess didn't believe in her, who would?

"No…" Bess started to explain.

Marissa wasn't listening. "I'm *not* lying, and I'm *not* making this up." She glared at Bess. "Why would I do that? I don't even like babies, really."

Marissa froze.

Where had that come from? She hadn't meant to say that.

Her aunt looked at her in amazement.

"I do like babies," Marissa insisted guiltily, her eyes darting between David's sleeping form and her aunt's face. They were a lot of work, and she was always happy when their mother's returned, but she did like them. "Really."

A Sunday in Hell

Libby pushed the scrambled eggs and sausage Jeff insisted on making for her around her plate.

"You should eat something." His plate was empty of everything but butter and jelly smears. "At least take a bite or two."

She lifted a forkful to her mouth. The smell reminded her of the breakfasts she used to make for Jenny's family, and it carried with it all the feelings of loss. First, she'd lost Jenny, then the kids, and now David. Her eyes filled with tears, and she lowered the eggs back to the plate untasted.

"I'm sorry. I just can't."

"It's okay. You told me you weren't hungry, I just hoped…"

"It's not your fault. It's…" She shrugged. "I don't know."

Jeff looked like he was in as much need of comfort as she felt.

"What I think I really need is to go to church." She looked at the clock. She had plenty of time to shower and change and make it to 10:30 Mass.

"I'd love to go with you. I just need to run home quick to shave and change clothes."

Now that he mentioned it, she noticed that he did look a bit disreputable, with his stubbly chin and cheeks and wrinkled shirt. Was that lipstick? Were those black mascara smudges? She'd probably made those smears when she'd sobbed on him.

"You don't have to go to Mass with me. You probably had a whole day of your own planned. You should go do whatever. I'll be fine."

He shook his head. "I'm not leaving, Libby. Just going home for a bit to change. I will be right back. We'll go to church together. 10:30 at Saint Mary's, right?"

"You don't have to. I'll be fine."

Jeff's look said he didn't believe she'd be fine. "Do you want me to go?"

"Yes. I mean, no. I mean, I don't want you to feel you have to stay. This is my problem. You've been great." She tried to look normal and strong, but she wasn't. Her eyes filled with tears again. "I just don't want you to feel you have to, is all."

"Come here." He pulled her from her chair into his lap. "I don't feel I have to. I want to. I want to be with you."

She pressed her face into his shirt and let him hold her. His arms shouldn't feel this good. She shouldn't need him this much. Her breath was a shaky sigh.

He squeezed her tight. "Say, why don't you come home with me? I'll change, we'll go to church, and then we'll stop somewhere on the way back and pick up lunch."

She shook her head. "I need a shower." He didn't smell quite as good as he had last night, either, but she didn't want to let go. Her nose must have wrinkled because he laughed.

"So do I, I know." He hugged her again. "Okay, this is what we are going to do. I'm going to go home, shower, and change. You're going to stay here and do the same. Then I'm coming back, and we're going to church and then lunch."

She shook her head and then eased off his lap. "I couldn't do a restaurant. Not without…" She wrapped her arms around herself and managed to keep back the tears. She wasn't going to make it through church without sobbing, but it didn't matter. "I need to go to Mass alone. Nothing against you. I just need to really pray."

"Are you sure?" He cocked his head and looked at her closely. "I still don't think you should go alone, but I'll respect your wishes. Just know I'm going to be back here before noon, and I'll bring lunch."

She saw him to the door and watched as he walked slowly to his car. He stopped every couple of feet to look back, as if waiting for her to change her mind.

"I'll be fine."

He didn't look convinced. "I'll be back."

As he backed out of her driveway, Libby changed her mind. The David-less silence pressed against her, urging her to call Jeff back. She stood in the open door watching until his car disappeared. Then she stepped back into her house, closed the door, and greeted loneliness by name.

The need to go to church pushed her forward.

She shampooed her head. Was that David? She froze, listening as the water fell around her. She poked her head out of the curtain, dripping suds on the floor as she strained her ears. Nothing. Of course, it was nothing. Marissa had taken David. Libby drew her head back into the shower. The warm water offered no comfort.

Wrapped in a towel, she checked David's room. Just in case. Nothing had changed. Still, the phantom cries continued in her mind. She stopped the blow drier twice to listen.

With no baby slowing her down, she was ready long before it was time to go. In the kitchen, she tilted the cold eggs and toast into the trash and washed the plate. The hands of the clock seemed frozen in place. She moved about the spotless house, picking up things and putting them down. Now and then, a sob would escape her tightly constricted throat. Too early, she put on her coat and gloves. She needed to go to church. She needed the hard pads against her knees and incense pulling her prayers to Heaven. She needed the congregation's voice joining hers. *Lord, hear our prayer.*

She froze at the door to the garage. What if Marissa called? What if the police found them and called? What if the police found out that David wasn't really hers? What if...

But she had to go. She needed church, the familiarity of Mass. *Lord, have mercy. Christ, have mercy. Lord, have mercy.* Any message the police had would wait an hour.

She rummaged through her purse for her keys, but found them on the breakfast bar instead. When had she taken them out? It didn't matter. She opened the door that lead to the garage, reflexively hitting the garage door opener button on the wall. The door rose grumbling and whining, filling the empty garage with light.

Emptiness slapped her. The car, of course, was gone. Marissa had taken it when she took David. Libby had known this, but she had somehow forgotten.

Oh, God. Libby fell to her knees, closing her eyes as the tears came. She was still kneeling in the doorway to the garage when Jeff returned twenty minutes later.

He gathered her into his arms. "I was in the shower when it dawned on me that you couldn't go to church because of the car."

Libby missed Mass.

It was a venial sin, but one she could ill afford.

§

She sat on the couch.

Sometime in the afternoon, Cheryl came over with the kids. Libby was sure Cheryl's intentions were good, but the sight of the kids was a knife to Libby's heart.

"Where's baby?" Devon ran around the house searching everywhere calling, "Baby Dawid," in his babyish lisp. Each adorable word twisted the knife.

Libby accepted the pain as penance. She prayed that her suffering would make it so David didn't. *Please, God. Make Marissa the world's best mother.*

The second hand of the clock ticked forward, but the minute and hour hands seemed fused in place. She'd take it in and get it looked at. Monday. Or Tuesday.

Cheryl and Jeff chatted.

Libby got off the couch. "You are all welcome to stay, but I think I'm going to take a nap." Maybe the clock hands would move if she were asleep.

Cheryl hugged her at the front door. "Call me when you wake up."

"If it's not too late. I'm planning on sleeping until tomorrow." If she could get to sleep. She was certainly tired enough.

"Call me whenever. There isn't a too late," Jeff insisted after he saw his sister-in-law out.

"I will." Maybe.

Silence descended in a thick cloak once Jeff's car left the drive. Seems she should have remembered that from earlier. She got into her nightgown and then started a load of wash for the comforting noise. She got the coffee ready for Monday and set the timer. Back in her bedroom, she closed the shade. The colors grayed. She lay in bed and listened to her heartbeat. Even with the whoosh of the washing machine, the house proved too quiet to sleep.

Wrapped in a blanket, she sat on the floor inside David's room with her back against the wall, clutching a teddy bear and staring at his empty crib. *Please, let him be safe. Please, let him be happy. Please.*

Where was he?

After the sun had set, she looked in the refrigerator for something to make for dinner. A bottle of formula sat next to the carton of milk. She closed the door, too sick to eat.

She dialed Mark's phone number, praying she wouldn't get the answering machine and praying she would.

Carrie answered.

"Can Mark pick up the extension, so I can talk to both of you at once?"

"Libby, is everything okay?" Carrie's voice was full of concern.

"No."

"Oh. Okay. Just hold a second, I'll get Mark."

Libby could hear Carrie call Mark.

Once Mark said hello, Libby wasn't sure she could talk. "The babysitter stole David."

"What?"

Tears choked her as she tried to repeat the words.

"Why? What happened?"

She couldn't say anything more. Couldn't explain. She just cried, muffling the phone so Mark and Carrie wouldn't hear her ugly sobs.

"Oh, Libby, I'm so sorry." Carrie's voice sounded more shocked than sympathetic.

Mark said the same thing or something similar. He sounded as if he didn't believe her. "Are you sure?"

How could she not be sure? It almost sounded as if he didn't believe there'd ever been a David.

Libby supposed it seemed unreal to them. *I got pregnant visiting Jenny's grave, and now a babysitter stole my baby.* One gigantic delusion.

Maybe she shouldn't blame them for sounding as if they thought she was making it all up. They'd never met David. He wasn't real to them.

Of course, they didn't say that. It was their tone of voice and their muttered platitudes. And their questions. "You called the police? What did they say? Did they have any leads?" *Did they believe there was a baby?*

David didn't matter to them. Libby didn't really matter, either.

What mattered was getting off the phone as fast as they could "… in case the police need to reach you."

"Of course." They thought she was lying.

After she hung up the phone, she got out a picture of David. She sat on the couch, clutching the photo to her chest. She wasn't crazy. He wasn't a lie. He was real.

Scenes of their life together ran through her head, starting with the moment she had found him. She wasn't delusional. She knew the truth; knew the birth story she'd told everyone was fiction.

Had Marissa been the one who left David? Had she reclaimed her son, or had she taken him for some other reason? Libby didn't know. The fact remained: David was gone.

Don't Lie to Me

Marissa sat with Bess in the dining room enjoying a chicken salad sandwich—well, as much as she *could* enjoy eating anything while someone looked at her with such heavy questions in their eyes. The sandwich was good, large chunks of chicken with bits of apple and chopped walnuts in a tarragon-basil mayonnaise loaded on thick slices of fresh, whole grain bread.

"Are you on drugs?"

Bess's question seemed to come out of nowhere. The sandwich turned to sawdust in Marissa's mouth.

"No."

Bess nodded. Her face was unreadable. "Mind if look at your arms?"

"Uh, sure." Shaking, Marissa put down the sandwich and pushed up the sleeves of her red sweater for examination. Bess didn't believe her. Gentle, loving, supportive Bess thought the worst of her. The knowledge tightened something inside her. Her lungs hurt, or maybe it was her heart. She swallowed the lump of half-chewed food.

Bess examined both arms without touching them. "I won't look between your toes."

"Between my…why would you want to look between my toes?" Shivering, Marissa pulled down her sleeves.

"I don't."

"But why would you? Why would anyone?"

Bess looked away. "It's a place to hide needle marks."

"How would you—"

"It's where your mother hid them, okay?" Bess's voice was angry and cold.

Marissa's eyes grew wide with disbelief. "My mother used drugs?" Marissa thought of her mother in the kitchen baking, at the table eating, in church. She was the perfect mother, smart, proper, clean house, high standards, a true get-your-elbows-off-the-table, don't-slouch kind of mom. Her mom, a drug addict? She shook her head. "No way. I don't believe it."

"It's true. You mother was a heroin addict. Probably still is." Bess's eyes brimmed with tears. "If she's still alive."

"Still alive?" Marissa repeated, confused. "Bess, my mom is alive, and she's definitely not an addict. You must be thinking of someone else." She looked carefully at her great aunt. Had the shock of Marissa's problems and the appearance of David triggered a stroke or something?

"I'm not. Your mom ran away from home her last year of high school."

Marissa shook her head again. "Not my mom. Not Tammy Fleming. She was an honor student."

"Tammy's not your mother."

She laid a hand on her great aunt's arm. "Bess, are you okay? Do I need to call a doctor?"

"I'm fine." Bess patted her hand. "And I'm not crazy. Tammy is not your mother. My daughter Mora is. My Mora." She looked at the framed photo on the mantel and sighed. "When Mora ran away in high school, she said Cliff was touching her. I didn't believe it. Not her own dad. Not my Cliff." Bess's voice broke. "I called her a liar, didn't protect her. It's because of me she left."

Marissa stared. The expression on Bess's face made her look old, far older than either grandma.

"She stayed in town at first, fell in with the wrong kind of people. After you were born, she didn't come see me. Didn't trust her own mother. I didn't even know she was pregnant. She sent baby pictures to Tammy—her cousin. I found out about you from Tammy."

Marissa shook her head. This was a faerie story, the nasty, unbelievable, bogeyman-eats-the-children kind.

"She moved away from Milwaukee and went from pot to heroin." Bess dropped her head in her hands. Marissa thought the story was over. But it wasn't.

"A year passed, and I didn't hear from her. No one did. Your sister was born an addict. Mora wrote Tammy that the baby, she called her Brat, was skinny and cried all the time. After Brat died, from neglect probably, Mora showed up on Tammy's doorstep with you. She had needle marks up both her arms, between her toes. You were dirty and hungry. There were cigarette burns on your arm and other places."

Marissa touched the round chickenpox scar on her arm. She had another on her chest and one on her upper thigh close to her...No. She didn't believe it. "Stop it!" she shouted. "Why are you telling me this?

It isn't true."

Bess nodded her head sadly. "But it is. Mora gave you to Tammy. Sold you for whatever was in Tammy's purse. She'd been living in Chicago and needed money. You were two years old, almost three."

"You're a liar!" Marissa shouted, waking David. "I don't have a sister. I have a brother. Mitch."

"Mitch is Tammy and Allen's son. You are Mora's daughter."

"No!" Marissa covered her ears with her hands to keep out the lies. Never mind that Bess's story explained why her grandparents always made more of Mitch than of her. David wailed.

"Tammy was pregnant with Mitch when Mora abandoned you."

"No!"

Bess stood and headed toward David. Marissa leapt from her chair, elbowed her great aunt out of the way, and snatched up David. "He's not your grandson. I'm not your granddaughter. I'm a Fleming, not a whatever your daughter's name is. You're a lying sack of sh—" she managed to stop herself from swearing. Why that was important, she didn't know. Maybe it was because her mother, Tamara Marie Fleming, had taught her better. She fled to the bathroom, slammed the door, and locked it. Tears streamed down her cheeks as she pressed her back against the door. Lies. All lies. Eventually, David's screams broke through the fog in Marissa's mind.

He had soiled his diaper. She could smell it. She put him on the bathroom floor and changed his diaper automatically. Her head hurt too much to think. David. Her. The shiny, perfectly round pock mark on her arm. Pock mark. Pock mark. She could almost imagine a big hand on a little arm. The sear of flesh, the smell, the pain, the tears. She'd always had too vivid an imagination. She picked up David and held him with one arm as she looked in the medicine cabinet for an aspirin.

§

Marissa refused to look at the pictures. She wasn't that little girl, anyway. Who took and kept pictures of bruised, underfed little girls in ragged underwear? Sick people, that's who.

"They're just copies. Tammy kept the originals in her safe deposit box in case your mother ever came back for you."

"Let's get this straight." Marissa stood, holding David against her shoulder as she rocked from one foot to the other. "Mora is your daughter, but she's not my mother. My mother, the woman who raised me from birth on, is your niece Tammy. Got that? My mother is Tammy Fleming."

Bess didn't answer.

The pressure built in Marissa until she wanted to scream. How had she thought being with Bess would help solve things?

"I can't stay here," Marissa announced.

"I know." Bess left the pictures on the table and walked back into the kitchen. "You're wanted by the police. You know that, don't you?"

"Of course, I know that. I'm not stupid." But she felt stupid; stupid and confused and lost. How had everything gone so wrong? Being reunited with her child was supposed to solve everything, instead it had turned into a nightmare about a past she didn't remember and doubted even existed.

Bess was in the kitchen puttering around. Marissa frowned. Her mother puttered in the kitchen when she felt stressed. Not that she felt stressed often. Her mother's life was the good fairy tale, where the beautiful girl marries the man of her dreams and raises 2.5 kids happily ever after.

Bess opened the bread box. "I'll make you sandwiches to take with you. How many do you want?"

"I don't care." Marissa wasn't going to get her dream come true, so what the hell difference did a couple of sandwiches make? She opened her mouth to tell her aunt not to bother, that she didn't need any damn sandwiches, but she shut her mouth. With the way her life was going, she'd probably be grateful for them later. She didn't have all that much money, and the baby used a lot of supplies.

Bess laid out the entire remainder of the loaf in pairs. There was enough bread for six sandwiches. Marissa's arms ached. David weighed a ton. She wasn't used to carrying him. Wasn't used to caring for him. She stood over the blanket. Would he prefer being on his belly or on his back? She should know. A real mother would know. Maybe she should—

"You should give him back." Bess's voice echoed the words in Marissa's head.

Marissa flinched. Had she finished the thought all by herself, she might have agreed with Bess. "He's mine."

Bess nodded. "You should still give him back."

"Are you going to call the police? Turn me in?" Marissa stared at her aunt's back. Great aunt, or not-so-great aunt, but definitely not grandmother.

"No." The older woman shook her head. "But you should. It would be better if you called and gave back the baby."

"He's my baby," Marissa insisted. She stared at the table. Angry tears fell, leaving damp splotches on the cheery, yellow tablecloth. "I didn't do anything wrong." Nothing wrong but abandon him in the first place. She didn't say the words and neither did Bess, yet they hung in the air like a noxious fog. "You can tell them that. Press your rights through legal channels."

"They wouldn't believe me." A sniffle filled with despair rent the air. "You don't even believe me."

Bess left the kitchen and was at Marissa's side in a heartbeat. She threw her arms around Marissa's shoulders.

"It's not that, honey," Bess said in a choked-yet-comforting voice.

She wanted to shove Bess away but found her aunt's touch soothing. Bess's hand smoothed over her head, gently petting her as her mother's used to when she was a child. Marissa sighed. If felt wonderful. Like home. It made Bess's words easier to bear.

"I just want you to be sure. You're not the only woman to ever give birth to a baby she didn't want. Maybe Libby wasn't the woman who found your baby. Maybe David really does belong to her, and your son is somewhere else. The police could help you find your son."

Marissa stiffened and pulled out of her aunt's embrace. "I'm not Mora. I didn't abandon my child. I knew he'd get turned in, and I'd get help. I didn't really abandon him." But she had, and now the police wouldn't help her. They wouldn't believe David was her son, even though he *was*. He *was*, wasn't he?

How could she tell? She dashed the thought from her head with a vicious shake that brought her headache back in full force. He was her son, but a part of her wished he wasn't or that she had never found him. But she *had* found him. And now, no matter what she really wanted, she couldn't let him go. She couldn't abandon him a second time. Not for forever. She wasn't Mora. She wasn't Mora's daughter.

"Could I borrow your car?" She prepared herself for the rejection, but none was forthcoming. She looked at her aunt. "You could say I stole it."

"No." Bess shook her head and looked into Marissa's eyes. "I'll tell them you knew you could use it any time you wanted. You don't steal." She said it strongly, looking pointedly at Marissa.

"I took Libby's car," Marissa admitted, challenging her aunt.

"Where is it now?" As if the fact that she no longer had the car meant anything.

"I thought that driving in the opposite direction from Milwaukee would throw off the police. I drove to Baldwin and left it in a field. There were other junkers there and…" She paused guiltily. "I didn't mean to steal her car. It was the only way I could think of taking David without him getting cold." It came out in a remorseful near-whisper. She really wasn't bad. She just wanted her baby.

The women fell silent, each entangled in her own thoughts, neither anxious to move from there.

"I'd better be going," Marissa stated reluctantly. "The longer I stay; the more risk you run."

"Let me finish making your sandwiches." Bess hurried back to the cutting board and the work in progress.

"I'll pack up David's stuff." His blanket and sleepers were in the dryer. She now wished that the convenience store she had stopped in that morning had sold baby clothes, as well. Maybe the mall would be a good place to hide out while she considered her next move.

§

Marissa pulled out of the driveway as the garage door closed electronically. Bess was to wait a half hour before calling the police. As Marissa turned the corner, she caught a glimpse of a state cruiser in the rear view mirror. Her aunt wouldn't get a chance to call.

She needed to disappear. The mall would be perfect. A lot of cars, a lot of people, a lot of chances to stock up on the things she needed to change their appearance.

In the mall parking lot, Marissa checked her cash. Bess had given her what money she had had at home, nearly two hundred dollars. But even combined with the ninety she had left it wouldn't get them very far. Marissa decided she would have to risk writing checks. It was Sunday after all, and the bank couldn't possibly get the check until Tuesday. By that time she would be long gone.

Since she was taking the risk anyway, Marissa decided to stock up. Never mind that she didn't have any money in her account. Her parents would cover it, so it wasn't like it was stealing, really. Her parents were going to be disappointed in her, but it wasn't as if she had another choice. David needed things.

She bought clothes for her and for the baby, bedding and toiletries, towels and things to set up house with. Her checks were going to bounce all over the place.

In Sears, she found adhesive numbers and letters meant for boat identification or whatever. She bought the kind she thought looked most like those on a license plate. She pushed her baby-filled cart through the aisles, grabbing bumper stickers and adhesive automotive detailing as well. She wasn't going to abandon this car. She couldn't.

Dying By Inches

Libby looked out the window at the crusty snow. She'd never gotten to make a snowman with David. He'd never been old enough to play outside. They'd never had a spring or a summer. There'd been no leaf piles or ice cream cones, no snowsuits or swimsuits, no training wheels, school books, First Communion...

Not much of anything. Still, the past three months had been the best in her life. She left the window and walked into David's room. The crib was new to them. She'd bought it used from an ad in the Shopper's Guide. They'd only had it a few weeks. She stuck her head inside and sniffed, trying to pick up his scent. Tears filled her eyes. It smelled like laundry detergent instead of David. His blanket would probably have carried his scent, but it was gone.

She walked around his room, touching everything, trying to remind herself that he'd been real. That he wasn't dead. That Marissa was probably his birth mother and not some insane kidnapper. She picked up a framed photo. Surely, Marissa would love him and take good care of him. If she were indeed his mother.

Libby held the photo to her chest. Marissa had abandoned David once. Would she keep him this time? What had changed in Marissa's life that made her want her son? That he was healthy and happy? That he was Libby's?

Tears flowed down Libby's face. She owed Marissa the best three months of her life. It wasn't that she wasn't grateful. She was. Still, she'd take David back in a heartbeat, even if it meant ripping him from Marissa's arms.

What did that make her? A kidnapper? She preferred "rescuer." She'd rescued David when he'd been left on the sidewalk. She hadn't gone into Marissa's home and taken him. She wouldn't take something that wasn't hers. If the cashier gave her too much change, she returned it. If she found a diamond ring on the ground, she'd have turned it in. David was different. She hadn't stolen him. He'd been abandoned, unwanted. She'd rescued him.

It was Marissa who was the thief. She had come into Libby's home and stolen David. Even if she were the birth mother, and Libby had no proof of that, she had no right. She'd thrown him away, left him like a bag of kittens. She, or whoever the birth mother was, had lost all rights to him when he was left on the pavement. He was Libby's. If only she had him in her arms right now.

Would Marissa keep him safe? Would she keep him warm and dry and fed? Or would she drop him off someplace when the going got tough again? Would whoever found him next time love and care for him?

Libby paced the living room, trying to convince herself he would be all right. Marissa was a competent sitter. She knew what she was doing. This time she'd care for him. This time…

Libby kept returning to every movie and television cop show she'd ever seen about kidnapping. They always seemed to end badly. The ransom didn't get paid, and the kidnapped person died; or the ransom got paid, and the kidnapped person still died; or the ransom got paid, but the kidnapped person never knew it because the kidnapper never said, never returned them; or the victim was returned, but was fearful and damaged and never the same again.

How would it end with David? What would Marissa do to him? Try as she might, Libby couldn't come up with a positive outcome. Marissa was young, homeless, and jobless. She was on the run. Where would she leave him this time?

Perched on the couch, arms wrapped tightly around herself, Libby fought the scream that threatened to bubble to the surface. The doorbell startled a squeak from her, alleviating some of the pressure.

She raced to the door, hoping against all reason that it was Marissa returning David: *"I'm sorry, Libby. I don't know what I was thinking. He's such a wonderful baby that I wanted him for my own."*

Of course, it wasn't Marissa. Libby saw Jeff through the glass sidelight.

She opened the door.

"It's just me."

"I wouldn't say, 'just.'" She moved aside. "Come in. You saved me. I was driving myself mad thinking of all the reasons Marissa might have taken him and what they might be doing now."

"I figured as much." He nodded, closing the door behind him. "I brought Chinese." He held a bag aloft. "You didn't eat breakfast or lunch, and I worried you'd skip dinner as well." He looked her up and down. "You didn't nap, did you?"

She shook her head.

"You didn't eat either, did you?"

She led the way into the kitchen.

"You need to eat."

"I can't." Her voice broke. "What if he's hungry or wet? What if she isn't feeding him? Sometimes, he gets so hungry he won't eat."

"Like his mother?"

Libby was in Jeff's arms. Had she raced there? Had he pulled her in? It didn't matter. She felt safe, as David had in her arms. The tears overtook her. Oh, please, let David be safe.

She must have said it aloud.

"He is," Jeff assured her. "I'm sure he is. She didn't take him to hurt him."

She squeaked in protest as terror hit her. She hadn't thought of *that* possibility. Maybe she wasn't his mother, just a child-hater. Or maybe she was his mother and had taken him to get rid of him permanently. Her heart raced and her breath followed it. "I have to find David." She needed to do something.

She pushed out of Jeff's arms, looking left and right in her agitation. She picked up the phone receiver and looked at it. She needed to call someone, but who? She set down the phone with a growl of frustration.

"Enough." Jeff gently grabbed her by the arms. "Panicking won't get him back."

"What will?" She looked at him, silently pleading for him to give her an answer.

He shook his head, pulled her closer and kissed her hair. "The police and the FBI. Prayer. I don't know, Libby, but I'm here with you. I'm not going to let you do this alone."

"Why?" David wasn't his. He wasn't really hers, either. She repeated his pretend birth story, the one she'd told herself over and over again. I didn't know I was pregnant. He came so fast…I had him in the bathroom…But it wasn't the truth, and she knew it. "Why?"

"I don't know." Jeff spoke into her hair. "I just…it just feels right. Ever since we met, being with you has felt right. If yesterday had been a normal day, I'd have wanted to see you today. I'd have wanted to be with you. But now, now that feeling is even stronger. I feel more protective, more…I don't know. I just need to be here for you." He loosened his grip and looked down at her with a worried look in his eyes. "That is, if you want me here."

She hugged him close. "I want you here. Being with you felt right to me too, but now I'm so confused. I don't know if the attraction I feel toward you is the result of my need to have someone to help me get through this. I don't think it is. I wanted you before, but…" She shook her head. "Jeff, I'm so confused." She looked into his eyes. "I want you here. I just want you to be here for the right reasons. I don't want you to feel obligated. This is my problem."

"Let me make it our problem, okay?"

She hesitated, trying to read his thoughts in his eyes. Did he really mean it or was he just being the extremely nice guy she knew him to be? She wanted him to stay. Needed *him* to. Jeff, specifically.

"Say yes."

Could she accept what he seemed to be offering? She could only take him at his word, knowing it would kill her if he changed his mind. "Okay."

Everything was surreal. This wasn't how she imagined having a family. This wasn't how she'd imagined falling in love.

News at Nine

Marissa sat on the greasy bedspread in a cut-rate motel room. The newly detailed car with the modified plates was parked outside, right in front of the closed drapes. On the television, the green-faced weekend anchor led off the news with her story.

It wasn't a flattering piece. Marissa was portrayed as a crazed, baby-starved, college coed who had convinced herself that she had a baby and then stole someone else's son. Clearly, someone had spoken to Bess. Her great aunt was the only one to whom she'd told the truth about David.

Marissa frowned as her roommate's face, also green-tinged, appeared. The same Jessie Tuttle who hadn't noticed that she'd been pregnant swore that Marissa hadn't been pregnant. "It's not something you can hide from your roommate, especially when that roommate is a nursing student, like I am." She told of Marissa's break-up with Paul and talked of Marissa's new mystery boyfriend who had gotten her thinking about babies. "My guess would be this is the new boyfriend's idea. Marissa babysat, but she was too into college to want to start a family now."

Marissa stood in front of the television, flipped open the front panel, and tried to adjust the color.

Her parents' next door neighbor's skin went from green to red, skipping over the normal flesh tone look. Crabby, old Mrs. Anderson told of Marissa's prolonged absence from home and hinted at an estrangement from her family. Her make-up looked fresh, and Marissa could almost smell the liberal squirt of Chanel Number Five she wore for dress-up occasions, like the block party.

Marissa turned the color back to green. Somehow, that sickly hue was more appropriate.

Next, Libby's boyfriend read a statement while a photo of David toothlessly grinning in Libby's arms filled the screen.

"Libby's main concern is David's safety. Her message to Marissa is one of understanding. Taking David is clearly a cry for help. Marissa, please, if you're listening. Please, leave David at any hospital or police station. Just pin his name to his shirt and hand him to the receptionist. Libby and I promise to help you get the help you need."

Marissa's lip curled. "Yeah, right." Too little, too late. Hot tears made mascara-black paths down her face. Her parents' faces appeared on the screen next as they made an impassioned plea for her to come home so they could help her figure everything out. Finally, a representative of the Eau Claire police department presented a recent photo of Marissa. He asked that any information viewers might have be directed to their local police department or the number on the screen.

As the station went to commercial, Marissa ran her fingers through her short, black hair and examined herself in the mirror. She compared her mascara-smeared face with the one on the television screen. Gone was the clean, all-American girl, the crimped hair, the healthy glow, the smile. But it wasn't just the heavy make-up and glasses with the new hair that made her look unrecognizable. It was the feeling she had inside. It was almost as if she weren't the girl she'd once been. Wouldn't be. Couldn't be. She wasn't Marissa anymore. Now, she was... Daria. The name came out of nowhere. Daria Dixon.

And David, in a pink sleeper and a matching headband with a little bow, wasn't David. Maybe he felt the same as he kicked and squirmed on a blanket on the floor, but he wasn't the same. He was now Chris, and he would wear pink in public for the next several months.

She allowed a tear to escape as she unwrapped her burger.

§

Snuggled close on Libby's couch, she and Jeff watched the news. Libby looked away from the television and said to him, "You sounded good. Do you think it will work? Do you think she's watching and will bring David back?"

Jeff hugged Libby even closer. "I don't know. I don't know why she took him in the first place. It doesn't make sense. Why would she supposedly claim David was hers?"

Libby said nothing.

"Maybe her family just said that. She didn't steal a baby. She thought he was hers. As if being nuts makes the crime understandable."

"Maybe it's like the newscaster said. Maybe she's obsessed with babies. Maybe she felt alone and thought a baby would fulfill her." Like David had for Libby. Had Marissa taken David for some of the same reasons Libby had? Libby closed her eyes. Her throat hurt. But Libby hadn't stolen David. She'd rescued him. "Do you think maybe she lost a baby somewhere down the line?"

"Maybe. Everyone seems agreed that she wasn't pregnant. I tend to agree with her roommate that there has to be someone else involved. Why else would she turn from being Cheryl's ultra-dedicated babysitter into a baby-napper? It just doesn't make sense."

Libby nodded. It didn't make sense. None of it did. An abandoned baby, a concealed pregnancy, theft, and kidnapping. Had the roommate been wrong? Was David really Marissa's? Was there something else going on? A new boyfriend who wanted a baby enough to get Marissa to steal one for him? Why? Why not just make one? Every scenario she imagined was worse than the one before it.

She knew she'd found David in a duffle bag outside a store and taken him home. She knew her tale of having conceived him in the back seat of a car with a man she didn't know and then giving birth to him on the bathroom floor was strange and unbelievable. Heck, Mark and Carrie thought she was delusional.

Her story and Marissa's. Which seemed most likely? Which would the world perceive as truth, which as fiction? Libby knew the truth to her side of the story, knew exactly where to place the blame. She'd taken David. If this pain was the punishment she'd earned for keeping him, she'd take it just as long as David was safe and loved.

Just Missing You

At 4:00 in the morning, Libby woke to the gravelly grate of the plow. She rolled over and pounded her pillow envisioning the snow she'd have to shovel to back out of her drive.

Or not.

Why did she keep forgetting her car was gone?

Her bed was a cocoon of warmth, but she left it to look out the window. The sky was milky. Clearly visible against the backdrop of evergreens, large fluffs of snow floated to the ground. The wood floor was cold beneath her bare feet. Was David warm enough? Where had Marissa taken him?

Cheryl and Jeff expected her to stay home from work, but she couldn't. If she stayed home, she'd spend the day in David's room crying. Besides, she had bills to pay.

She made the bed and pulled off her nightgown, shivering for a moment before pulling on jeans and a sweater. The shovel seemed lonely in the empty garage. The garage door opened to reveal five fluffy inches of snow. Beautiful.

Push, lift, toss.

Some foster father, she didn't remember which, had taken the time to teach her how to shovel efficiently; how to make nice edges that didn't collapse and dump the snow bank onto the clean driveway. She employed that technique now. Push, lift, toss.

The monotonous rhythm was as comforting as the creaking of a rocker or waves upon a shore. Snow cloaked her sleeves and mittens as it fell. Her body grew warm. She unbuttoned her coat. Deliciously cool air bathed hot, sweat-coated skin. Scrape. Plop.

She stopped three quarters of the way through to catch her breath. The snowflakes were loud as they hit the ground. She closed her eyes and listened. Snowflakes fell on her heated cheeks and melted instantly. Somewhere out of sight, car wheels spun seeking traction. Libby lifted the shovel. The plow's drift waited.

Back inside, she called the bus company to find out how to get to work.

§

Libby hung her coat on the employee's coat rack at the clinic. Thanks to the bus, she was ten minutes earlier than usual.

Marsha gasped as she walked into the break room. "Libby, I saw the news. I'm so sorry." She pulled Libby into an awkward hug. "What are you doing here?"

"I work here." Libby clocked in.

"But you shouldn't be here. You should take a week, or at least a couple of days."

"I can't."

"Of course you can. We'll call the temp service if we have to."

Libby shook her head. "No, I mean *I* can't stand to sit at home and do nothing. It's too quiet. It's too..." Dog-gone-it, why did she have to explain her need to work? "I can't just sit there without him. I need to be busy. I have bills. My insurance isn't full coverage, so it doesn't cover theft of the car." She knew she was speaking a little too loudly, but she couldn't seem to help herself. What made Marsha think she knew best? Had *she* ever lost a child?

"Uh, sorry. I just thought you'd need some time off."

Libby winced at Marsha's affronted tone. "I'm sorry, Marsha. I didn't mean to be short. I know you mean well, but I'm struggling here." Her eyes filled with unwanted tears. "Maybe you'll be right and I'll need time off, but right now I feel that if I spend one more minute looking at his empty crib I'll go nuts."

Marsha's scowl changed to an understanding smile. She patted Libby's arm. "I can't imagine what you're going through, Libby. You just do what you need to. If working helps, you work. Just let me know if it gets to be too much, okay?"

"Okay." Libby escaped into the restroom to splash cold water on her face and blow her nose. Handling her own emotions was hard enough. Why must she handle everyone else's too?

Libby was on the phone taking an appointment when Cheryl walked in late. Cheryl's eyes were red rimmed and damp, her eye make-up was smeared. She looked like a prize fighter after a losing bout. Libby was glad she'd decided to go without make-up today.

Once the phone was back in its cradle, Cheryl launched herself at Libby and hugged her so hard it took her breath away. *Come on, Cheryl, please don't.* She'd only just recovered from the last scene. Besides, they'd done this all weekend long.

"I'm so sorry."

Libby shook her head. "Please, don't." They'd had this conversation a hundred times, already. She couldn't do it again.

"But it's all my fault."

Libby shook her head.

"It is," Cheryl insisted.

Now it was Libby's turn to say "No it wasn't," and "You couldn't have known..." They'd done it before. She couldn't do it again. "Fine, then I think you should turn yourself in."

Cheryl gaped at her. "What?"

"If David's disappearance is your fault, then you should turn yourself in." She picked up the phone and handed it Cheryl. "The number is 9-1-1." Cheryl just stared. "Or better yet, give him back. Return him, and we'll forget everything."

"I didn't take him." Cheryl's voice shook.

Libby nodded, the hardness in her voice melted. "I know you didn't. And you didn't make Marissa take him, either. You couldn't have guessed that she would. No one could. So will you just quit with the apologies? You didn't do it."

Cheryl turned beet red, but Libby continued.

"I'm tired of telling you I don't blame you. I don't. This is Marissa's fault, not yours. So can you shut up about it so we can move past it and be friends? I really need you to be my friend now, not another victim. I need *you* to comfort *me,* not the other way around. David is my son."

Cheryl struggled to her feet, took one look at Libby and burst into tears.

Libby closed her eyes against her own tears as Cheryl ran off. "Great. Just great." This was just what she needed. She'd lost her son, and now she was losing her best friend. Why did she have to be the strong one?

David had brought everything good in her life and now that he was gone, everything else that was good would be leaving too. Jeff would be next. She fanned her face with a sheet of paper in the vain attempt to dry the tears before they fell. She understood what Cheryl was feeling. She really did. If the situations had been reversed, she would have felt the same, but they weren't. This was *her* loss. David was hers. Not Cheryl's, not Marissa's. Hers.

She managed to get herself back under control before it was time to unlock the door and let in the first mother and her sick child.

For the Love of *David*

She let herself go on autopilot: Get name. Confirm birth date and complaint. Pull chart. Check for labs. Double-check insurance. "Have a seat. The doctor will be right with you."

Cheryl still hadn't returned, so Libby ignored the insurance and billing, her assigned task for the day, and focused on reception. Mondays were always busy. Libby checked in people, fielded calls, made appointments and pulled charts.

She was on the phone setting up an appointment for a well-baby checkup when Cheryl returned. She should have finished the call and stood, yielding the seat as they did when the receptionist of the day returned from a bathroom break, but she didn't. The phone rang again and she answered it, immediately feeling guilty.

"Gunderson Pediatric Clinic, please hold." She turned to Cheryl. "Do you want to handle this?"

Cheryl shook her head, but she didn't look at Libby.

Libby's stomach cramped. Darn it all. Was Cheryl too upset to talk to people? Or was she just too mad to talk to Libby?

She wanted to scream, "This isn't my fault!" But apparently Cheryl thought it was, so she was going to have to apologize, anyway. It was like Marsha all over again. She couldn't do this. Why wouldn't anyone just let her work? She took a deep breath and let it out before pressing the hold button again.

"Thank you for holding, how may I help you?"

Cold waves of silence poured from Cheryl. The harder Libby tried to ignore it, the deeper and heavier the silence became. It wasn't that she and Cheryl usually talked when it was this busy. They didn't. Still, there was normally a tone of joyful camaraderie that was conspicuously lacking. Even as she smiled at patients and their parents, she felt the silence behind her.

By the time her lunch break rolled around, the silence was nearly solid. Libby glanced at the clock, but she kept working. Her stomach ached, more sick than hungry.

Had her comments been that out of line?

Her hand hovered over the phone. If she called Jeff, would he be impartial or would he automatically take his sister-in-law's point of view? It didn't matter. She would live. She'd been alone before. Her stomach clenched. The thought made it hard to swallow. Bile rose from her empty stomach to burn her throat. Darn it, she needed Oreos.

§

After work, she walked to the bus stop grateful for the cold that bit her cheeks and made her toes ache inside her boots. The icy squeak sent shivers down her spine. Cold occupied her mind.

A block from the stop, a black pickup truck pulled up beside her. The window rolled down and Jeff stuck his head out. "Hop in."

Libby looked left and right, but no one else was there.

He pushed open the door. "Libby, hop in. I'll give you a ride home."

She couldn't help smiling as she reached for the door. Growing up, she'd seen other kids' parents and friends pick them up, but she and Jenny had always taken the bus or walked. She sat on the seat and closed the door.

He pulled away from the curb. "I didn't know you were going to work today. You should have called me. I told you I'd pick you up."

"I know." She didn't know why she hadn't. "You don't have to drive me everywhere until the police find my car."

"They found it."

Libby turned abruptly in her seat. "They what? Where? Was David in it? Is he all right?" A ball of anger warmed her. "Why didn't they call me?"

"Relax, sweetheart. I'm sure the police left a message. Nobody expected you to go to work today."

"I had to."

He reached across the seat and held her hand. "I know, honey. I can't say I blame you. Being alone in the house is too much. That's why I'm going to be there as much as I can." He squeezed her hand and then released it to signal a turn. "Anyway, according to the news, the police found it abandoned in a field near Baldwin, just where Marissa told her great aunt they would find it."

"But no sign of David?" She knew he hadn't been there, but she still needed confirmation that he hadn't been left to freeze.

"There was a frozen diaper, but that's all."

She nodded, releasing the breath she'd been holding. "Good." As long as David was with Marissa he'd be fine, right? She looked out the window. *Please, God.*

"How was work?"

Her stomach tightened. "Horrible. Cheryl wouldn't talk to me. She started off telling me how sorry she was, again, and I guess I snapped at her. She didn't say a word to me the rest of the day."

Jeff nodded. "I heard. She called the office this morning and talked to Jack. He told me everything. I felt like I was in junior high."

"Sorry." She winced.

"Not a problem. Trouble is, Cheryl doesn't know what to say. She feels like she's let you down on so many fronts that she's afraid to say anything."

"I didn't think I was that harsh. I told her…"

"I heard. You weren't harsh. You were honest. David is your son, and she's been mourning him like it was Devin. Worse, because she still has Devin. According to Jack, she didn't think you were harsh. She'd probably have handled it better if you had been." He shrugged. "Whatever *that* means. Anyway, they're coming over with pizza."

Her eyes grew wide and her mouth got dry. "I don't—"

He squeezed her knee and interrupted her protest. "I know you don't want to, but you need to. You and Cheryl need each other, so you're going to make nice tonight, cry in each other's arms, and get your friendship back on track. Jack and I have decided. No way we're going to play middlemen in this."

"Seems to me that's exactly what you're doing." She grinned. "Explaining motives. Arranging pizza."

He turned and grinned sheepishly. "Maybe, just this once. This is too important not to."

"Okay." Her smile faded.

He opened his door, got out, and closed it. Libby continued to sit there. Tears blurred the closed garage door. Jeff opened her door. His face softened. "It's the car, isn't it? I know that getting it back is going to be hard because she used it to take him, but getting it back is just the first step. David will be next. Really. You'll see."

She shook her head.

"Sure, you will. It's only been a couple of days. You have to give the police a little time."

"I know." He was so sweet and caring, how could she tell him it wasn't the news about the car that started the tears? It was pizza and spending the evening with friends. David was gone, but life was moving on. David was gone and there was a good chance tonight there would be laughter. How could she have fun with David missing?

Homeless

"Damn." Marissa tossed the newspaper to the battered linoleum of the coffee shop table. She didn't have enough money for an apartment. She had enough money for rent for a month but not enough for the security deposit and the first and last month's rent every landlord seemed to require. Sure, there were rent-by-the-day (or the hour) places, but she wasn't *that* desperate.

In the booth beside her, David rumbled into his pants. Marissa sighed. He didn't sleep the night through, he drank bottle after bottle of formula, and he spat up and crapped all the time. He'd be more fun when he could do stuff, like roll over and crawl. More fun. And more work. She needed an apartment before that. An apartment and a job, which meant day care.

She picked up the newspaper. Job first, day care second, and apartment third. She thought of her supply of diapers and formula. She needed to eat, too. The apartment dropped down the list to fourth or fifth.

She looked out the window to the greasy slush the cars had shot onto the sidewalk. Not so long ago, her only worry had been classes. Room and board and spending money had all been taken care of. She didn't have to take sink baths in public restrooms. She used to tip waitresses and never contemplated skipping out on a bill. She never considered that one day she'd live in a car.

§

"I don't know why you think I should kiss you when you hit my guy and send him to the bar," Libby protested as Jeff took her backgammon checker and set it on the bar in the middle of the game board. "Seems to me, you should kiss me in apology."

"Okay." Jeff pulled her close. "If you insist."

His lips were the perfect combination of firm and soft. When he pressed them against hers, coaxing hers to part, all thoughts temporarily evaporated. One kiss lead to two. "I'm sorry I'm whooping your butt."

Libby pushed him away and laughed. "You are not."

He grinned. "That's right." He handed her the dice. "I'm going to get another beer. Do you want some more wine?"

"Sure." She drank the last sip and handed him the empty glass.

As soon as he left, she rose to her feet as well, heading to the bathroom. The vacant silence of David's room pulled at her. She stood in the doorway, unwilling to enter. It had been only two weeks, but it felt like a lifetime. Every night she woke, thinking she heard him cry. Every morning she stood in the doorway and prayed as if she were at a shrine.

"So this is where you went." Jeff's arms reached around her from behind, drawing her back against his chest.

She leaned against him trying to absorb his strength.

"You're doing it again."

She nodded. "I know." Every time she caught herself having a good time she felt compelled to stop, as if she shouldn't be able to enjoy life while David was gone. "I don't mean to."

"I know you don't, and it has only been two weeks, but I think you should talk to someone."

"I'm grieving."

"Of course you are." He pressed a kiss behind her ear. "This isn't a normal situation. David isn't dead. In a lot of ways, that's worse."

She snorted. "Gone is worse than dead?"

"I think so. If he were dead, we'd have a funeral. Everyone would come at once to express their sympathy. We'd know he wasn't hungry or cold, and we'd know he wasn't coming back. Now, you worry. I see it. You aren't sleeping or eating properly. You stand in this doorway and look in, but you don't go in."

"I know."

"Why don't you go in?"

She hugged his arms to her belly. "I don't know. It's like if I don't go in, he isn't really gone."

"But he is gone."

Libby's throat felt tight. "I know."

"I worry about you. Every time we get close or you start to enjoy life, you pull away."

She nodded. There were times she worried about herself as well. "I miss David." She sniffled.

"Of course you do."

She shook her head. "No. Sometimes, I don't think I miss him enough. There were moments, brief moments, mind, but moments nonetheless, when I forget about him. When I forget to miss him."

"That's when you pull away."

He understood. She nodded, grateful he was so caring and patient with her.

"Do you feel the need to punish yourself for forgetting him? For feeling happy?"

She nodded, then leaned her head against him and let the tears wind their way down her cheeks.

"You shouldn't. It's normal. People don't grieve forever. They aren't supposed to grieve forever."

A sob rose and choked her words. "But it's only been two weeks."

"I don't think that's abnormal. I would think it was strange if you weren't moving on."

"But it's only been two weeks." What kind of a mother was she when two weeks after her son's disappearance she needed a picture to remember exactly what he looked like?

"That's why I think you might want to see someone. A professional who will tell you that what you are going through is normal. That you shouldn't punish yourself because your life hasn't ended."

She shook her head. "I don't know."

He turned her so she faced him. "Think about it, Libby. There's a whole lot of future in front of us. It's good that we grieve for David and work for and pray for his return, but his absence shouldn't be what defines us. What defines you."

"I know you're right, but it's too soon."

He nodded.

She forced a smile. "But it's not too soon for me to whip your butt at backgammon."

"That's my girl."

§

"You're losing too much weight, and it's starting to worry me," Cheryl told Libby as she picked Libby up for work. The police considered Libby's car evidence and nearly a month after the kidnapping, they still kept it impounded. "You need to eat more."

"I'm just not hungry." It wasn't true. She was always hungry. She dreamed of Oreos. At night, she chased David through the house while giant Oreos pursued her. Last night, the cookies cornered her in the kitchen. David's cupboard had been emptied of bottles and filled with

Oreos. Package after package tumbled from the cabinet. Each one that touched her melted into her, becoming huge thighs and rounded belly. She'd screamed for David to come back and rescue her, but he disappeared, crying. Jeff appeared, took one look at her fat and left. She woke with a stomachache. She didn't eat breakfast. Couldn't eat.

Cheryl shook her head. "It's not healthy. You're going to make yourself sick."

Libby shrugged. What could she say? Her relationship with food had always been dysfunctional, and now it was even worse. She was afraid to eat for fear she wouldn't be able to stop.

"Well, you'll eat tonight. I expect you and Jeff at 6:30."

Libby nodded. It was far easier to pretend the problem didn't exist. "What can we bring? You never said."

"A bottle of white zin. It doesn't really go with lasagna, but it's what I like."

"How about we bring a merlot too? Jack will drink a red, won't he?"

"He'd rather have beer. We've got some in the fridge, but it wouldn't hurt to have Jeff pick up a six pack of something. I know he prefers beer as well."

§

After work, Libby climbed into Jeff's truck. He smelled delicious, like vanilla and spearmint. Her mouth watered.

Once inside, he pulled her into his arms. "Hi, sweetheart," he murmured, as his mouth descended toward hers. Libby's lips parted when they came into contact with Jeff's, and their normal greeting peck turned into something much more. He'd been eating Nilla Wafers and was trying to mask it with a fresh piece of gum. She could see the cookie wrapper sticking out of the glove compartment. With a hunger that had nothing to do with food, Libby wanted vanilla and spearmint.

A horn beeped beside them. They broke apart and turned to the source of the noise. Cheryl's station wagon was alongside Jeff's truck. He rolled down the window.

"You're fogging up the windows. Don't get distracted and forget you're coming for dinner."

It was only one kiss. Still, Libby felt her face heat. She'd forgotten they were in the parking lot at work.

"We won't," Jeff assured Cheryl.

"You better not. I know where both of you live, and I'll send Jack to get you if you aren't on time."

Jeff laughed, but Libby wondered if they couldn't just hide out somewhere.

Cheryl drove away.

Jeff rolled up the window and turned to Libby. "Darn that Cheryl."

She grinned. "It's probably for the best. I was getting a little carried away."

"You can get carried away anytime you like. In fact, I'd like you to get carried away again, real soon."

"I'd like to get carried away now, somewhere private."

He groaned. His eyes reflected the heat she felt. "Then let's do it."

"What about Cheryl and Jack?"

"Who?" His thumb was making seductive circles in the center of her palm.

"They're expecting us."

He groaned again. "I know. And I haven't picked up the wine and beer yet. We better get going. Darn it."

She smiled.

They held hands as he pulled out of the parking lot. His hand was solid and warm as it wrapped around hers. A strong anchor to keep her grounded when she was drifting. She swayed. Longing for him made her dizzy.

"Did you eat today?" His voice was gentle, but his tone was mildly accusing.

She blinked at him. It was desire, not hunger that made her weak. Of course, she couldn't say that. She shrugged.

"I'm not sure about lunch, but I think I had breakfast." Actually, she wasn't sure about either. Hunger pangs masqueraded as the sick stomach she got when she thought of David and Marissa. If she kept busy enough, she could distract herself from her sick stomach and ignore her hunger. Sometimes meal time would pass, and she would forget she'd been hungry.

"I'm worried about you, honey. You're losing too much weight."

"Losing too much weight? Is that possible?"

"Yes."

She didn't agree. All her life she'd been pudgy. Now, she knew it was partially because she'd tried to swallow her hurts, fears and feelings of inadequacy with food. Now, she was trying to do what the books said and experience her emotions rather than swallow them. It was more difficult than she'd imagined.

"Well, you'll eat tonight," Jeff said, breaking into her thoughts.

Libby smiled. "You sound just like Cheryl. The two of you are becoming food pushers." She looked left and right as if to make certain they wouldn't be overheard. "Isn't that illegal?" She smiled so that Jeff would know it was a joke.

He smiled back. "Not in Wisconsin, but I'm not certain about Wyoming. All the 'W' states aren't the same."

She laughed, and with the laughter came guilt. How could she feel happiness when David was missing?

Jeff squeezed her hand. "Have you given anymore thought to talking with a therapist? I think the food issue and the guilt you feel about enjoying life during David's absence are related."

"I don't know." Maybe a therapist could help her deal with her loss without knowing of her guilt. Maybe he could help her untangle all the emotions. But what if she let something slip? Would her therapist be required to turn her in?

"Let me call someone, please."

"You think it's gotten that bad?"

He nodded. "What can it hurt?"

That's what she was worried about.

§

Marissa, as Daria, sat in the front seat of the car with her paycheck. She counted her tips twice before adding them to the small stash in the car seat lining.

"Crap."

Three weeks on the job, and she was nowhere near having a security deposit, much less first month and last month rent.

"I didn't think it would take this long," she told David as he watched her from the car seat. She was working long hours, leaving David at daycare as soon as it opened and picking him up moments before it closed. They knew him as Chris. She had to be careful not to slip up. On her skimpy little paycheck, she was able to keep up with daycare, diapers and formula, but not much else. Living out of a car wasn't free, especially in Chicago. Parking was expensive. She had to feed the meter or move the car. Good daycare was expensive. Even lousy daycare was expensive.

She picked up David and shoved his car seat aside so she could lay him on the seat. "You need a bath, kiddo." She did, as well. What she wouldn't give for a ten minute shower. The memory of being at home and showering until the hot water ran out was like a fantasy. There weren't gas stations with showers in downtown Chicago. Showers at the YWCA weren't free. Laundromats made a killing and were frightening at night. Nothing was free.

She changed David's diaper and got out of the car to go to the back seat. Once inside, she put David in the footwell and double checked that each door was locked. Only then did she begin the contortion act of removing her shoes and changing from her regular clothes to the sweat suit she slept in. Man, she hated living in a car.

Once she was dressed for bed, she carefully folded her day clothes and set them on the front seat. David fussed.

"Just a second."

She sat with her back against the door and stretched out her legs. She hated sleeping in the car. Sleeping curled up on the hard, lumpy seat her legs cramped. All of five minutes had passed since she'd turned off the car, and already it was cold.

She climbed into the sleeping bag they shared and plucked David from the floor. His bottle, made with hot water from the diner's restroom, was waiting in her coat pocket. The windows fogged and dripped, but she didn't wipe them. There were crazy people out there—scary people who pressed their faces to the windows, and banged and yelled obscenities and propositions. She snuggled lower into the sack, drawing David and his bottle with her.

This wasn't how she'd imagined things would be when she'd taken David. She imagined what she knew–suburbia. Warm house, clean clothes, plenty of food, love. She longed for home, for her mother.

David finished his bottle and fell asleep. She shifted his warm bulk onto her chest. He was heavy, but at least he helped keep her chest warm. If only she could put him on her feet. Sleeping bags never kept her warm no matter what they promised. Maybe it was the zipper leaking cold air. Maybe it was condensation slowly seeping in. Maybe it was the damp of that leaky diaper two days ago.

Marissa closed her eyes. Sleep came slowly, as if wary of its reception.

The room was shades of gray, like the picture on the small television in the corner. Across the room the baby was crying. The baby was always crying. Probably hungry. Marissa was hungry too—and cold. Momma was gone and so was the man. There was always a man when Momma was around.

Her tummy rumbled. The pizza box smelled spicy and enticing, but it was cold and empty. She'd eaten the crumbs earlier, along with the little black ring. There was nothing now but the wet spot on the box where the pizza had been. Maybe it would taste like pizza.

The baby screamed. "Okay, okay." She'd taste the box later.

There was a baby bottle on the table next to the other bottle. The floor was cold and sticky. It pulled at the skin on the bottoms of her feet. She didn't like the feeling, so she walked on the mattress as much as she could. She ran from the edge of the mattress to the table and climbed up on the wooden chair. It was sticky too. She didn't like sticky.

The bottles sat in the middle of the table out of reach. The table shook so hard as Marissa crawled across it that a bowl of stinky cigarette butts fell to the floor. The baby bottle fell over and the other one too. Marissa grabbed the bottles before they fell to the floor.

Across the room, the baby cried and cried.

"Coming, Brat!"

Marissa twisted the top off the other bottle. It smelled like Momma. Marissa took a drink and coughed. It was hot in her throat, but warm in her tummy. Warm was good. The baby was probably cold too. She opened the baby bottle and poured some in. A lot spilled. She wasn't good at pouring.

§

A rattling sound jerked Marissa awake. Someone was outside trying the car door. She'd locked the car. She knew she'd locked the car. The keys were in her right pocket where she always kept them. She pulled them out and held them so the end of a key sat between her first and second fingers of her fist. She unzipped the sleeping bag and slid David from her chest and herself from the bag in one rapid motion. In another, she was diving into the front seat.

The black woman at the door screamed and jumped back.

Marissa scrambled into the driver seat. Her hand shook so much that she missed on her first attempt to jab the key into the ignition. There was yelling outside, and David woke up with a scream in the back seat. She hit the key hole on her second try, but the key didn't go in. Was it the wrong key? Upside down? She fumbled in the noisy dark, nearly dropping the keys. She found the square one and jammed it home. Please, please. The engine roared to life.

She hit the gas. The car shook as it hit someone or something, but Marissa didn't stop to look. She didn't turn on the headlights until she'd driven a block.

She drove straight and then right and then left, searching for a sign for the highway. David wailed in the back seat. She cried in the front. Dashing the tears with her sleeve, she followed the signs to I-94. North or south didn't matter. She needed to get out of the city.

The traffic was steady, light for Chicago. The clock on the dash said it was 12:18. Not so late. She drove. In the back, David found his fist. She heard him slurping on it as his cries decreased. His car seat sat on the seat next to her, which meant he was still tangled in the sleeping bag. On the seat? On the floor? A quick glance over her shoulder didn't show.

Some mother she was.

The dream was still with her. Bess had told her she was two when her mother abandoned her. Two. No one had memories of being two. The earliest memories she and her friends could place for certain were from kindergarten. She had picture memories of earlier times, but they were just that, memories of pictures. She didn't actually remember holding Mitch when he came home from the hospital.

She'd seen her baby book. There were baby pictures in it and a list of firsts. Bess lied.

Marissa took an exit, thinking of the pictures. There was a newborn shot, one baby photo, and then pictures of her as toddler on up. She'd never found it strange that Mitch had a million baby pictures. Hers were lost when her parents moved to the house just before Mitch was born.

So the dream was just a dream, not a memory. She'd only called the baby Brat because of Bess. She'd only dreamt of cigarettes and booze because of the details Bess had fed her. She'd been hungry and cold in the dream because she *was* hungry and cold. It half surprised her that she hadn't seen drug paraphernalia in her dream, as well. Thanks to Bess's fictional details, she should have seen needles, powder, spoons, and an elastic tube.

Marissa drove to a car dealership and parked in the back next to the trade-ins and repairs. She and David would be safe there. She turned off the ignition and crawled into the back seat. The car was warm, thanks to the heater. David was damp with sweat in his little pocket of the tangled sleeping bag.

Marissa dried him off, located his bottle and pulled it into the sleeping bag with them. He didn't like cold bottles.

Had she really been about to feed the baby liquor in her dream?

§

Marissa was up at the break of dawn. She used to be able to sleep until noon unless someone woke her. Her mother called her sleepy-head and quoted nursery rhymes: "Mistress Mary, quite contrary, how did you wake so soon? You used to rise at 10:00 and now it's only noon."

Now she was up before the sun, moving the car, trying to find a new place to sneak a sink-bath for her and David. Today, there was traffic. She worried as she drove into town. If she didn't get to daycare early enough, they might not have spaces, and as hideous as work was, she didn't want to be late. She needed the money.

Somehow, she had to get enough money to quit living in the car.

§

"He's really bad today," Latisha said when Marissa clocked in.

Marissa didn't need to ask who. Joey was the owner's brother and cook. Latisha, Wendi, Nora and the rest of the waitresses had warned her about Joey when she started working for Ben. They'd gathered in the tiny waitress station and whispered fervently.

"Don't ever go in the walk-in cooler alone. Always get one of us to go in with you or ask Ben," skinny, caramel-skinned Latisha insisted on Marissa's first day. "It's better to have your tables never get their coleslaw than to get caught in the cooler."

Wendi, the heavyset brunette, nodded emphatically as she tossed out an old coffee filter and replaced it with a new one. "Joey's a sex fiend."

"He's majorly disgusting, but if you're low on cash, they say he pays well," Nora, the faded blonde with the strung-out look, hissed as she filled glasses with water.

"You'd know," Latisha sniped, giving Nora an ugly look, which was promptly returned along with a shove.

Marissa took the warning to heart. She might be struggling, but one look at the greasy cook with the crazy eyes and the snaggle-toothed leer made goose flesh appear. She tossed her orders onto the counter like the rest of the girls and made certain she never reached for the plate he was closest to.

She endured, with sweaty palms, his questions about her orders, questions directed to her chest. She stayed out of the kitchen unless absolutely necessary.

Joey hadn't gotten any less creepy over time, but she had gotten better at ignoring him.

"What's his beef today?"

Latisha laughed. "Oooh girl, you nailed it. He's got his beef out, and he's looking for somewhere to stick it."

"Eww." Marissa winced. She needed money to get an apartment, but there was no way she'd get it whoring. She'd sell the car first.

"Ben's on the phone now, trying to get him help."

Marissa shivered. "What kind of help."

"Drugs, I hope." Nora pulled her card out of the pile and clocked out.

Latisha sneered. "He won't share the drugs, girl."

Marissa gave the stringy blonde a once over. Nora looked particularly shaky this morning. The circles around her eyes appeared deeper and darker.

"Or maybe he will. I'll bet Ben would give you enough to score if you took on Joey." Latisha had obviously looked Nora over as well. "Should be fast. He looked ready for action when I saw him."

Nora flipped them the bird. "I'd do a two-fer in the alley before I'd do Joey. He's nasty."

Marissa felt sick just thinking about Nora's list of options. Latisha just shrugged.

Nora headed for the door.

"Wait a sec, Nora. Do either of you know where I could sell my car?"

"The Buick?" Nora asked.

Marissa nodded.

Latisha shrugged. "Nice car. Should be able to drive it to one of them used-car lots and make a deal. Unless it's not quite yours."

Marissa felt her face grow hot and hated even more how Latisha smiled whenever it did. "It's not."

"I know a guy," Nora volunteered. "Just give me the keys, tell me where you stashed it, and it's as good as gone."

"She don't want it gone, junky. She want it sold." Latisha turned to Marissa. "How much you need for it?"

Marissa knew exactly, first month, last month, security deposit, and some for cushion. She padded the cushion, knowing that she'd get less than she asked for and far less than Bess's car was worth.

"That all?" Latisha said. "Girl, you are so green. I get you that myself. You got any papers on the car?"

Marissa nodded.

"In the car?"

"I'm not an idiot." They were in David's car seat lining with everything else important.

"You got papers, I'll help you change em for two hunerd. You can sell it legit. Get twice what you was asking."

"You get me twice what I was asking, I'll give you three hundred."

"Deal."

Nora screwed up her face. "Bitch, if you can get her all that, why ain't you just giving her what she asked for and taking the rest?"

"Karma. Daria's got a kid. You fuck a mama, and you fucked when *you* a mama. My mama didn't believe in no karma. She fucked a mama, and now she's fucked up bad. Why you think being a mother-fucker is so bad? It's all karma, junky. All karma."

§

Two days later, Marissa moved David and their small collection of belongings into a small, furnished efficiency apartment within walking distance from his daycare and her work. The apartment was in a neighborhood Marissa would have avoided a few months ago. Everything about Marissa's life was something she would have avoided several months ago.

She carried David into the bathroom. Their very own, disgustingly dirty bathroom. She turned on the hot water and stuck her hand into the stream. It was hot. She grinned. It would take a lot of work to scrub the place clean, but then she and David would get to take a nice, hot bath.

She carried David back into the living room/bedroom combo and sat on the plaid hide-a-bed couch. "Life will be better now."

David watched her with the serious look he often wore now.

"We won't have to worry about safety." The past two nights she'd driven to the suburbs and barely slept. She kept envisioning some druggy taking a baseball bat to the windshield while she and David were sleeping. "I got the old caretaker's apartment."

She smiled. The landlord had told her it had only had two tenants, and both had been elderly couples. As if it were a car he was claiming had only been driven to church on Sundays. She put David on a blanket on the floor and then walked to the window.

It had a lousy view, thanks to the bars, but it was those bars, the steel door, and the dead bolt that made the dingy apartment feel like an oasis of safety in a moral desert. The rest of the apartment was crap. The standard, rundown hide-a-bed couch, a coffee table, oversized dresser, cheap laminate table, and two kitchen chairs. Still, Marissa didn't regret paying extra for the security. She checked to make certain the dead bolt was engaged. In this neighborhood, bars on the window and a solid door with a good lock meant a good night's sleep. No wacko with a baseball bat could pound in the door or come through the window to hurt her or David.

Maybe she couldn't afford a better part of town, but she could afford the extra twenty a month to make sure they were safe.

She made certain David was still okay on the blanket and handed him a set of oversized plastic keys. "You hang out there, kiddo. Mommy's going to clean this place." She hummed as she broke out the cleaning supplies. Maybe they would manage, after all.

The bathroom smelled of bleach and toilet cleanser when she stopped the bathtub drain and turned on the water.

"You're first, stinky boy." She stripped him naked, wrinkling her nose at the ammonia smell. His bottom was red from too infrequent diaper changes. A small economy that had taken its toll. Daily baths would help, the newly purchased baby care book said. Airing his bottom would, as well.

His rubber-doll body was as slippery as it had been during the first bath at Aunt Bess's house, but Marissa was an old pro at it now. David lay on his back in the tub, kicking his legs and burbling. A hearty splash hit his face. Marissa laughed as his eyes grew wide and his lower lip quivered. "You're okay, baby. Chris." She had to remember his name was Chris.

When he was clean and dry, she laid him on his belly on the new bathmat to look around as she showered.

"Heaven, I'm in Heaven," she sang as the hot water sluiced over her. She shampooed her hair. Twice. Then conditioned it. It was forever since she'd had a real shower. Even longer since she'd had the chance to take a look at herself. Her hands skimmed over her body. She'd lost weight. No surprise there. With the meals she'd skipped, it was a wonder she wasn't skin and bones. Her breasts were back to normal. No one would know by looking at her that she'd ever had a child. She felt a pang of guilty pleasure at the thought.

But she was a mother.

Dressed again, she transferred David to the living room floor and wiped down the kitchen while his bottle warmed on the stove. This was home.

She looked around. "It's not so bad here. It just needs a fresh coat of paint, the use of a carpet shampooer, and something to hang on the walls."

If she were making a wish list, she would have added a telephone, a television, and a crib—but who was she to complain? Until a couple of hours ago, they'd lived in a car.

She tested the temperature of the formula on her wrist. "We'll be happy here, you'll see. I'll line that big bottom drawer with a towel and it will make a nice bed. Much better than your car seat or the back seat of the car."

Marissa sat on the couch and talked to her son as she fed him his bottle.

"I probably bought more than we need today, but the baby book and film for the Polaroid Aunt Bess gave me are important. You're not always going to be this little, and you'll want to see what you were like as a baby. I always did." Her heart cramped. What if the stories about her as a baby were a lie? Had Tammy made up the stories, seeing what Mitch did and changing them just a little for her? She pushed the thought aside. This moment was about her son.

"I don't know that I'll always call you Chris. You really are more of a David, but I can't call you that for a little while. We won't stay here forever." She wasn't sure why they were there now. Did she go to Chicago because that's where Bess said Mora had been? She didn't believe Bess, but here they were anyway.

"Come spring, we'll move from here, and I'll finish school." She thought of her days at Eau Claire. "Well, maybe not college. I'll probably take night classes on legal or medical terminology and be a legal secretary or a Med-Tech or something. I don't know. Something that pays better than waitressing. Then we'll get a house with a yard. You'd like a yard. I'll build you a tree fort, though that's usually a dad's job. Maybe I'll meet someone and get a dad for you."

David looked into her eyes as she spoke. A wave of love warmed her, and she hugged her son a little closer.

"Someday I'll tell you about your birth daddy. I'll skip the leaving you for three months part. Let's just say that never happened. We'll just say your daddy wasn't ready for fatherhood. We'll say that I was, but that when you're big, you should make certain both you and your girlfriend are ready before you have sex, cuz it only takes just once." David's eyelids were getting heavy. He was losing the fight to keep them open. "I love you, little man," she told him. "You go right to sleep. You're safe here. We're both safe here."

She held him long after he fell asleep, even though she had the kitchen floor to wash and the carpet to foam clean. She'd worry about a vacuum cleaner later, after she'd saved enough from her checks for rent. Maybe Ben would let her borrow the restaurant's vacuum cleaner. If she got off early, she could race home, vacuum and run the machine back before she had to pick up David—she meant Chris.

"Why is it I have such a hard time remembering that I registered you as Chris at daycare?" she asked her sleeping son. "I don't seem to have any trouble remembering that I'm Daria. Maybe because I'm not who I used to be, but you are. Who knows?" She eased off the couch. "Enough philosophy for one night. Welcome home, little man."

Half Truths

Two months and three days after David's abduction, Libby sat on the therapist's couch. It was just a couch, not a fainting couch like they had in the movies, and she was sitting, not lying prone. It wasn't her idea to be there, but she'd given in to Jeff's urging.

"Why don't you tell me why you're here today?" Dr. Day set the chart, containing the sheets Libby had filled out, face down on the table next to her chair.

"It's like I wrote, I feel so torn. I don't know how to act since David was stolen. Most of the time I miss him so much it's like a part of me has been ripped away. Then sometimes, I catch myself smiling and having fun, and I feel guilty. It's like I should be miserable as long as David is gone."

"Why?"

Libby shrugged. "I don't know. Because he hasn't been gone that long, and I seem be moving on."

"You don't want to move on?"

Libby's hands wound around each other in her lap. She didn't know how to answer. "I do, but I don't. It's like I can't remember how to act without him."

The doctor nodded. "That's not uncommon. Children change everything."

"It's more than that." She looked at her hands, noticed their movement and held them still. "How do I explain?" She looked back to the doctor. "I used to be heavy, but after David came, I lost weight. Now, I don't know how to eat. I don't know how I lost the weight or how to keep it off. It's like David's mother was slim, and Libby Armstrong isn't. I'm afraid to eat."

Dr. Day looked at Libby, picked up the chart and checked what Libby expected was her weight. "Your weight is a bit low for your height, but not seriously below what is considered normal. How much did you weigh before you got pregnant?"

Libby shrugged. "I don't own a scale. The thing is, I was so heavy that I could pass for pregnant. David surprised me." It bothered Libby how she could omit enough information that she misled without actually lying.

"I see." The doctor wrote a note on the chart. "I think we can help you with that. I'll have you talk to the nutritionist when we're done here. Diane will help you figure out your ideal weight and develop a life plan to maintain it."

Libby's heart sank. "A life plan? You mean diet and exercise?" Calorie counting diets didn't work for her. It wasn't a proven formula. Despite the logic that calories consumed minus calories burned in exercise yielded a certain weight, it didn't work for her. Those formulas didn't take into account metabolism or something. When she and Jenny had eaten, bite for bite, the same food and done, step for step, the same exercise, Jenny, who hadn't needed to lose weight, lost weight, while Libby who did need to, hadn't. Still, that was an issue for the dietician, not the therapist.

"Basically, but research has found that diets don't work for most people in the long run. Changing habits and philosophy of eating tends to give better results," the doctor said.

Libby was still afraid that if she ate, she'd gain weight again and, without David, not be able to lose it again.

"But that's just an example," Libby said. "Everything I do and think is affected. Jeff and I are close and getting closer, but how can I fall in love while David is gone?"

"So you think you shouldn't feel good while David is missing. Is that right? Why do you think you feel that way?"

Libby sighed. If she knew the answer, she wouldn't be there.

§

"So, how did it go?" Jeff was waiting outside her house with a bag of groceries when she got home that evening.

"You were right," she said as she hit the garage door opener to close the garage. "It was worth it. We talked about the stages of grief. She said that even though David wasn't dead, I was still grieving. Everything I'm feeling is normal, the anger, the guilt, the sadness...everything. I'm supposed to allow myself to feel, without judgment." She took off her coat and hung it on the hook by the door. "If I feel happy, I'm supposed to go with that and not ruin it by thinking I should be feeling something else."

"What about eating?" Jeff set the bag of groceries on the counter.

"She said the out-of-control feelings I'm having could be connected to not eating. That I'm starving myself in punishment for going out to eat while Marissa stole David. I don't buy it. Anyway, she sent me to a dietician who worked up something she called a 'life plan,' but it's really a diet and exercise program. It has a minimum and maximum. I must eat three meals a day, but six would be better."

"Six?" Jeff pulled steak, potatoes, mushrooms and a bottle of red wine from the bag. "That's going to be quite a change. You eat, what? Once now?"

She ignored his question. "The dietician recommended eating small meals. I guess grazing is in." She smiled at Jeff's choice of dinner fixings. "Oh, and food combinations are important."

He raised a brow.

"Fruit gets eaten alone. Vegetables go with starch or with protein, but starch isn't supposed to go with protein. And I can't remember about dairy. I think that went with vegetables too. There's a book I'm supposed to get that explains everything in detail."

"I didn't understand what you said. Some foods are supposed to go together and others aren't? What does that mean?"

"Well," she picked up a t-bone, "this can't go with," she picked up a huge baking potato, "this, but," she put the potato down, "it can go with this." She picked up the mushrooms.

Jeff picked up the bottle of Merlot. "What about wine?"

"I'd have to check the papers she gave me, but I think it's no tolerance for wine or sweets."

"And this is supposed to be a *life* plan?" He looked as disgruntled as he sounded.

Libby smiled. "I think the real message is moderation. It always is with diets. And I've seen enough come and go to know that dieticians don't know any more about what causes a person to be slim than the average Joe. They keep coming up with something new because the old diet was proven unhealthy or didn't work or couldn't keep the weight off."

"Or was impossible to follow." He set down the bottle, took the food from her hands and pulled her into his arms. "I'm not worried about you gaining weight, honey. I'm worried about you losing it."

She took his hand and led him into the living room. "See this?" She picked up a picture of Jenny, the kids and her old pudgy self. "That's what I looked like."

"But you're pregnant in that picture. You're supposed to be bigger."

Libby shook her head. Her stomach gurgled sickly, and she felt the beginning of panic. This was it. He'd see how she really was and want out. "No. I wasn't pregnant. That's just how I looked. For years. I didn't change size until after David came. I looked pregnant for years."

He stared at the photo. "And that's why you didn't know you were expecting him."

Libby wished she could read his mind. Was he disgusted? She was. She'd been fat and could be again. She could wake up tomorrow and find that her metabolism had slowed to such a crawl that she'd gain weight on the little she consumed now.

He set down the picture and reached for Libby, pulling her close. "It doesn't matter."

She gave him a look that said, "Liar."

"Well, it might have at first. I might not have looked at you as closely when we met."

Libby pushed at his chest. Tears burned her eyes. She'd thought so.

He held tight. "And that would have been the biggest mistake of my life because I would have missed you."

She looked at him through brimming eyes. "What?"

"I'll admit it. I was first attracted to your face and then your body, but even then that wasn't it. There was more. I can't explain it. I've said this before. I felt a connection between us from the start. Physically, I was probably attracted to your eyes first, the rest of your face second, and your body third. All in rapid succession. Almost more the whole package than individual parts."

She didn't know what to think. Like every other person in the world, he was attracted by looks. Slender and sexy sold, while nice but chunky didn't even enter the running. She couldn't blame him. She'd been attracted to his looks first, too.

"I'm making a mess of this, I know," he admitted, looking worried. "The thing is, skinny or not, it's *you* I'm attracted to. *You* the person. That doesn't mean I don't care about how you look. I'd be lying if I said that, it's just that even if you looked like you did in that picture, I'd still want to be with you."

She looked at the picture and cried, "I wouldn't."

He laughed. "What I meant was, the important thing is for you to be healthy—feel healthy. If you think the food combining thing is the way to go, I'll pitch the wine and potatoes and we'll just have steak and veggies."

She smiled despite herself.

"The thing is, *not* eating isn't healthy, either. There's a book I heard Barbara Walters talking about on TV about some condition called Anorexia something-or-other, where girls starve themselves, and it isn't attractive. I'd rather cuddle up to a soft, round body than a skin and bones one. Either way, though, it's *you* I want to cuddle up with."

"You say all the right things." She gave him a deep, grateful kiss. His shirt was hot and sweat dampened. She'd worried him. The thought that he worried about losing her, the over-emotional, could-be-fat-tomorrow her, made her heart soar. But what would happen if he knew she was a liar? If he knew the truth about David?

§

The first morning in the apartment, Marissa awakened on the couch. She'd pulled it out the night before to find that it had obviously been well used by the previous tenants. One look at the stains that discolored the mattress changed her mind of using it as a bed. Even covered with the new sheets she'd purchased, she wouldn't feel clean. She'd even flipped the mattress, which only proved that the good side had been up. It was just as easy to make up the couch as a bed.

Marissa looked through the barred window at the sidewalk several floors below. It had snowed overnight. The April flowers were covered by snowdrifts. It would have been miserable in the car. She grinned as she folded the sleeping bag and crammed it into a drawer. They were warm and safe and dry.

§

"Daria, how's the new digs?" Latisha asked as Marissa clocked in a couple of hours later.

"Wonderful. Dav—I mean…Chris and I slept like the dead. He slept the night through for the first time in…" she stopped a second to think, "…forever. I feel so good. Thanks again for your help."

"Not a problem, girl. I got me a new coat thanks to you, and with the weather like it is, I need it." She shook her head. "I still can't believe you'd been living out of a car all these weeks. I'd of done something, had I known."

"Like what? Thrown your boyfriend off the couch?"

Latisha laughed. "Who says he's on the couch?"

Marissa put her hands on her hips and struck a mother-scolding-child pose. "You best be careful, girl. I didn't make my man sleep on the couch either, and I've the baby to prove it."

Latisha got serious. "What happened to your man?"

Marissa shrugged, but she felt her face grow stiff with regret. "He turned out to be less of a man than I'd thought. First hint that I was expecting, and he bailed. Wanted me to get an abortion, but I couldn't." Her frown curled into a smile. "Now, when I look at Chris, I'm glad I didn't."

"You got a picture of him? Your Chris, I mean?"

Marissa shook her head. "Not enough money, so far. But I got some film for my Polaroid, so I'll be taking some soon."

"You gonna sue for child support? You should. Get a better apartment in a better neighborhood. Get a better job, too. You're smart. You could go places if you got a little help with the expenses."

Marissa's smile faded as she looked away.

"He owes you." Latisha pushed on.

Marissa nodded. He wasn't the only one who owed her, but in order to get financial assistance, she'd have to admit where she was. Then she'd be arrested. The authorities wouldn't believe the truth. And when it was proved that he *was* her son, they'd take him from her because she'd left him on a sidewalk. No, better to go it alone. She thought of David's toothless grin. She couldn't leave him again. Ever.

Lent

Libby waited in line by the confessional examining her conscience. That was what the church called preparing the mental list of sins prior to confession. It was something Libby had been doing for months. Her palms were wet, and her damp shirt stuck to her back beneath her coat.

The door to the confessional opened, and a man walked past her on the way back to the pews. She didn't make eye contact with him or the lady in front of her whose turn it was to confess. Like everyone in the other five lines, she kept a polite distance so that, even in the silence of the church, confessions were not overheard. It was the old-fashioned configuration of confessionals, with three booths connected in a line. The priest sat in the center booth on a chair. When a penitent entered a booth and knelt on the kneeler, a light went on outside the booth and inside the priest's cubical to show occupancy. When it was time to confess, the priest slid open a small twelve-inch or so square door to reveal a heavily-screened partition. The partition allowed priest and penitent to see a vague shadow of the other, but nothing distinct. The priest generally sat in profile, inclining his head to listen. When the confession was finished, the standard prayers recited, and absolution and penance given, the priest would slide the screen closed and transfer his attention to the other side of his booth where the new penitent waited, head bowed in prayer.

Times were changing in the church, and many congregations were starting to offer face-to-face private confessions or general absolution options, but it hadn't really caught on yet. Besides, Libby wanted the intimate anonymity of the old way.

There usually weren't lines at confession on Saturdays, but during Lent was different. The lines for the lenient Father Paul and deaf Father Michael were much longer than that for Father Ryan, whose reputation of weighty penances kept his lines short. She chose him on purpose.

When Libby's turn came, she was tempted to step out of line and make a beeline for the door outside. Instead, she took a steadying breath, entered the small booth, and knelt on the padded kneeler.

For the Love of *David*

In the stuffy dimness of the wooden box, time seemed to stop. She could still leave. Pretend she'd already confessed. Just think her sins really loud and hope God heard them, knew she was sorry and would forgive her. That's what Protestants did, wasn't it? Why did Catholics have to say their sins aloud? It was the same God.

Just as she was about to get off her knees and leave, Father Ryan opened the little door on his side of the screen, signaling her to begin.

She felt a burst of panic that had nothing to do with not eating. Sweat trickled down her cheek. Her voice shook.

"Bless me, Father, for I have sinned. It's been six months since my last confession." She took a breath and rushed on in a small, choked whisper. "I stole a baby." She kept her head bowed.

"Excuse me? Could you speak a little louder, please?"

She took a ragged breath. Why, oh why was she Catholic? She cleared her throat and spoke a little louder. "I stole a baby. Well, actually, I found an abandoned baby and kept it."

Sweat trickled down her back and soaked into the waistband of her dress pants.

A waiting silence seeped through the screen from the priest's booth.

Father Ryan had been hearing confessions for an hour and a half, Libby knew, and was scheduled for another half hour. She could only imagine, based on her average confession, what it must be like for him or any priest. He had probably been half asleep, numbed by a litany of venial sins such as lying, judging others, not attending Mass regularly and swearing, spiced infrequently with the odd petty theft or infidelity. To hear someone had stolen a baby would be, to say the least, stunning. She expected him to gasp and tell her to give the child back or turn herself in. She expected some reaction, but the silence continued.

Maybe she'd given him a heart attack.

"Father?"

"Yes, child. I'm listening." His voice was gentle and kind, far more loving and encouraging than she'd expected. He didn't sound like the no-nonsense Father Ryan she knew, but his words were an invitation.

As if a damn had broken inside of her, thoughts and feelings rushed out. All the fears, all the guilt, all the lies she'd told. What she'd done and what she had failed to do. She handed the whole, mangled, convoluted, soggy wad of tissue of an emotional mess to God, through the priest. And He took it.

Love and forgiveness poured through the grate and into her soul.

She wasn't talking with Father Ryan. He didn't know, had no way of knowing, the things about her this man did.

She was like the woman at the Biblical well. "He told me everything I ever did."

She left the confessional absolved and lighter than she'd ever felt, despite the hefty penance Father Ryan had assigned—forty hours volunteering to minister to at-risk mothers, homeless shelters, or sick babies suffering from withdrawal of their mother's addictions. Forty hours—the Biblical number of testing—one hour for each day of Lent. Lighter, despite knowing that she'd only taken the first step on the road to forgiving herself.

Now, she remembered why she was Catholic and why Reconciliation was a sacrament.

§

Only a few tables lingered at the end of the lunch rush. Marissa and Latisha had worked it without Nora for the third time that week.

"That girl's gonna get herself fired." Latisha set three more catsup bottles on the counter for Marissa to fill.

"What do you think happened to her?"

Latisha shrugged, and the beaded ends of her braids clacked. "She's a junky. They disappear."

"Disappear?" Marissa tossed brown, catsup-crusted lids into the bowl of hot water and tried not to appear too interested.

"Where you from, girl? They disappear. You know, go on a bender, OD, get whacked by a john, find a sugar daddy and move on. Disappear." Latisha's Chicago cant always got thicker when Marissa asked stupid questions. "Why you so interested in junkies, anyway?"

Marissa shrugged and up-ended one catsup bottle over another, balancing it perfectly. "Just never knew one, I guess."

She didn't look up. She knew Latisha would be looking at her as if she'd sprouted horns, or pearls and a twin set. "I mean, sure they were in high school, but we didn't hang out, you know?"

"What high school you go to?"

"One in Minnesota."

Latisha narrowed her eyes. "White one?"

Marissa nodded.

"Knew it." Latisha scooped a lid out of the hot water and wiped off the softened catsup with a stained cloth. "You don't belong here, Daria. Why don't you take your baby and go back to Minnesota?"

For the Love of *David*

Ben poked his head in the waitress station. "Daria, I put a four at twelve, and Latisha, table six wants coffee."

Latisha grabbed a thermal carafe and stuck it under the spigot of the coffee maker to fill. "Your momma kick you out, didn't she?"

Marissa scooped ice into four gold, plastic water glasses, thinking of Tammy and Mora and wondering what they would think if they saw her now. "Something like that."

Holy Week

It was the Thursday before Easter. Holy Thursday, the start of Eau Claire's spring break—not that Marissa was keeping track.

A chill, damp wind propelled Marissa from work to daycare. Inside, paper chicks and flowers were taped precariously to the pale green concrete block wall. David lay on his belly inside the nearest of the four playpens where the younger kids were corralled while the older kids played.

He squealed as she crossed the room and waved hello to Kara, the only staff member there. Kara was handing out crayons to a table of six squirming preschoolers in the corner.

"Hey, baby." She lifted David free. His diaper was heavy, sagging at his hips, and his waistband was damp. "Did you have a good day?" He grabbed her hair as she kissed him and pressed his gaping mouth on her cheek. "Ooh, a kiss. Thank you, sweety." She repositioned him in her arms and disentangled her hair from his fists.

"You're early." Kara crossed the room with David's diaper bag. "I was just going to change him."

Marissa nodded. "I'll do it." She took the bag and headed to the changing table next to the door of the bathroom. The paper covering the table was soiled, so she balled it up and pulled a length from the roll before setting David down.

Kara looked over Marissa's shoulder. "I didn't expect you for hours. Something wrong?"

Marissa shrugged. "Business is slow." She pulled off David's pants. His round little belly was too tempting to leave alone. She tickled it. He squealed in delight. "Did you have a good lunch? I'm glad you're still awake. It's almost time for your nap, isn't it?" She always talked to him when she changed his diaper. She taped the new one in place and pulled his pants back on. They didn't reach much past his diaper. His little belly stuck out of his shirt. "Have you got cereal and peaches in there?" She blew a raspberry against the warm white mound and was rewarded with another squeal.

"We close Friday at noon for Easter."

Marissa picked up David and carried him into the bathroom to wash her hands. "Noon? I work until two."

"Sorry." Kara picked up a little girl and put her on the newly vacated changing table without replacing the paper. "And don't be tempted to just leave him, neither. The fifteen minute rule stands."

Marissa didn't comment. Corner Care had three rules posted at the door by the desk, and probably carved in stone somewhere. One: If you don't bring it for your kid, he can't have it. That meant food, diapers, wipes, bottles, bibs and changes of clothes. Corner Care had toys and playpens to share. Two: Payment due in cash at pick up, no excuses. And Three: If you are more than fifteen minutes late, your kid isn't welcome back. Ever.

They had policies about sick kids, who could pick up whom, and what they did for discipline, as well. But those policies, like the number of kids one staff member could watch (six) and sanitation issues like prompt changing of diapers, hand washing, and replacing the paper on the changing table between kids, were enforced loosely at best.

She counted out the money due and made certain Kara marked David's account as paid before pulling David's winter coat out of his bag. "I guess Mommy will have to figure something else out for you for Friday, won't she?" She caught her son's arm and guided it into the too-small coat sleeve.

§

At one o'clock on Good Friday, the clinic closed. Libby walked across the highway bridge to Sacred Heart Hospital. She meant to go to services in the hospital's chapel, but somehow she ended up taking the elevator to the third floor maternity/neo-natal wing instead. Three days a week she volunteered there after work, rocking babies. What had started as part of her penance had turned into so much more.

Carol, the head nurse on duty, looked up and smiled. "I didn't think we had any volunteers coming in today."

"I'm not scheduled. I was on my way to church from work and thought I'd stop in for a few minutes."

"Well, if you can stay, we can use you. We had a CA mother deliver yesterday." CA stood for chemically addicted.

When Libby said she could stay, Carol handed her off to Kim in the nursery and disappeared down the hall.

Kim led Libby to an acrylic bassinet where a tiny baby flailed beneath a heat lamp. Through the clear, acrylic bassinet, Libby could see the poor little girl's heels were covered with tape and tubes. Her big toe was stuck in an oxygen monitor. A clear tube was stuck up one of her tiny nostrils and taped across her cheek. "What's her name?" Libby asked.

Kim scowled. "We certainly aren't going to call her any of the things her mother suggested. Of course, the mother doesn't have any say in the matter. Social Services and the police are already involved. I hope they lock the mother up for good. Her little girl is going to have a rough couple of days ahead, if she survives."

It pained Libby to look at the tiny infant. Through no fault of her own, the poor little girl was going through the same detoxification and withdrawal as her mother. Holding, rocking, and monitoring the vitals after her medication had been administered was all that could be done. It was time-consuming and not an efficient use of labor to assign a nurse to comfort the poor unfortunates. In times like these, Libby knew she was truly helping.

Libby sat in the rocker next to the newborn's acrylic bassinet as Kim carefully picked up the baby.

"Hold her tight, or she'll squirm out of your arms. Here's a pacifier, and there's a bottle beside you, if you can get her to take it. She has an I.V., so it doesn't matter much."

Kim carefully placed the newborn in Libby's arms. "Nancy is monitoring her from the desk, and I'll be in and out. We've another two moms in delivery."

Libby nodded and turned her attention to the purple-faced infant. It hurt to hear the little girl scream herself hoarse. "You're safe, peanut. I've got you."

She rocked and rocked while the baby wailed. Poor little thing. What would prompt her mother to continue to take drugs when she must have known she was pregnant? Libby pushed away the thought. Who was she to judge? She'd kept a baby not her own and was thankful that Marissa had abandoned him. She regretted the pain she'd caused Marissa almost as much as she regretted Marissa finding David. Had Marissa been looking for David all along, or had she just stumbled on him? Had she planned to take him, or had it been a spur-of-the-moment decision? Was she happy now that she had him, or did she regret it as before? Did she love him?

Her thoughts were like poison burning through her system as she rocked the baby. In a way, they were both detoxifying, only the babe in her arms was an innocent victim and Libby knew she wasn't.

She prayed for the baby. She prayed for David and Marissa—and for herself. She sang little songs to her small charge. "Hush, little baby, don't say a word…" The song grew as she made up new verses. Whispering about David, Libby picked up the bottle and gently jiggled the nipple in the baby's mouth to try to entice her to suck.

She kept the motion up for a full minute before the little girl clamped down on the nipple and began to suck. She took one ounce before spitting out the bottle and vomiting the sugared water.

Libby set aside the bottle and wiped up the mess with a burp rag as she continued to cradle the baby.

The padded chair she was in was more of a glider than a rocker. It squeaked in a quiet but satisfying way each time it rocked forward. Libby rocked. Her patience with her little charge was a deep, calm pool. She picked up the pacifier and repeated the jiggling motion she'd used successfully with the bottle.

Poor little thing. The tiny mouth closed around the pacifier. The little girl's face was wet with sweat. Libby rolled the baby to her chest for a moment to wick it away. The miserable child whimpered, but the pacifier stayed in place.

Another baby cried, and Nancy left her paperwork to attend to it. That baby was nearly twice the size of Libby's.

Nancy efficiently changed the little boy and returned him to his bassinet. "You're amazing," she said as she wheeled the child toward the door for his afternoon feeding with his mother. "First time she's stopped crying."

It didn't last long. Within fifteen minutes the baby was screaming again, shivering in Libby's arms as her little legs and arms twitched uncontrollably.

The agony the poor child was going through sickened Libby. Her sorrow for the child scoured her clean of her own problems. Nothing was more important than comforting this child.

Later, as she took the last bus home to her empty house, the sounds of the baby's cries still rang in her ears. Being at the hospital, and holding that baby had filled her more than the piece of chicken she'd eaten for dinner. Her penance wasn't penance, but grace. She knew what her real penance needed to be. Somehow, no matter what the cost to her, she needed to clear Marissa's name.

§

There wasn't a lunch crowd on Friday, so Marissa had no problem picking up David at noon, even though Nora hadn't shown up for her shift again. She opened the door of the daycare to the sound of crying children. It was like one of her nightmares. Three preschool kids sat in a puddle of juice eating an explosion of Cheerios from the floor. One left the mess and ran to her.

"It's okay, now. It will be okay, now," she reassured the little boy as he grabbed her legs. The younger kids, confined again to playpens, cried their neglect. David was pressed into the meshed side of his playpen. His face was red and streaming. Dual rivers of snot coated his upper lip and slimed his cheek. A red bump the size of a large chicken egg stood out above his left brow. The other child in the pen was rocking herself, crying with her fingers jammed in her mouth. A small wooden mallet and cobbler's bench meant for older children sat on the padded floor.

Taking the little boy's hand, Marissa took him with her to rescue David. He was in her arms in an instant. "It's okay. Mommy's got you." He pressed his face against her shoulder as his sobs changed to whimpers.

Holding David close, she scanned the room. The sole attendant, a black girl in a company shirt, was slumped against the wall with rubber tubing still around her arm, a syringe, lighter and spoon lay next to a small, powder-dusted plastic bag. The little girl in David's playpen was the only other infant. She pulled that girl into her arms as well. Balancing the two babies, hindered by the boy clinging to her leg, she made her way to the desk and sat down. Emergency numbers were taped beside the phone.

She was still situating the children when the door opened and a woman entered.

"What the hell?" She looked around, focused on Marissa, and blazed her way over. "What is going on here? Where's Micah!"

The little boy clinging to Marissa's side began to wail.

The woman plucked up her son and pressed him to her chest. "What did you do to my son?"

Marissa held the two little ones close. The raised voice had started them both crying again. "It wasn't me." She jerked her head toward their stoned babysitter. "I just came to pick up my son."

"Stoned. My God. Well, if they think I'm paying for this, they're whacked."

Marissa didn't know what to say to that. "I was just trying to figure out who to call."

"The police. I want her ass in jail, leaving my kid…"

"I know." Marissa interrupted. "But the rest of the girls here seem okay. If we call the police, they'll close this place down, and where will you bring Micah come Monday?" She patted David's and the little girl's backs with shaking hands. She couldn't believe she was thinking this way. "I don't know about you, but I need to work."

That shut up the other woman. They looked at each other for several minutes, comforting the children.

David had fallen asleep in Marissa's arms, and the little girl was down to a whimper.

"Is there a number for the owner there?" the other woman suggested, calmer now. "Her name is Formica or something strange like that."

A *Phonesia* was listed. Marissa shifted the little girl into a more stable position, picked up the phone, and dialed.

Two other mothers came in to collect their children while the owner was en route. Shantelle's mother took her from Marissa's arms and also claimed one of the toddlers on the floor. They all waited.

§

Marissa carried David's limp weight against her shoulder. The voucher for two week's free childcare burned in her pocket. Something died in her when she took it. Phonesia wouldn't give more. "If you close me down, who you gonna have watch your kids while you at work?" Her words had echoed Marissa's. It was the way it was. Hating it didn't help.

The business sector where she'd planned to work, back when her life had a plan, had all but shut down. Even in her part of Chicago, several blocks off the glamorous Miracle Mile, the streets seemed deserted. She didn't delude herself that everyone was in church, Good Friday or not. The homeless shelter and soup kitchen were doing a thriving business. They always did on holidays, Latisha told her.

Echoes of Latisha's advice played in her head. "You know, that money you got from the car ain't gonna hold you forever. You need to sign up for assistance. They don't give it out right away. It takes a month, minimum. You cut it too close, you gonna have to figure out how you gonna feed Chris on what you get here." The trouble was, Marissa didn't know if she could do it. It wasn't that she was too good to take assistance. Raised to be self-sufficient, the concept chafed and burned. But that wasn't it, entirely. She could accept assistance for David. The problem came when she found out that to get Welfare, she'd have to lie again and again.

"You can't tell them you're working. You say you're unemployed. You say your jerk of a boyfriend ran out on you. You say you're about to lose your apartment. They ask about savings, you lie. You tell them you have less than nothing and are about to be tossed out on the street. Keep David up from his nap, delay his lunch. Crying babies speed things along. Still, it will take a while. You're lucky it's spring. There's always more people looking for help when the weather turns bad. Maybe it won't take so long in spring. Still, you sign up now before you *have* to, or you will end up using all your cash to keep you off the streets."

Somehow, David seemed heavier when he was asleep. Marissa's back began to ache, and she shifted him to relieve the pressure. The diaper bag slipped from her shoulder and caught in the crook of her elbow.

Two more blocks.

The sky was ashen and heavy. She wished it would rain and melt the dirty snow banks. Instead, a sleety drizzle fell, making everything damp and miserable. No, the streets were no place for a baby. They were no place for anyone.

A block from their apartment, a living pile of rags huddled in an entryway. Inside it, a wild-eyed and wild-haired, sickly-pale person clutched a half-empty bottle. Marissa stared as she passed. This was a new one. Well, new to this spot, anyway. That was strange in itself. The homeless were as territorial as stray cats.

She itched to get closer, to exchange a couple of dollars for a name. Pat, Jill, Jenny, Lisa…she only checked the white women of a certain age. Unfortunately, there was no way to tell the age of the person in this pile without getting closer, and she wouldn't, not when she had David with her. Still, this one didn't have a beard, and, even though she couldn't afford it, she was tempted to step nearer and drop some coins or, if there was a cup, tuck a dollar or two inside.

It was stupid, taking food from her meager table to give to someone who'd use it for alcohol or drugs. Somehow, every time she saw a middle-aged, homeless woman, she thought of Bess's daughter. Was Mora still living on the streets of Chicago?

Even a sidewalk width away, Marissa could smell the woman, and her nose wrinkled automatically at the stench.

For the Love of *David*

The smell wasn't much better inside the broken door of her building. Food, urine, cigarette smoke, and the sour stench of poverty was made worse by the cold humidity. She walked up the stairs. On the ground floor of her apartment building someone—or more likely several someones—lived on the back side of the stairs. She'd never seen them, but she heard them. At the moment, the sounds of passion were unmistakable. Bile rose in her throat.

She hurried up the stairs to her apartment on the third floor. Her door was the second on the right, underneath the light. She pulled out her key as a mob of kids barreled past. They played in the halls when the weather was bad, running up and down the worn carpeting. It was no life for a kid. Upstairs, a door banged open, and a man yelled. Harsh voices and harsher words. It reminded her of her nightmares. She closed the door and threw the deadbolt. Safe.

Holy Saturday

At 8:30 on Saturday night, Jeff waved at Libby through the nursery room glass.

Baby in arms, Libby caught the motion and slowly lifted her head. Jeff. Her heart caught. A wave of sadness swept over her, and she wished it were Jeff's baby she rocked. The thought startled her. She should be wishing she was rocking David, and she did, but not as much as she wished David was Jeff's son. Not as much as she wanted to be the mother of Jeff's son. Libby swallowed heavily and smiled at Jeff.

The addict's daughter in her arms was doing better than yesterday and was now limp with sleep. Slowing her rocking to a gradual stop, Libby stood. She eased the little one into the acrylic bassinet and propped a cloth diaper against her back so that she would remain on her side while she slept. She stroked the petal soft cheek in farewell and left the nursery.

"'Night, Carol."

The nurse was checking charts at the desk inside the enclosed work area adjoining the nursery. She looked up at the words.

"You heading out, Libby?" She looked from Libby to Jeff, who stood waiting in the hall. "Have a Happy Easter. Thanks for the help."

Libby smiled her good-bye and quietly left the glassed-in room.

She grabbed her coat and purse and then rushed to Jeff's arms for a hug. His lips were firm yet soft as he gave her a welcoming peck. He held her close. "You're an angel."

She shook her head. "Not really."

"Someone steals your son and you minister to other's babies. That's near sainthood in my book."

She shook her head, holding his hand as they walked to the elevator. She knew that's what it looked like, but how could she tell him that it was penance? At least it had started out that way. She'd passed her forty hours nearly two weeks ago. God had forgiven her, but she couldn't seem to forgive herself. And how could she ever make it up to Marissa?

"I'm not so good. Marissa is not so bad."

"Are you kidding? It almost sounds like you've forgiven her." He sounded surprised. "I still want her head on a platter."

Libby's eyes filled with tears. The world tipped on its axis when she thought of Marissa. People would see Marissa's crime to be abandoning David. And Libby understood that. She, personally, found the concept of abandoning a child completely incomprehensible. Still, she didn't condemn Marissa for it. Rather, she thanked her. Had Marissa not left David in the parking lot, Libby would never have been able to pick him up. What Libby blamed Marissa for was the very thing she should have understood—taking David back. Retrieving David, taking him from a loving home, was the real crime in Libby's eyes. If the world knew the whole truth, it wouldn't condemn Marissa for taking David. That was Libby's crime, not Marissa's, and, as the good priest had said, it was really up to Marissa to forgive her.

"I just want David safe and happy." She didn't wish Marissa harmed, but she stopped short of wishing her well. The girl had abandoned David once. Was she caring for him now? "Father Ryan seemed to think I need to work on letting go."

Jeff frowned. "I'm siding with Dr. Day. You should let go when you feel ready to, not when some priest says it's time. I've never liked Father Ryan. He's mean."

The elevator door opened, and Libby stepped in.

"Mean?" She shook her head. "I'm going to go to him for confession from now on. He's…" She shrugged. "I think he's got a direct line to God. Anyway, I think he's trying to prepare me for the future."

Jeff punched the button to the ground floor. "He doesn't think you'll get David back?"

Libby shook her head. She didn't think she'd get David back. "The police don't think so, either. Remember what Sergeant Wells said? 'No note, no ransom…'"—no chance of return.

Neither said it, but both thought it.

Jeff shook his head. "Gotta love their optimism." The bell sounded and the door opened.

A sigh moved Libby's chest. "I don't like their pessimism either, but there isn't anything I can do." She sighed again. "They're releasing my car on Monday. That's how certain they are that he won't be found. At the beginning, they said if they found my car, they'd keep it until the trial." In the main lobby, she let go of Jeff's hand to pull on her coat and button it.

The doors opened with a whoosh, and they walked outside. Jeff pointed toward his truck. "They are only returning it because there wasn't a lot of evidence in it. I got the impression that they found a hair or two. No evidence of foul play. Nothing they could really use in a trial." He got out his keys and unlocked the door, her side first. "Besides they know you only have the one vehicle. I think they consider it a hardship catching the bus or hitching a ride. Personally, I kind of like it. It would save you money: just park the thing and let me pick you up."

She smiled as she climbed in the truck. "Speaking of angels."

§

On Easter, the wind blew warm and sweet as Marissa walked around town. The restaurant was closed, so she had the day off. She shifted David to her other hip, wishing she had a stroller. The balmy breeze reminded her of spring breaks spent on Florida's beaches. What should have been happy memories became images of regret. The Easter Bunny hadn't come. Sure, David was young for coloring eggs and Easter egg hunts, but there hadn't been the time or the money, either.

Ready for lunch, David fussed in her arms. She turned the corner and headed home. Their path took them by the Sixth Street Mission. The door was propped open with a felt covered brick, and a sign stood in the middle of the sidewalk.

Easter Dinner. All welcome.

The smell of smoked ham was moist and thick in the air. Marissa's stomach growled. She stopped and poked her head inside. Just looking. She wasn't homeless. Besides, she had lunchmeat for sandwiches in her refrigerator.

"Come on in. Everybody's welcome." A perky girl not much younger than Marissa beckoned her inside.

In high school, the youth group at Marissa's church had spent Christmas at a mission in downtown Minneapolis serving the poor and indigent. Never in Marissa's wildest dreams had she imagined being on the receiving end. Her face was hot with shame.

"You can sit anywhere. I'll get a highchair."

Marissa wanted to turn tail and run, but David was hungry. He chewed on his fist and whined. People sat in small groups or by themselves at long, cafeteria-style tables. The walls were papered with lily-decked crosses and signs announcing "Jesus saves."

The girl from the door pulled a highchair to the end of one table. "How about here?" She took off the tray and waited for Marissa to cross the room. The table was set with blue paper placemats, white paper napkins and silverware. Easter lilies in purple-foiled pots sat in the middle of each table section. Marissa got David situated, tying on the McDonald's bib, and sliding the tray onto the chair. A basket of crackers sat on the table. She tore the cellophane off a couple of soda crackers for David. He stuck the first one in his mouth as she took her seat. The metal folding chair was two down from a mother with three kids under the age of ten. The kids were chewing with their mouths open.

Marissa and the woman exchanged embarrassed smiles and mumbled a greeting. They were here for the kids.

Old people, all gray and overdressed from street living, sat alone or in small groups around the room. Funny how living rough did that, made people gray. Not their hair—their skin. Black or white, it didn't matter. Street people seemed gray, as if they were chameleons blending with the sidewalk to avoid detection. There was the buzz of casual conversation, mostly between mothers and children, but some between what appeared to be the mission's regulars—small knots of people who at least knew each other and the workers by name.

The girl appeared with a plate full of ham, mashed potatoes and gravy, corn, pureed sweet potatoes and canned pineapple. "How old's your baby?"

"Almost five months."

"Mrs. West said we don't have baby food, but maybe the sweet potatoes and mashed potatoes and gravy would be okay for him."

Marissa picked up her spoon. "It'll do just fine, thanks."

She scooped up a little sweet potato and delivered it to David's gaping mouth as the girl watched. She shot the volunteer a smile. "Thanks."

She wanted to say, "I really don't belong here," but then she remembered her black hair with the inch of light brown at the roots, her empty fridge, her pitiful tin of money stashed in the cupboard, and her son banging his little hands on the tray to urge her to hurry up. She turned back to the plate and scooped up more sweet potatoes. The girl wandered back to her position by the door. When the mission closed, the girl would tell her friends about Marissa, a girl not much older than they were. She'd comment on Marissa's hair, her baby, her stained sweater. She'd speculate what happened to put her at a mission on Easter. What mistakes she'd made. The youth minister would advise her not to judge, but she would anyway. Marissa knew she would because she'd been that girl three years ago.

§

Back at the apartment, Marissa sat on the floor and checked her purse. $12.96. The restaurant had been slow lately, and the tips nearly non-existent. When meals were served for $2.95, tips were never all that high to begin with. Ten percent of three bucks is thirty cents. If she could work nights at a nice restaurant, she'd do much better, but who would watch David?

She took out the empty tin for powdered formula that she kept in the cupboard as a crude sort of bank and emptied it. Thanks to the car, she had enough for two month's rent and daycare with $23.70 to spare. She'd been so relieved to get off the streets and find a safe apartment that she hadn't done the math. Her plan had been to earn enough to stay at least one month ahead of expenses, but she hadn't counted on heat, electric and water bills with their hook-up fees and deposits. In this neighborhood, forced prepayment made sense, but it didn't help her budget. David's ever-growing needs were another budget breaker. Even shopping at Goodwill was expensive since she either had to spend all her time running back and forth on the bus or pay for a cab.

She needed a better job, and for that she needed an education. But she had to work to live. When was she going to have the time or the money to take the classes she needed to get ahead?

David lay droopy-eyed next to his mother, chewing on his fist, the sleeve of his new sleeper damp with drool.

Marissa rubbed his back affectionately. He was doing everything the baby book said. He could roll over and sit supported. She'd introduced him to rice cereal and all the vegetables. Baby food made him sleep better, but it was messy and expensive. She frequently gave him smashed canned vegetables, mostly because it was cheaper.

He kept growing, and he had to wear something. Maybe she shouldn't have gotten him so many outfits, but she was washing them all the time as it was, and six wasn't really that many.

David's eyes closed, and she pulled a blanket over him. It filled her heart to look at him. Who would have thought she'd love him so much? Love hadn't really factored in her decision to take him. Neither had thought. Taking him had been a knee-jerk reaction. She'd spent more time contemplating leaving him in the first place.

She scooped up her savings and put it back in the formula tin.

A moment later, she stood in the hall, locking the apartment door behind her, leaving David inside. She was never alone. Never free of responsibility.

She leaned against her door. The kids were running the halls again. Up and down, playing tag. The grumpy man on the fourth floor was yelling as usual: "Go outside, you hellions!"

Outside. As if there were a yard. As if there were a park nearby to send them to. Outside was a sidewalk and city street. Where did he expect the kids to play? Three pre-teens walked by her and paused at the head of the stairs. They pressed the side of their faces against the wall, looking in the gap between the stair rail and the wall to the first floor and then put their heads together to confer in whispers. They looked a second time before tiptoeing down the stairs. They were clearly off to spy on the residents beneath the stairs. Marissa wanted to ask them to tell her what they found. As bad off as she was, as those kids' families were, none of them lived beneath the stairs. What kind of a life was that? Marissa sighed, remembering her canopy bed, her mother's kitchen, and the huge yard she'd grown up with. She and Mitch had their own playground in the back yard and a pool.

David had nothing. An explosion of raised voices preceded the thunder of footsteps as the kids barreled their way back upstairs. Marissa pressed herself against her door as they rushed by, laughing and screaming. Shouts and profanity echoed from below, trailing off to nothing.

She unlocked the door and let herself back in, hoping that the noise hadn't awakened her son. He slept on, oblivious. In a few years, he'd be one of the hellions. The thought stopped her in her tracks. She had to get out of there.

Truth

The following Friday, Jeff met Libby as she walked out the clinic door. He grabbed her and gave her a smacking kiss on the lips.

"Let's go get a pizza. I've been hungry for pizza all day—thin crust with sausage, mushrooms, onions, and, of course, green olives."

"Hello to you, too." She grabbed the lapels of his spring jacket and kissed him back. What she'd meant to be another smacking kiss turned hot as their lips met and parted. He tasted like spearmint gum and Jeff, hot and delicious. She loved the feel of being in his arms, his strength, his love, but they were in the parking lot. Libby stepped out of Jeff's arms. Her cheeks were hot.

His grin was that of a man confident of his appeal to his woman. "You ready? I've been thinking of nothing but you and pizza all day. I'm starving."

Pepe's Pizza was filled with families. The hostess seated Jeff and Libby in a small booth across from a table of five. The family's pizza had just arrived, and the dad was serving slices to the older kids while the mother cut a slice for the youngest in the high chair. David would be sitting in a high chair now. At five months, she wouldn't have given him pizza, but he would have had Cheerios to finger.

"Are you okay?" Jeff reached under the table and grabbed her hand. She forced a smile. "I'm fine. I think of him a lot, but I'm okay." No need to explain whom she was talking about.

"You're supposed to think about him. It wouldn't be natural if you didn't. You've come a long way."

"Sometimes it hurts so bad, and other times I wonder if I haven't gone too far. Healed too much. Part of me says I should clean out his room. Put the crib in the basement. But then, there's the part of me that is afraid he'll come home and find it missing."

Jeff squeezed her hand. "What does Dr. Day say?"

She shrugged. "That I need to do what feels right. If I need to keep the crib up, then I should. The thing is, I don't know if I need to or not. It's like I'm afraid to put things away because then he'll really be gone."

"Cleaning out his room isn't going to change the way things are. It's not going to make Marissa return him, and it certainly won't make her keep him."

The waitress arrived and Libby watched Jeff as he ordered their beer and pizza. He was so good to her, always willing to talk, to explore her feelings and to share his own. The trouble was she still hadn't told Jeff the truth. She was in love with him, knew he wanted to take their relationship to the next level, but she wasn't ready. And she wasn't being honest with him.

She turned the conversation to other things: work, weather, plans for the weekend. He made her laugh. Their focus changed again once the pizza came.

"What is it that makes Pepe's the best?" She picked up a slice and looked at it before taking a bite. "The crust?"

Jeff's mouth was too full for him to answer.

She took a bite. "Mmm." The crust was the perfect consistency, crisp but not brittle. The sauce was hot and savory, but not too spicy, nor too salty. She sighed, savoring the one piece she allowed herself. One piece of pizza; one mug of beer.

Her weight was holding steady, but she still didn't know why.

"The sausage," Jeff said, once he'd swallowed. "It's real Italian sausage. It's even got the little banana seeds in them."

"Banana seeds? What are banana seeds?"

He dug into a piece of sausage and pulled out a small, black crescent. "These."

"I think that's fennel."

"Fennel, banana seeds, whatever. It's what makes it the best."

She laughed, slipped her left shoe off, and slid her toe up his pant leg. She wanted to be close to him. Intimate, without being too intimate. She was the reason they hadn't made love. She was the one who wanted to wait.

It was almost 8:00 when they pulled into Libby's driveway. Just in time to watch the latest "Movie of the Week" on TV.

Inside, Libby flicked on the lights and headed to the kitchen to start popping the popcorn. She thumbed through her mail and felt a momentary wave of disappointment tinged with sadness. No messages from the police about David. They would have left a note for her if she hadn't been home.

She pulled out the popcorn popper and warmed it up.

"Do you wanna beer?" She walked into the living room so that she could hear Jeff's answer.

"Sure." He looked up from the television. "No messages?" He knew the ritual as well as she did. Neither expected news, and yet both were disappointed when there wasn't any. And there hadn't been any for weeks. The police had lost Marissa's trail long ago.

Libby shook her head. "Nope, nothing."

"I'm sorry." He hugged her close.

His arms felt like home. Libby sighed. There was so much promise in their relationship. So many good, strong, loving things that should have allowed them to take the next step, but always there was the pall of David's absence.

Libby snuggled close to Jeff on the couch while the movie began. He lowered his lips to hers, and they kissed. Tender and sweet at first, the kiss intensified.

Libby was conscious of the guilt. Yes, there was the guilt Dr. Day said was normal—the guilt over enjoying herself and falling in love with Jeff while David was missing. She acknowledged it, experienced it and let it go. It was normal. Missing David shouldn't be her life, couldn't be. She closed her eyes and focused on the kiss, on the firm, yielding softness of Jeff's lips, on the contours of his mouth, on the intricate movements of his tongue as it caressed hers, on the taste of him.

He cupped her breasts with his hands. "I love you. I want you."

His hand skimmed to the waistband of her jeans, popping the button open. She wanted to continue, but she couldn't. It was more than just Catholic guilt. She wanted the whole "happily ever after" and premarital sex, despite popular opinion, didn't seem to yield that. Look at Marissa.

Besides, she hadn't told Jeff the truth. He couldn't find out like this. She had to tell him. She had to confess.

"I can't." She gently pulled out of Jeff's embrace. "I thought I could." She looked into his warm, brown eyes. They were so filled with concern and desire that she almost recanted. "But I can't."

His eyes asked the question before his voice. "Why? Is it me? Is it David?"

Libby reached down and buttoned her jeans while she answered. "Neither. It's me."

"Oh." His face grew stiff and still. He stood awkwardly and tucked in his shirt.

"I love you, Jeff." She watched him, panic and loss cascading over her. He was going to leave. She was going to lose him too, and she hadn't even told him yet.

"You do?" He stopped adjusting his clothes and looked her in the eye.

"Yes, I do." Her eyes brimmed with tears, her look one of loss and fear. "Believe me."

"But," he prompted. "There's a 'but' there, isn't there?"

"But—" There were so many *buts:* but I haven't been honest with you; but I'm not really David's mother; but I never even made love before. "But I won't make love with anyone but my husband. I promised myself I'd save making love for marriage." It wasn't what she should have said, but it *was* true, or at least a fantasy she'd had since she was little. One man, one woman… weird in this day, impossibly old-fashioned. Could he possibly understand?

His jaw dropped. "You're married?"

"No." The tears that had threatened before, spilled out of her eyes, though her lips smiled. "I'm not married. I just meant I wouldn't until I was married." Her face flamed with embarrassment. David's existence made a lie of her statement. Or at least, the appearance of one.

"But, David—"

She didn't let him continue. "David just happened." How true that was! She should tell him everything. Now was the time. But she couldn't. She was too afraid. Delaying sex was a big enough issue. If they couldn't get through this, there was no way they could get through the truth of David's presence in her life.

"David just happened." She looked away. She wanted to tell the whole truth, but she couldn't.

"I love him so much, but how I got him…" She looked Jeff in the eye, but saw David in the duffle bag. "I promised I would never do that again."

"Until you are married," Jeff clarified. "You haven't sworn off sex permanently."

His statement jarred Libby from her mental image. He'd asked her something. What was the question?

"Libby?"

"Right." It was a distracted response.

"Libby." He grabbed her arms to force her attention back on him. She looked at him, making herself focus her attention on him. "I'm sorry." The tears that had wet her face earlier were joined by more. "I was thinking of David, for a minute."

"I know. There's no need to apologize." He smiled into her eyes, and she returned a tentative smile.

"Libby, I need to be sure you aren't swearing off sex for good." His eyes were serious.

She blushed crimson. "No," she stumbled over her tongue. "I…" she lowered her voice to a whisper. " I want you."

"Good." He took her firmly in his arms and kissed her deeply. She returned the kiss, leaving them both breathless. "Then we'll just have to wait a while."

She stared at him, her jaw gaping slightly. A while? Did that mean he was planning on proposing? She hardly dared to hope.

"Maybe we should find something else to watch. It looks like we've missed a good chunk of the movie." He turned his back on her and walked to the television.

She blinked at his back, certain she'd just missed something more important than a few scenes in a movie.

§

Marissa left the restaurant and forced her body down the damp sidewalk. Left foot, right foot. It seemed to take a conscious effort to walk. Her arms were sodden noodles and her feet tenderized brisket, throbbing with every heartbeat, pounding with every step. She hoped David hadn't taken much of a nap and would be ready for an early bedtime.

She didn't often work a double shift, but one of the waitresses had called in sick, and they'd been short handed. She patted the deep pockets of her black and white polyester waitress uniform and felt the reassuring crush of bills. Tips had been good, real good for a change.

The blocks passed slowly. It was only six blocks from the restaurant to daycare and then another four to their apartment. Most days it seemed like nothing, but today, with the sky threatening rain again and Marissa's aching body, it was miles.

One of the daycare employees met Marissa at the door.

"We were about to call you. We know you had to work late and all, but Chris is sick. He's fussy and feverish."

She stared blankly at the woman for several long seconds until she finally remembered David was Chris to them. She threaded her way around the short tables and play area to the sickroom in the back of the building. Marissa followed silently.

"Oh, and he has the runs. We used up all the diapers you sent and three of ours. You'll have to pay for those today, too." Marissa had used the last of her free hours and was back to being nickeled and dimed.

David fussed in the arms of the sickroom attendant. His eyes were red-rimmed and puffy, and his little nose was runny. He looked as miserable as Marissa felt.

She reached for her son. He was hot and damp and seemed heavier than usual. She shifted him on her shoulder. David whimpered and laid his head in the crook of her neck.

She listened to a detailed description of "Chris's" afternoon because she knew she should, but all she really wanted to do was leave.

"You can't bring him back until he hasn't been feverish for twenty-four hours," the attendant chirped at the end of her lengthy description.

The reminder irritated Marissa. This was the same place that left a junky in charge.

Marissa sighed with irritation. David had gotten sick at daycare and had probably already infected all the other kids. So what would it matter if he came back tomorrow or the next day?

Damn it all, now she would have to miss at least a day of work.

The four blocks home were even longer than the six to the daycare had been. David whimpered and fussed as he pressed his little face into Marissa's neck. She tried to walk rapidly, but the jostling made David cry. They stopped a block away from home. Marissa shifted him to the other shoulder, and he threw up all over her, screaming his discomfort and fear.

She knew he was afraid and sick and that's why he screamed and cried, but she didn't care. She couldn't handle vomit, and there she was covered with the remnants of strained something or other and curdled formula. Anger as hot as fire coursed through her veins. Her fingers squeezed his little arms tightly.

David wailed all the louder.

Somehow, she resisted the temptation to throw her child to the ground and leave him squalling. Somehow, she made it home to their cramped, untidy apartment before he splattered her again.

He was sick. She knew that. But it didn't matter.

"Damn you, ya little brat! Look what you've done to me."

She pried her clinging, stinking, crying son off her chest and tossed him into a laundry basket filled with dirty clothes. The basket tipped as his weight slammed into its side and fell over, burying him in soiled clothing.

Marissa was halfway to the bathroom when she heard the thump. She froze as silence filled the room. She held her breath and closed her eyes until her son's cries of outrage and fear rent the air.

What had she done? Oh, dear God! What had she done?

Marissa spun around and pushed the overturned basket off the pile. She pawed through the dirty clothes until she uncovered her feverish child. Snatching him from the floor, she held him close to her breast, rocking and crooning to him.

"I'm sorry. Oh, baby. Mommy is so sorry."

David continued to wail his distress.

Marissa continued to croon.

Tears ran down her face. What had she done? David couldn't help it that she was tired. He didn't mean to be sick.

She thought of all the times she had been ill as a child. Colds, chicken pox, flu, ear infections, strep… Her mother had always taken care of her. She had been coddled and cared for, pampered and loved. Treated to sweetened tea and buttered toast. Allowed to watch all the television game shows she could stand. She was read to and sung to, cajoled out of the sulks that often accompanied missing things due to illness. But never—never—was she hit or punished for being ill. Her mother had never yelled at her or made her feel like a burden. Surely, her mom must have missed things and changed plans because Marissa was sick, but Marissa never knew it. Her mother never complained or made her feel guilty.

And what had she done? The first time her little boy was sick, the first time he had really been any real trouble at all, she screamed at him and tossed him out like so much dirty laundry.

What kind of a mother was that?

He deserved better.

David's screams had quieted to sobs.

Marissa carried him into the bathroom and turned on the water in the tub. She held him snug to her chest as she adjusted the water temperature and plugged the drain. Then she gently peeled the sodden sleeper off her son and removed his soiled diaper. She wiped him down with a warm, wet washcloth and removed her own clothes. A pacifier sat next to the sink. She grabbed it and her son before slipping into the warm bath.

The water acted as a balm, soothing David's hurt and terror and his mother's frazzled nerves. He sucked on the pacifier and quieted.

Marissa finally relaxed enough to examine the damage. An abraded lump swelled on David's forehead at the hairline. Red fingerprint bruises dotted his back and arms. If they darkened, as she feared they would, they would be clear signs of the kind of mother she was turning out to be.

"Damn it!" she whispered violently.

David's little body grew tense as if he knew the meaning of the words and the threat of the tone.

"I'm sorry, baby." Marissa rocked and soothed him until she felt him relax once again.

His eyes drifted closed.

"I'm a horrible mother." She was careful to keep her voice down and her tone calm. Tears that had dried on her face began again. "You're such a good baby. You deserve so much better than me."

She began mentally inventorying their life together. Work and daycare. Crummy work. Crummy daycare. Crummy little apartment. Cheap clothing. Stress. They didn't really cuddle or play all that much, either. There was never any time. She was always too tired.

She rarely sang to him. Or read to him. Or played with him. She worked at a crummy job for crummy wages so they could live in a crummy apartment where she could be a crummy mother to him.

He deserved better.

He deserved what she had as a child. What he'd had with Libby.

Guilt, heavy and painful as molten lead, scoured the ragged remains of her self-worth, and her body sagged under the weight.

Hot tears dripped into cooling water.

Her son would be better off with Libby.

David sneezed and shot a stream of diarrhea into the bath.

Marissa sighed and pulled the plug. Another mess to clean.

She showered using the last of the shampoo to clean his tender skin. There were two clean towels in the drawer. She dried herself with a hand towel and used the bath towel to wrap him in as she searched for a clean sleeper. It wasn't a very successful search. The one clean outfit she found would no longer snap closed in the crotch. She shook her head in disgust and vowed to hand wash what she could in the sink as soon as David was asleep.

Sitting on the couch, Marissa rocked back and forth with David in her arms. As his eyes drifted closed, angry voices came through the wall from the apartment next door. Or maybe it was the one above. It didn't matter. Both couples fought, sometimes violently. Kids ran wild in the halls. People lived under the stairs. The door to the alley was chained shut. Teens made out in the halls and spray-painted graffiti on the walls. Someone was dealing out of the apartment down the hall. Her son had finger shaped bruises on his arms. There was never anything to eat in her fridge. She'd thrown her son in a basket of dirty laundry.

The entire building stank with dead dreams and vibrated with anger and frustration. The fire escapes were ragged and rusty.

She paid extra for a window with bars.

House of Cards

The buzz of her alarm clock jarred Marissa awake. She sat up so fast, her neck complained. David hadn't wakened her. He always woke her. She flew out of bed to David's drawer on the floor.

She knelt over him her heart pounding loudly in her ears. He lay sprawled on his stomach, head turned to one side. His back rose and fell rhythmically. She let go of the breath she'd been holding. He was okay. Her hand shook as it brushed his cool forehead. He hadn't gotten up at all last night, not even for a midnight bottle.

She pulled on jeans and a sweatshirt. His fever was gone, but she couldn't take him to daycare. She needed to call work, and that meant a trip down the block to the convenience store payphone.

§

David was still asleep when she left the apartment. She locked the door and hurried down the stinking stairs. Once outside the building, she felt the urgency to rush back home disappear. Instead of trotting down the street, she stopped and breathed deep. Freedom. The air was a warm prelude to summer. This was the type of May day that emptied the dorms. Students lounged in the grass outside the resident halls and Davies Center.

Marissa strolled down the street, walking past the convenience store before remembering her errand.

She gave Ben her excuse and hung up the phone. Time to go home. She took a step toward the door and stopped. The smell of fresh coffee filled the air. She stopped and inhaled. Coffee and something yeasty and sweet. The scent reminded her of her mother's kitchen. Her mouth watered. A covered tray of bakery rolls that sat beside the coffee pot.

A glazed donut called her name as she poured herself a large cup and added cream. It had been forever since she'd had a chance to enjoy a cup of coffee and even longer since she'd read *Cosmo*. She grabbed the magazine from the rack. It felt thick and polished and oh so good in her hand. She had a subscription. *Cosmo* and *Business Week*. They were probably stacked behind the counter at the dorm. She put the *Cosmo* back. It was half the price of a bag of diapers.

"Where is the closest park?" she asked as she paid for her purchases.

"Lincoln Park is ten or twelve blocks north. Take the Brown line. It takes maybe ten minutes."

If it had been just her, she'd have been on the bus already. If it had been just her, she'd be working in the Loop and having coffee and donuts at her desk. If it had been just her, she'd be in Eau Claire, preparing for finals. She'd have a summer internship lined up.

But it wasn't just her. She bit into her roll, determined to savor these last few moments of freedom before she had to be Mom again. The donut was gone before she knew it. The apartment building looked marginally better on the outside than it did inside. Tufts of weeds and a lone dandelion sent scrawny shoots reaching skyward from a crack next to the building's foundation.

Inside, David was sure to be up now, hungry and wet and crying for attention. Sighing, she dragged herself into the building and up the stairs. As she reached the third floor, David's cries became audible through the door. She slipped the key in the lock and wished it were just her.

The room smelled like a dirty diaper. She wrestled opened the window, propping it open with the handy dowel before rescuing him from the drawer.

"Feeling any better?" She carried him into the bathroom. Despite last night's bath, he didn't smell better. It was the diaper. He'd had the runs again, diarrhea soaking all the way up his back.

He cried while she changed him. Marissa knew he wanted a bottle, but there was no way she was holding him close when he smelled this bad. She stripped him and, using two fingers, dropped the soiled outfit in the toilet to soak. She wiped him clean. Thank goodness, the finger mark bruises on his arms weren't as dark as she'd feared they'd be.

The day stretched before her in an unbroken vision of boredom. While David ate, Marissa looked around the tiny apartment. The laundry she'd spread out everywhere last night made the place look tired and dumpy. She'd fold the clothes, wash the outfit he'd just wrecked, and then what? She could clean, but the stained linoleum wouldn't look any better. Cigarette burns couldn't be scrubbed out.

The soft breeze flowed through the open window. Was he well enough to take to Lincoln Park? She shook her head. He hadn't kept anything down yet. How did she know he wouldn't be vomiting up his bottle in two minutes? She was a horrible mother for even thinking of taking him out after how sick he'd been last night. Bird song mixed with the sound of traffic. If she knew anyone to leave him with, she would be on the bus headed to the park herself.

Her mother had skipped bowling when Marissa was sick. She'd brought sweet tea and buttered toast to Marissa on a tray. She hadn't hopped on a bus and gone away for the day. Marissa looked at her son. No, she was not like her mother at all. An icy chill froze Marissa. Or was she? If what Bess had said were true, she might be just like her mother. Sold for the money in Tammy's purse.

She didn't understand, yet she did. This wasn't the life she wanted. She hadn't imagined the endless days of work and worry or the living conditions…or the smell. She meant to have better. To do better. But how could she rise above this life when she lived here and worked in a two-bit restaurant?

David looked at her. Instead of holding him close, Marissa wanted to set him on the ground and walk away.

What was wrong with her? This was her son. She loved him. He deserved so much better.

Dissolving Daria

The sun was gone the next day, hidden behind a thick, gray mat of clouds. Yesterday's sweet, warm breeze had a sharper, colder quality, and somehow that made everything easier to take. Marissa put on jeans and a sweater and carried her uniform to work.

The smell in the daycare center was so strong it nearly brought tears to Marissa's eyes as she dropped off David.

"What happened?" Marissa asked. "Someone spill the bleach?"

"No. We had to close yesterday. Everyone got what David had. Inspector said food poisoning."

"Food poisoning?" It struck Marissa as strange, since everyone had to send their own food.

"That's what he said. So we got here early today to wash everything with bleach."

No one said so, but Marissa suspected that someone had used the same rag to wash the changing table as the high chairs and tables.

§

It was slow at the restaurant. Again. The city outside the window was so cold and gloomy that Marissa didn't blame people for not venturing out to eat. The breakfast crowd had been so thin that Ben had sent the other waitress home. She'd worked a double yesterday because of Marissa's absence. This was just payback.

Marissa didn't mind. Daycare and rent had to be paid, regardless of how slow the restaurant was. The lunch rush came and went, leaving few tips.

"Miss, there isn't any lettuce." An elderly couple stood next to the salad bar.

"Really?" Marissa glanced at the salad bar. There was a space where the bin of lettuce should have been. Stocking the salad bar was Joey's job, but the customers were from her table. Marissa headed to the cooler without thinking it through.

Intent on getting the lettuce and getting back to the dining room, Marissa hurried through the kitchen. Joey was in his usual place in front of the grill.

She yanked the cooler door open and flipped on the light—a solitary bulb enclosed in a protective cage positioned in the middle of the ceiling. A row of shelves ran down the center of the room. The bulb cast a bright and glaring light on the laden, aluminum shelves lining the walls.

Marissa looked around the cooler, a short, wide room with a heavy, insulated door.

Looking straight ahead at the part of the wall visible from the door, Marissa saw boxes of half-and-half, flavored creamers, and pats of butter. To the left, large tubs of coleslaw, potato salad and assorted pasta salads lined the near side of the island shelves along with cold minestrone, split pea, and French-onion soup, and five-gallon bottles of salad dressing. Farther left still, on the shelves lining the wall, her gaze flicked past cold cuts, thawed steaks, loaves of processed cheese and leftover spaghetti sauce.

Marissa didn't spot the lettuce. It must be on the far side of the island shelves. She stepped into the cooler and turned into the second aisle.

She realized her mistake when she heard the door close for a second and then open again. Shit. Joey. She darted further into the aisle.

Marissa froze as she heard the door close again, her body tightly coiled, poised for flight. Which side would he appear from?

She listened. There were no footsteps. She wanted to hear footsteps.

Joey popped out at the end of the aisle nearest the door, his crazed hair and eyes looking like Jack Nicholson in *The Shining* when he popped out around the corner saying "Daddy's home."

A frightened squeak escaped Marissa's tight throat.

"It's cold in here, baby, but we can warm it up, can't we?" His voice was almost as greasy as his hair.

Marissa dashed down the aisle. She grabbed the metal bar at the end of the shelving unit and spun around the corner. Halfway to freedom. On the other side of the unit, Joey began pushing containers of food off the shelves. They fell in front of Marissa's feet in an explosion of goo, spraying their contents—potato salad, French dressing, blue cheese, chili.

She gasped and jumped back. A hand reached through the now-empty shelf to grab her shirt.

"No," she shrieked. Buttons flew as she pulled out of his grasp. She started for the door again, but she slipped, coming down hard amidst the slime that covered the floor. She scrambled to her feet in time to see Joey round the corner.

He was on her before she could react. His hands tore at the remains of her blouse. Her nipples pebbled in the cold. "Just look at you. You want this," he said as his mouth came down hot and wet on her breast. He nipped and tugged, first on one nipple and then the other, hurting her.

She fought, pummeling him with her fists, but she only managed to slip and fall, once again, in the filth.

She heard the rasp of a zipper as she struggled to her knees.

"Come on baby. I know you want this." He tangled his fingers in the hair on either side of her face and drew her near his huge erection.

Later, as Marissa stumbled from the cooler, sobbing, she spotted Ben. He was rushing toward her, his face lined with worry.

Too late, she wanted to say. You're too late. Instead, she shot him a frantic glance. Her hair was flecked with food, and she was smeared with tomato sauce. Her hands clutched the soiled remains of her untucked blouse, holding it closed.

She sobbed as she staggered past Ben on her way out of the kitchen. Marissa figured that he would know exactly what had happened when his brother appeared in a moment, equally food-splattered, but zipping his pants and smiling.

The thought of Joey's leering grin made her stomach lurch. The memory of his teeth and how they'd felt on her breasts made her gag. She refused to think of his cock with its unwashed smell and worse taste.

Her bag of clothes sat in the cubby beside the time clock. She grabbed it with slimy hands and held it to her chest as she dashed through the dining room. Desperate for the bathroom, she crazily thought of the lettuce. Where had it been? Had Joey hid it to trick her into his lair?

Her hands slipped on the bathroom door as she tugged it open.

In the locked ladies' room, Marissa sat in a heap on the floor. Sobbing, she emptied her stomach into the toilet. Her hands shook violently as she peeled off her sodden work clothes. She tried to clean herself with the caustic, lotioned soap from the wall dispenser. The slime coating her breasts and thighs was cold and greasy, not easily removed using paper towels that dissolved to gray globs with minimal scrubbing.

For the Love of *David*

The towels were completely ineffective at removing the mascara and eyeliner that had made black rivers of her tears. She shivered despite the hot water, rinsed her hair as best she could. Another pile of paper proved inadequate to dry her hair.

She vomited again in the sink, thick viscous fluid. Saliva probably, but it reminded her of other things, and she retched until her stomach was raw. Marissa left the water running as she dropped the soiled uniform and ruined hose in the trash and yanked jeans and sweatshirt over damp, sticky limbs.

Her hair was a wet tangle. The comb caught in greasy remnants of tomato and ground beef as she tried to rid her hair of the mess.

Greasy, dirty, sick, and shivering violently, she crossed the dining room. There were gasps. Someone called out, "Daria," asked if she was all right.

She didn't answer, didn't stop, just headed directly to the waitress station to grab her tips. A fifty-dollar bill sat amongst the singles and change in her cup. The tears pouring down her face accelerated. She was tempted to rip it into shreds, but she needed the money too badly. Her stomach cramped and her bowels turned to water. Ben didn't quibble when she held out her hand and said, "Pay check."

He gave it and more to her in cash. She pocketed it and left the restaurant in the middle of her shift.

Cold and shaky, she took the short cut through the parking lot in back. When she passed the back door, it opened. Joey stuck his greasy head out and called to her.

"Hey, Daria! You're a tasty suck. Get me a rubber and let's have us a fuck."

Bile rose as she took off running. Joey's laughter chased her out of the block.

Without consciously realizing where she was going, Marissa found herself walking into the drugstore. She shivered when she passed the condoms. Joey's gap-toothed smirk rose in her mind's eye, and she shook her head to clear it.

Making her way to the hair care aisle, she stopped to contemplate dye colors. A shock of different colored synthetic hair hung on a chain attached to the front of the display. She fingered through the samples and quickly settled on the color that she thought would most closely match her roots. She couldn't be Daria anymore.

§

Libby stood in front of her open closet door. She had work clothes, casual clothes and fat clothes, but nothing nice enough for the restaurant where Jeff had made reservations.

"Are you almost ready?" Jeff called from the living room. "We've reservations for 6:30." He had picked her up from work wearing a suit and tie.

The crushed velvet dress hung in the back of the closet. It was the only thing she owned that was nice enough, but she couldn't look at it without thinking of the night Marissa stole David. Not that she needed visual reminders to remember. "In a minute. I can't decide what to wear."

"I thought you were going to wear that dress I like." His voice came from the hall outside her bedroom.

She closed her eyes. "I can't. It's velvet. It's too heavy for spring." Besides, she'd lost and then gained enough pounds since then, she had no idea if it would still fit.

"Really?"

"Yes, really." It was only May fourth. She could probably get away with wearing it because of its cut. If she could stand to wear it. She opened her eyes. Just the sight of it brought back the guilt she'd felt by the end of that evening. That vision of an empty crib. She'd been out, dressed to the nines, and her baby had gone missing. "Maybe we should just stay in tonight."

The door made a swish as it swung over the carpet. Jeff looked in, his eyes narrowed with concern. "I'm sorry. I wanted tonight to be special, and I didn't think. I should have given you warning so you could have gone shopping."

Her heart melted. "You are such a wonderful, thoughtful man. Can I keep you?"

He reached for her. "I hope you do."

It was always heaven in his arms. It seemed every time she was close to him, she had to remind herself why she was waiting, why she didn't just tackle and ravish him. The warmth in his eyes made her melt. His eyes said he loved her and wanted her and thought she'd hung the moon.

"I want to." Why were they waiting? Oh yes, commitment. She was *not* going to be one of those women with three kids from three different fathers. Two were inevitable, but not three. Her head remembered, even if her body was screaming "to hell with commitment." Caught between the warring factions of desire and morality, Libby knew if she and Jeff waited much longer, she'd need to be committed.

"About the reservations?" He continued to look into her eyes. "It took a while to get them, but we *can* cancel."

She stepped out of his arms. "Don't be silly. I'll find something. Go wait in the living room. I'll only be a couple minutes."

§

Libby smoothed the floral skirt with the safety pin altered waistband and allowed the waiter to seat her. She'd never understood how having someone pushing a chair in helped one be seated. There must be a trick she didn't know or timing she hadn't figured out. It didn't matter. She wasn't likely to practice enough to perfect the move.

She smiled at Jeff and opened the menu. No prices. How was she supposed to know what to order? Normally, she selected a couple of things that sounded good and then let price narrow the selection. Here she could accidentally order the most expensive item on the menu. She looked at Jeff. "There aren't any prices."

The corners of his eyes creased as he smiled. "They do that on purpose so you will order what sounds good without considering the cost."

"I know. I just don't like it. I'd feel better if I could look at your menu for a moment."

He laughed. "Honey, relax and pick whatever you'd like. Pick two things if you want. I can afford it, I promise."

Her face grew hot. She knew he was talking about the money, but his words chased the original worry away and left another in its place. Two entrees? She'd gained a little weight, but not enough for anyone to think she could eat two entrees.

Stop it. She scolded herself. This was Jeff. Her weight was fine. She was obsessing over nothing. She took a deep breath and held it a moment before breathing out the tension.

He reached across the table and squeezed her hand. "You look especially beautiful tonight."

"Thank you." She smiled at him as the remaining doubt slipped away. He always knew the perfect thing to say to her. Not just beautiful, especially beautiful.

Having decided to get the veal Oscar, she set the menu aside.

He put his menu down, as well. "Libby, have I told you how

beautiful you are to me?"

She grinned. He was so cute. "Maybe once."

He fidgeted in his chair. "Well, you are. Not just outside, but inside as well. You are kind and thoughtful, always thinking of others, me in particular."

"Uh…thank you." Her smile grew a bit stiff. He seemed nervous all of a sudden.

When he pushed back his seat and stood, her heartbeat accelerated and her eyes got wide.

"Jeff, are you okay?"

In a heartbeat, he was beside her chair on one knee with a small, green velvet box in his hand. He took her suddenly cold hand in his large warm one. "I need to ask you something."

Her eyes skittered off the box in his hand to his serious eyes. All moisture disappeared from her mouth. She licked her lips, watching him, hardly daring to breathe. "Okay."

"I love you, Libby. Will you marry me?"

Her heart skipped a beat. "Yes. Oh, Jeff. Yes."

She was in his arms with no memory of leaving her seat. His mouth was hot and moist and so wonderfully Jeff. She forgot they were in public until he ended the kiss. It surprised her that they were both kneeling on the floor of the restaurant and that he was shaking as much as she was.

"I love you, too."

He fumbled a diamond solitaire onto her finger. Gold band. Huge rock. She gaped a moment as her eyes filled with happy tears. She was engaged.

Seated again, though she really wanted to be in his arms, she stared in turn at the huge round solitaire on her finger and at Jeff. He'd asked her to marry him. Her smile was so wide her face hurt.

They were getting married.

"Could you pinch me, please?" she asked.

Jeff laughed and handed her his handkerchief. "You're awake."

As she dabbed her eyes, the wine steward arrived with a bottle of wine Libby didn't remember them ordering. He pulled the bottle from the ice bucket, wrapped it in a white towel, and presented it for Jeff's approval.

Jeff nodded.

"Shall I pour it, sir?"

"Please."

The champagne cork popped. "And may I say, congratulations."

Libby beamed. "Thank you."

When the waiter returned for their order, she had no idea what she'd decided on earlier and had to look at the menu again to remember.

She ordered the petite filet, and he ordered the lobster. She memorized the details. His irrepressible smile. The way the melting look in his eyes embraced her. The way the champagne tickled her nose and was drier than she'd thought it would be. How they talked about the future.

"We'll build a house and fill it with children. What do you think of four kids? I've always wanted four or five." His heart was in his eyes. Hers was in her throat.

"Four is good. Or five."

All dinner long they touched. Feet beneath the table. Hands above the table. Eyes locked. "How soon can we get married?" This was a dream come true.

His thumb traced little circles in her palm. "Depends on what we want."

"I want you forever." The words slipped from her lips.

His gaze turned her bones to jelly. "You're getting me forever. And I'm getting you. Somehow, that makes waiting easier."

"And harder."

He nodded. "But you are worth the wait. We are worth the wait."

His words made her feel cherished. She'd never felt cherished before.

The bill came. Jeff handed the waiter his credit card, barely glancing at the bill. They floated out of the restaurant and into the star-filled night.

They walked hand-in-hand to the car, for the moment not talking, not kissing, just being together.

His eyes promised this was only the beginning.

"Tell me about your dream wedding," he said as he merged into traffic.

"You, me, Cheryl and Jack, a priest..."

"Father Ryan?"

She laughed. Ever since her confession about David, she really liked that priest. Confession. Her heart fell. The ring weighed heavily on her finger. She couldn't get married. She hadn't told Jeff the truth about David.

The food rolled in her stomach.

Could she march down the aisle and promise to love, honor and obey Jeff if she couldn't tell him the truth about David? Could their marriage last "'til death do us part" if part of their relationship was built on lies?

A part of her wanted to deny the truth and repeat the initial lie like a mantra: David was her son. She had him in the bathroom…But it was a lie.

Dear God.

Her stomach protested and her head hurt. She needed to purge herself of the lie. She had to tell him. But she wanted to vomit.

He was talking about white dresses and tuxedos, her brother-in-law and his family, how thrilled his folks would be. "My mom loves you."

It wasn't until they pulled into her driveway that he noticed her silence or at least commented on it.

"You're thinking about David, aren't you?"

"A little." She forced a smile. If only it were that simple. "You're coming in, aren't you?"

The look he gave her was as odd as her question had been. "I'd thought I would."

He unlocked the door as usual. She flicked on the light. Though they'd repeated this action a hundred times since the night of David's disappearance, she couldn't get that night out of her mind. She should have told Jeff then. Should have told the police. Then she'd be in jail, or maybe on probation, and Marissa and David would be somewhere known. Not on the run.

"You want coffee?" She headed to the kitchen. Everything was normal. Except it wasn't.

"Please." He picked up the phone. "I'm going to call my folks, share the good news."

She wanted to tell him not to. The fewer people who knew about the engagement, the easier it would be when he asked for the ring back after she told him the truth.

The normally comforting scent of coffee added to her nausea. Her right hand worried the ring on her left. She loved Jeff and wanted nothing more than to enjoy these last few minutes of them together, but her stomach wouldn't let her. She needed to tell him.

But did she? The devil on her shoulder suggested she could live the rest of her life without saying anything. Truth was overrated when you knew it would cause nothing but heartache. Telling him would bring on rejection. She'd be alone again, like she was before David, only worse because this time she'd know what she was missing. Now, she'd know she didn't have to be alone. That it was her fault she was. Her fault for clinging to the truth.

What was truth anyway? David had surprised her. She didn't think she was pregnant. Those were truths.

The rest of the story contained details better left unexposed. She could get away with saying nothing, especially if it allowed her to keep her happily ever after.

But it wouldn't, and she knew it. Happiness was incompatible with living a lie.

The clock ticked on the wall. She remembered how loud it had been the night of David's disappearance. The living room was bright. She could easily see David's baby picture through the arched doorway. He wasn't coming back. At least, he wasn't coming back to her. Would Marissa keep the secret, or would the police show up at her door to arrest *her* for David's kidnapping? How much harder would it be to tell Jeff then, after months and maybe years of lying?

She was swallowing feelings again, she knew. Her weight was inching up because she was swallowing her fear. If she faced it, if she admitted the truth aloud to herself with Jeff as a witness, would she feel whole again like she had the day she'd confessed to Father Ryan? Would she be free of the guilt that ate at her heart?

Libby carried the coffee into the living room as he hung up the phone.

"They're even more excited than I thought they'd be. Did you want to give Cheryl a call before it gets too late?" She shook her head and set the mugs on the coffee table. "Not yet. Let's talk some more first."

"Libby, honey, what's wrong?"

Love and fear roared inside of Libby. She'd lost David, but she had so much more to lose. "I just…" She didn't know what she had meant to say. The lie battered at her teeth. Unwanted tears cascaded down her already tear-stained face.

Jeff crossed the room to join her on the couch. "What's the matter? Are you having regrets about saying yes?"

"No, no." She shook her head and wrapped her arms around him. "I love you, Jeff. I want nothing more than to be your wife."

"Then what's the problem?" He held her close. It was heavenly. For how much longer? If she told him, would she lose him? What if she didn't? "Being with you, loving you, is more than I ever hoped for. More than I deserve."

"Hush." He kissed the top of her head. "That's not true. You deserve every happiness."

The words battered against her heart. Should she confess? Could she live with herself if she didn't? Could he live with her if she did?

Jeff held her close. His heart matched the irregular rhythm hers was keeping. "Is this about David?"

She nodded against his chest. *Please, God, help me.*

"I know you miss him, honey. I know we can't replace him, nor do I want to. But I'll give you other children. I promise."

Libby hugged him tightly. He was such a good man. She didn't deserve him. "That's not it. I need to tell you something."

"Okay." His voice was hesitant, as if he feared what she was going to say and was anticipating a blow.

Libby sat up. As much as she wanted to cling to Jeff, she knew she couldn't. Chances are, he'd push her away once he knew. She twisted her hands in her lap. Her engagement ring sparkled in the lamp light.

"Honey, whatever it is, we can work it out. Whatever it is, I'll still love you."

Her heart ripped open, and she started to cry in earnest. "You can't say that. You don't know. You'll hate me. I hate me."

"Let me be the judge of that." He kissed her forehead.

She took a deep breath, held it for a moment. She wanted to pray, but she couldn't come up with more than *please, God, please.*

"I'm not David's natural mother." Her breath came out in a rush. There. It was out. Funny how it didn't make her feel any better.

"What?" He sounded confused. "What did you say?"

Libby wept into her hands. The truth hadn't set free. She felt, if possible, worse than before. It was as if giving voice to the words had made it so. David wasn't hers.

Jeff gathered Libby into his arms. "I don't know what you said. You said it so fast. I couldn't hear you."

She sobbed. She couldn't say it again. Couldn't. This was far worse than confession had been. There, she'd been certain God would forgive her. God always forgave the truly contrite. Man wasn't as good at it.

"It almost sounded like you had said you weren't David's mother, but that doesn't make any sense. You couldn't have said that you weren't a good mother because that's just nuts. You're a wonderful mother," he murmured, gently stroking her hair.

"No, I'm not," Libby croaked. "I'm not a mother at all. I found David in a duffel bag outside of Kerm's and kept him."

"You what?" Jeff grabbed her by the arms and held her away from his chest to look at her.

Libby longed to bury her head in Jeff's shoulder and once again feel the comfort of his arms around her, but she knew that that was impossible. Now, she would lose Jeff, too.

"That's nuts. You're upset. You don't know what you are talking about." Jeff shook her gently, as if trying to jar her out of the delusional world she had obviously entered.

Libby shook her head while the tears streamed down her face. He didn't believe her.

"I love you, Libby." He pressed her head against his shoulder. "You're upset about life moving on without David, that's all." Jeff pulled her close and held her, murmuring reassuring nonsense into her hair. He rocked her, smoothing her hair while she sobbed. "You're a good mother. We aren't leaving David in the past. He'll always be in our hearts and in our prayers even if he isn't physically in our house. Everything will be okay."

Even through her tears she heard the worry in his voice. He didn't believe she was a kidnapper. He thought she was crazy.

Saying Good-bye

Marissa's hair was its normal color before she went to bed that night, or as near as she could get it with a bottle. She lay on the couch, listening to the wind howl outside the window. She'd already turned up the heat and used a towel as another blanket for David.

It didn't matter how much her electric bill went up. She wouldn't be here tomorrow night. David's diaper bag held her identification, their stash of money, a change of clothes, and enough baby food, formula and diapers for several days.

She stared into the darkness. Tomorrow, she'd spend a final day with David. Tomorrow evening, she'd hop the bus back to Eau Claire.

Chicago was too hard. It had beaten her. Tears dampened the hair at her temples. Like her mother before her, she'd failed at motherhood.

§

Marissa awoke to screams of, "Fire!" She sat up, wet with sweat. The sleeping bag slid to the floor. No fire alarm wailed. No sirens blared. She blinked in confusion. Screams weren't all that uncommon in the building, but "fire?" Raucous teens often woke her with their laughter and squeals. Had she dreamed the screams?

Disoriented, she struggled to her feet. Her apartment was hot, much hotter than the electric heat ever made it, and the air was tinged with smoke. Hurrying, she tripped over the sleeping bag on the way to the door. She pressed her palm against the door as she'd been taught in elementary school fire safety class and pulled it away a fraction of a second later—burned. Smoke seeped under the door.

A hot door meant the fire was in the hall.

Marissa felt herself grow oddly calm, as if she were on the outside looking in.

She couldn't run out the building using her door, but there were things she could do. Call for help. Wet a cloth and press it in the crack beneath the door to block the smoke. Fill the tub and cover herself with wet towels. Open the window. Call for help. Wait to be rescued. Do not jump. She backed away from the door and tripped over David's drawer, waking him.

David.

She picked him up and carried him to the bathroom with her. She'd forgotten about him.

She had a wet towel pressed in the crack under the door and another dripping one draped over David and the diaper bag when they reached the window. She'd doused herself and David from head to toe before the water had stopped. She'd have used toilet water if she'd had to. Now, Marissa pulled aside the ratty curtains and looked beyond the bars to the commotion on the street outside.

She'd paid extra for the bars.

§

Libby awakened in Jeff's arms. The clock on the living room wall said it was just after 4:00. As always, her first thought before she was even awake enough to think, was of David. A prayer for his safety and well-being. Her mind turned to Jeff. They were still engaged. She touched the ring to reassure herself. His arms were warm and safe and strong. She soaked in the comfort for several moments until the memory of what she had told him came back to her and her heart became lead.

She fingered her engagement ring. The truth hadn't set her free. He hadn't believed her. Should she insist on the truth? Pretend it had been a dream? Ignore her confession entirely? She couldn't think clearly wrapped in his arms. Her mind kept going to what she had to lose instead of what was right. Her love for him was an ache in her chest. Or maybe that was fear. Tears filled her eyes and slid into the couch cushion. She had to go, but she wanted to stay.

She must have moved and awakened Jeff.

"Libby?" Jeff tightened his arms around her just enough to prevent her departure. "Are you okay? You were a bit confused last night."

She shook her head. "I wasn't confused. I was telling the truth." Here she was blurting it out when she hadn't even decided what to tell him.

"The truth? Honey, you're David's mother. You delivered him yourself in the bathroom."

"No." How could she make him believe her? "That was the lie I told to keep him. I really found David outside of Kerm's." A sob broke free from the tightness of her throat.

"Don't cry, honey. Please." Jeff hugged her to his chest and gently kissed her lips.

The kiss surprised Libby. She hadn't expected that he would still want to kiss her. She returned the kiss with relief and gratitude, focusing not on the problem at hand, but on the safety and acceptance she found with Jeff. She focused on the kiss. His lips felt so good. So soft and warm that it quickly intensified from the calming, reassuring kiss that Jeff had probably intended to something much more intimate. For a moment, she was tempted to distract him with the physical, but that wasn't her. It was ridiculous. She ended the kiss.

Jeff looked at her, bemused or was it confused? Hard to tell. "Tell me what happened."

Her whisper was rough with emotion. She was reluctant at first, and then, since he didn't condemn her or leave, she spoke more easily. While she talked, the burden slowly began to lift. The problem didn't disappear, but the guilt of lying lessened.

"Is Marissa David's mother?"

"Birth mother?" Libby clarified the question. Whether Marissa had given birth to him or not, she knew now that she, Libby, had been his mother for three months. Still felt like his mother. "I don't know. But he's still my son."

He nodded, but he looked away. Libby could almost hear him think. But *what* was he thinking? Libby found it hard to breathe. Did he see her as a kidnapper who had stolen Marissa's baby or did he see it the way she had? The longer he stayed silent, the longer he looked into space, the more anxious she became.

Finally, he looked at her. "The way I see it, Libby, you found an abandoned baby and took him as your own to love and raise. That wasn't wrong. You didn't steal David from anyone anymore than someone steals a kitten that's been put in a gunnysack with rocks by a rising river. You rescued him."

"You don't hate me?"

Jeff furrowed his brow. "Hate you? For rescuing a child?" He pulled her close. "Never." He squeezed her. "Never. But I *am* worried about Marissa. If she's his biological mother, we can't charge her for kidnapping her own son."

Libby nodded. "But we don't know she's his biological mother. How would she know? There was no one in the parking lot. I looked. Even if she is, she can't be sure he's her child. He doesn't have a birthmark. She guessed he was and took him."

He shook his head. "It's too much of a coincidence, her stealing

David. No, she must have seen you even if you didn't see her."

Her stomach turned. Had Marissa watched her take David? "Then why didn't she do something earlier? Get help?"

He shrugged. "She probably figured you'd turn him in. Who knows? I don't think it makes any difference."

Tears ran down Libby's cheeks again. She turned her head to look at the photo of David she had on the table beside the couch. One glance at her little boy, and she lost all pretense of being relaxed and under control. "I didn't mean to steal him."

"Hush, hush." Jeff pulled her close again. "Libby, this isn't your fault. No matter what Marissa or whoever thought she was doing when she set him on the sidewalk, she was abandoning him. No one forced her. She made the choice. She had options. You've seen her family on television. She was loved, supported. She wasn't alone. She had parents, relatives, friends, and a boyfriend. She went to a university where she could have gotten free health care, free counseling, all kinds of help. But she chose to abandon her son, and in doing so, she threw away any rights she ever had to him."

Having him agree with her made her cry all the harder. "That's your opinion. Sometimes, I think I'm a monster."

Jeff shook his head. "If there's a monster in this story, it's Marissa." He pulled a handful of tissue out of the box on the end table and gave it to Libby. "First, she abandoned her newborn, and then she kidnapped him. If she wanted him back, there were things she could have done legally instead of stealing him from his bed in the middle of the night. Not to mention stealing your car. Once she reached her aunt's, she had another opportunity to seek legal recourse, but instead, she stole another car."

"Her aunt said it wasn't stealing."

Jeff snorted. "Her aunt just wants to keep her out of trouble, but with the type of decisions Marissa has been making, I don't see how that is possible. She took a baby, cleaned out her paltry checking account, wrote bad checks all over Milwaukee, and ran to God knows where. How is she living? She needs daycare to get a job, but she doesn't have enough cash to afford that and housing. She's probably living in some homeless shelter somewhere. She stole David from a good home and a loving mother to live in a box."

Libby listened to his words and cried. She'd spent days praying that David was safe and well, agonizing that he might be cold and wet and hungry. She'd never shared her fears with Jeff, with anyone. The fact that Jeff held the same fears ripped at her.

Jeff stopped his diatribe and looked at Libby. "Shit." He looked stricken. "I didn't mean it, Lib. David's fine. I don't know how she's managing it, but you've got to believe David's fine."

She needed to believe it, but she didn't. Diapers and formula were expensive. She had a job, a house and savings, but she'd still had trouble getting all the things he needed. She couldn't begin to imagine how Marissa would do it.

"Do you have any way to prove that David is yours?" His abrupt change of focus startled Libby. She didn't know what to think.

She swabbed her eyes and blew her nose. "Prove he's mine? I told you I found him."

"What about his birth certificate? Does he have a birth certificate?"

Libby nodded, disentangling herself from his arms to leave the couch. David's baby book was in a dresser drawer in her bedroom. She walked there, pulled it out and retrieved his birth certificate from a special pocket made just for that purpose.

When she returned to the living room, Jeff was still on the couch. She couldn't help thinking how blessed she was that he was still here as she gave him the small piece of paper. She perched next to him while he looked at the certified copy.

He smiled at her. "This is it." He held up the certificate. "This is all the proof we need. With this in hand, Marissa can claim whatever she wants to claim, but legally he's yours."

He looked happy, but Libby couldn't share his joy. "Unless Marissa has a blood test done which would prove I'm not David's mother. We have the same blood type, but they can always test for that HLA thing. I've heard the doctors at work talk about it being an indicator of biological relationships." Tears filled her eyes again. "And, of course, we can't forget the fact that she still has him."

His smile faded. "That's right." He looked at the birth certificate. "I guess I was thinking about how this is a legal document, and I didn't think about how paternity blood tests could be used to test for maternity." He looked at Libby with his heart in his eyes. "I was so thrilled, thinking that David was yours that I forgot for a moment that she still has him."

Libby nodded. She might not think of David every waking moment, but she never forgot he was gone. Every morning it was her first thought. Every night, except maybe last night when she'd nodded off in Jeff's arms, it was her last prayer. Still, Jeff looked so devastated, she forced a grin. "It's okay. I'm sure he's okay. He has to be."

"This reminds me of that Bible story where King Solomon is asked to decide which of two women is the mother of a disputed baby."

"The one where he's going to cut the baby in half and one woman says 'go ahead'?"

He nodded. "Yes. But the second woman says, 'No, don't harm the child. Give him to the first woman.' And that's how Solomon knows who real mother is. Because the real mother wants what is best for her son. You are David's *real* mother."

"Because I don't want him cut in two?"

"No, because you want what is best for him. You don't sleep worrying about whether he's warm, fed and dry. And Marissa wants him because she thinks he's hers and not because it's what is best for him."

Tears trickled down her cheeks. "He deserves to be well cared for and loved. He deserves..." She took a ragged breath as images of all the everyday events she'd never see passed before her eyes and a second set of images of him dirty and hungry and poor. "Jeff, I could maybe let David go, in my heart, if I thought being with Marissa was what is best for him."

"But you don't." It wasn't a question.

She shook her head.

Fire

Marissa put David on the floor to open the window. She shoved, lifting the ancient, double-hung pane. It fell back down until she propped it open with the dowel from the ledge. She screamed for help and grabbed David again, making certain the wet towel covered him before pulling her shirt over her nose. The zippered diaper bag banged against her side. It really didn't matter that she had it. Locked behind bars, she wasn't going anywhere. Still, having it at her side calmed her. She'd die with all her money.

Behind her, the walls were smoking. It wouldn't be long before the flames were in her apartment.

She'd paid extra for the room with bars. Extra for the solid door. Extra to keep them safe.

Turning her attention to the window, she yelled for help.

She couldn't die now. They were going home today. She was taking David home.

The fire was loud, like the roar of the heater inside a hot air balloon. There were people screaming. A group of men held a blanket taut between them, calling to the people hanging out the windows to jump. The building was only five stories high, but the jump from that height into a cheap blanket was frightening. Still, people were doing it, throwing what little of value they had onto the sidewalk and leaping after it. She saw a man miss the blanket and hit cement. The fire was too loud to hear the thud.

Marissa wished jumping were an option. Caught behind bars, she and David were doomed to die unless someone helped them.

Her screams joined others.

Sirens added to the cacophony as police and fire trucks finally came.

Marissa didn't recognize many of the people milling outside. The fire doors were chained against vandalism. She didn't know how many had access to fire escapes. She'd paid extra to deny access to the rickety one bolted outside her window. In choosing her apartment, she'd been more worried with keeping others out than getting out herself.

They were going to die.

Beneath the wet towel, David squirmed and cried.

Desperate, Marissa held him with one arm and shoved her other shoulder into the bars.

She almost fell out the window when they let loose and fell to the ground, taking the rusted fire escape with them. Marissa gaped at the tangle of metal three stories below. She didn't know whether to be happy or angry. The firefighter it almost hit looked up and saw her. David's towel slipped. She grabbed it before it got away and draped it back over him, covering his face. She pulled the collar of her wet shirt back up over her mouth and nose.

The firefighter grabbed a megaphone to yell to her. "Stay right there. Hold that baby tight and stay right there. I'm coming up for you. Stay right there." He repeated the words over and over as if afraid she'd climb out the window at any moment and jump. A ladder bounced off the wall to her left and then settled.

The heat behind her was blistering, but she didn't turn to look.

"Stay there. I'm coming. Hold onto the baby. I'm almost there." Her clothes were steaming, scalding her.

"Hurry," she urged the firefighter.

David wailed as she pressed him into the firefighter's arms. She started climbing onto the window ledge as he handed David down the ladder.

She was shaking when her turn came. "It's just a ladder." He told her to turn to face the building and climb down. The heat from the fire made her flinch when she turned toward it. Her apartment was burning. The ladder was painful to touch. Hot and hard, its metal rungs were slippery from her sweaty palms. He was behind her on the ladder. His arms framed her on each side. He wasn't going to let her fall. Hands grabbed her off the ladder before she was even on the ground.

"Come on. It's going to go."

Going to go? It didn't make sense. It was already burning. How could it go worse than that?

"David? Where's my baby?"

Someone had their arms around her and were running with her to an ambulance. She glanced back. Her apartment glowed like the rest. Someone showed her David crying in his oxygen mask. She coughed up smoke as the EMT strapped an oxygen mask on her and checked out her hands and back.

"You were smart to wet yourself and your little boy," he told her as flames shot out her window. "You're both in really good shape. That wet towel saved his lungs."

She took David when the EMTs had checked him out. Held him close as ambulances full of people drove off, only to be replaced by new ones. The building collapsed in a sudden roar that was echoed in the voices of the crowd of bystanders. Ash filled the air and sparks rained down, sizzling as they hit the damp towel she still held around David.

Stunned, it was all she could do to continue breathing. She'd been in there. She and David. Just moments ago. If the bars hadn't given way. If the firefighter hadn't raced up the ladder. If...

She sat on the damp ground with David in her arms and shook. It seemed a little late for her life to pass before her eyes, but it did. All the mistakes. All the dreams she'd once had for the future. David. All the things she meant to do for him tomorrow.

Several minutes passed. Her shaking was down to occasional tremors. She breathed oxygen until her breath came easier.

The EMT had said they were in good shape, that she'd saved David's lungs. Any minute someone would offer to transport them to a hospital. They'd need information, identification and payment. She took the mask from her face. Her lungs felt fine. For a moment, she was tempted to leave him there, write a note identifying him and leave him behind. It would be so easy.

Just put him on a gurney and walk away.

She meant to return him to Libby, but she couldn't. Not in that manner. Maybe it was Chicago. There were so many throwaway kids here. Too many. But not David. Not while he was watching her with tears in his eyes.

Pulling the elastic strap, Marissa unhooked the mask from David's wide-eyed face. She put the oxygen mask carefully on an open equipment box next to the gurney and shifted her son to her shoulder. Her left hand patted the diaper bag at her side.

The sun inched its way over the horizon as she turned her back on the rubble remains of the smoldering apartment. She hurried away before she could change her mind.

§

Marissa sat at a table in the Sixth Street Mission and stuck a bottle in David's mouth. She should have left him behind. It would have been easier without him. She could be gone, already.

"You from the fire?" a plump, middle-aged woman said as she slid a cup of coffee and a donut in front of Marissa.

"Yes."

"Smelled like it. Them, too." She nodded her graying head at a knot of people huddled in one corner. "We got showers you can use."

Marissa looked up. "I'd like that."

"Your baby need to see a doctor?"

Marissa shook her head. David was calm now, sucking his bottle. He was damp and sooty, but cleaner, by far, than she was.

After her shower, wearing someone's cast-off jeans and sweater, she helped in the kitchen. David slept in a donated car seat in donated clothes. In another room, hers and David's things were thumping around in a drier.

A girl came in with a toddler. She had black hair, plenty of eye make-up, and too tight clothes. She reminded Marissa of herself a few days ago.

"You get many like them?" she asked Kim, the mission's matron, when she returned to the kitchen having delivered coffee and a donut. "Like me?"

Kim lifted the plastic off another box of donuts and put two on a plate as a heavy man waddled in the door and headed to the serving counter. "Here you go, Jim." She handed him the plate.

"Thanks, Kim." He took the donuts from the plate and turned back to the door.

The woman turned her attention back to Marissa. "Young mothers like you? Girls on the run? Too many." She shook her head. "Far too many."

"What becomes of them, us?" Marissa knew the answer, but still she asked the question.

Kim looked Marissa up and down. "You using?" She shook her head and then held up her hand to forestall Marissa's answer. "Never mind. I don't need a lie. You don't have the look—yet. Don't mean shit, I know, but all I got to say is—if you're using—stop. If not for you, for your baby."

She shook her head, as if she knew her words were falling on deaf ears but hadn't been able to hold her tongue. "But you asked a question." She took a sip of her coffee. "Some girls disappear. I like to think they go back home. Like you. I'd like to see you go back home. But most get into drugs, either before they hit the street or once they get there. Drugs change everything. You see a lot of junkies working the street. Then pretty soon, it's just the kids that come in."

Marissa picked up her coffee cup and mumbled into it. "I'd like to go back home. I just don't think I can."

Kim nodded. "That's what they all say." She looked from Marissa to where David slept. "Bet you lost everything in the fire."

Marissa looked at David. "Almost everything."

"We've got stuff in the back I can set you up with. Clothes, shoes, purse and such."

"Uh, thanks." Her mother used to donate Marissa's old clothes to Goodwill. Things that were in good condition, but weren't stylish enough. She'd never thought where it ended up, if someone else ended up wearing her cast-offs. Another thing she hadn't wanted to think about.

"How long have you worked here?" Marissa asked Kim.

Kim sipped a cup of coffee so cold that the cream was a thin, dirty slick at the top. "Forever. Fifteen years this October."

"That's a long time. You must be really dedicated."

Kim shrugged. "You could say it's my calling."

Marissa couldn't relate. She couldn't minister to the homeless. Even now, when she was one, she didn't want to be around them. Not really. Her eyes were drawn to a skeletal woman who sat at a table staring at the wall. She was white and old, but Marissa couldn't tell how old. Living on the street aged people. Marissa had had an apartment most of the time they'd been in Chicago, but the last few months had aged her a dozen years or more.

"What's her story?"

"Her?" Kim nodded to the flannel-clad woman. "Not a happy one. Been coming here forever, when we can scrape her from the street. Used to be, she had kids. Don't know what happened to them. She's too stoned to say."

"What's her name?" Marissa asked before she could stop herself.

Kim looked at her. "You looking for someone in particular?"

The donut became a stone in her stomach. Marissa nodded. "Mora Frost."

"Mora, huh? Frost you say?"

Marissa nodded. Her heart beat faster. "You know her?"

Kim didn't answer. "Why are you asking? What is Mora Frost to you?"

Tears stung Marissa's eyes. "Nobody."

"Nobody, huh?" Kim's narrowed eyes said she didn't believe Marissa. "Why should I tell you about a nobody?"

Her heart was lead and her stomach stone. She stared at Kim, willing her to answer. "Do you know her?" The words squeezed their way through a too-tight throat.

"Maybe. Depends on who you are. Why you're asking."

Marissa shot a glance at David and then looked back at Kim, swallowing hard. She could leave her son, but she couldn't do this? "I'm told she's my mother."

"You'd be Marissa, then."

Good Decisions and Bad

Libby admired her ring as she poured the coffee.

"Careful there, you're going to spill all over."

The mug was only halfway filled. She laughed. "I can't help it. The ring is so beautiful." She handed Jeff a mug.

"It fits you."

She smiled. "You say the nicest things."

He took a sip of coffee. "We'll call the church today and set the date. I want to make it official, so you don't change your mind."

Libby laughed. "Like I'd change my mind. I'm more worried about you. I'm not the girl you thought you were getting."

"You are exactly the girl I thought I was getting."

"But I lied, I stole a baby. I lied to you."

"You rescued a baby and were living a lie. Now, you aren't living that lie any more. There's nothing you've done that I don't understand or can't forgive. And you say you've confessed all this to Father Ryan and got absolution?"

She nodded, her eyes misty.

"I like that man more and more."

She smiled. "I'd really like him to officiate the wedding."

"Me, too." Jeff kissed her cheek. "The sooner the better."

"About David," Libby began. "Are you sure you're okay with it? I mean. Not everyone would be. I bet if you took a poll, most people would think I was horrible for not turning him in. Crazy or something."

He hugged her close. "Most people didn't spend half a childhood in foster care."

"I know. You didn't. And even those who did. Foster care is not a bad thing, really. Everyone means well. I'm sure it's a wonderful thing for most kids. Gets them out of bad situations. Gives them a sense of stability. Allows parents a chance to get their act together, if they can. It just didn't work for Jenny and me."

She shook her head. "But there's more to it than that. If I had turned David in, they might have found Marissa, and she could have gotten help. Maybe she would have gone home, and her parents would have helped her. Maybe her boyfriend would have stepped up, and they'd have lived happily ever after."

"And maybe they wouldn't have found her, or she'd have felt forced to take him and wouldn't have treated him well." Jeff took another sip of his coffee. "Look at the decisions she made." He stuck up one finger. "First, she had unprotected sex when she wasn't ready to become a mother."

"We don't know they had unprotected sex." Libby interrupted, pointing a finger. "Maybe the condom ripped or whatever they used failed. Somehow, I can't judge her. I don't know what road she was walking. And without that, there'd be no David. And David, wherever he is, is a definite good."

Jeff grabbed her finger and kissed it. "I can't deny that. Still." He kissed her finger once more before releasing it. "Now, where was I?" He held up two fingers. "Second, she denied the pregnancy which meant no prenatal care. Third, she probably starved herself to hide it. Fourth, she had an un-assisted birth where a hundred things could have gone wrong." He held up a fifth finger. "She premeditated leaving him. She knew it was wrong, and she hid the evidence to avoid discovery." He had six fingers raised. "More than a handful of really bad decisions, and she hadn't even left him yet. I say you rescued him."

§

"How d-d-do you know?" Marissa asked, her voice shaking.

"I knew your mother." Kim's face was unreadable.

"You did? Where? When? Is she all right? Can I meet her?" Her hands clutched the edge of the table as the words tumbled out of Marissa's mouth.

Kim held both hands palm out. "Slow down. Slow down."

"At least tell me if she's all right?"

"First things first." Kim stood and got the coffee pot, splashing hot coffee in hers and Marissa's cups. "I need your story, first."

Marissa frowned. "Why?"

"Because those are my rules," Kim insisted. "And I want the truth. I'll know if you're lying."

She sounded like a mother. Like Marissa's mother. Like Tammy. Marissa pressed her lips together. Who was Kim, and how could she possibly know if she were lying?

"Who are you?"

"Not your mother, if that's what you're thinking." Kim glared at her. "You think you're the only one with secrets you don't want to tell? Everyone who's ever lived on the street has a past they ain't proud of. I knew your mother from when I was in rehab, and that's all I'm going to say until I hear your story and judge it true."

Marissa nodded once and told Kim everything. Paul, Libby, Aunt Bess, Joey, everything. Her coffee had grown cold long before she'd finished. David woke, and she fed him rice cereal as she talked.

Kim handed Marissa a wet washcloth for his face. "So, you've decided to give him back to Libby?"

Marissa nodded. "I want him to have the kind of childhood I had. I can't give him that now."

"You could if you fought for him. Surely, your mom would help."

Marissa's heart lurched. "Mora? Mora would help?"

Kim scowled. "Don't be an idiot. Tammy. She's more your mother than Mora ever was. Best thing Mora ever did for you was give you to Tammy."

Stubborn anger reared up. "Sold me. Mora sold me for whatever was in Tammy's purse."

"Bus fare back. Just like I'm going to give you bus fare home. You can take it to your mom's and get help, or you can take it to Eau Claire and give him up. Your choice." Kim took a key from her pocket and unlocked a cupboard. She opened her purse and took all the money she had from her wallet.

"Take it." She grabbed Marissa's hand and folded it over the small wad of bills.

"Why?" Despite Kim's words, Marissa searched her face for some resemblance to Bess or Tammy or herself. She saw nothing. Kim's eyes were hazel, like David's, not brown like hers.

§

"You didn't tell me about Mora," Marissa protested as Kim pulled her ancient Chevy into a stall in front of the bus station.

"There's nothing to tell. Our lives are just different versions of the same story. We met in rehab after your sister was gone and she'd given you up. We talked a lot, 'cuz I'd lost a baby too, a couple of months before she did. Pretty hard to keep a baby alive when it's born as stoned as I was." She shook her head. "I kept forgetting I had it."

Her eyes were hard as granite. "There's nothing quite like losing a kid to make you reassess things. Anyway, rehab don't take kids, so she gave you away. Got you safe. Gave you a chance." She sighed and shook her head. "Her rehab didn't take like mine did." She shrugged. "I got a job at the Mission. Saw her once, about a year later." She shook her head in silence, as if remembering. "Hard winter that year. Lots of people disappeared."

Marissa's heart was in her throat. "She froze?"

Kim shrugged. "Or moved on. Anyway, she's gone, and you're okay." Her eyes narrowed. "You'll be okay, won't you? You'll go home or give the baby up, but you won't let the drugs take you?" She grabbed Marissa's arm. "It's just temporary oblivion they offer. You know that, right?"

She patted Kim's hand and nodded. "I know that." She looked into Kim's eyes. "My life is a big enough mess without drugs. I'll stay clean. I promise."

The older woman's eyes reflected a combination of relief and skepticism. She'd clearly seen enough not to believe everything she heard.

§

It was early the following morning when the cab pulled up to a curb one block from Libby's. The city bus didn't run to the Greyhound Station this early in the morning, and Marissa wasn't willing to wait or make the necessary transfers. Once the decision was made, she wanted the deed done.

Same as last time.

She paid the cabby, begrudging ever dime. Then, she unbuckled David's replacement carseat and jostled it, the diaper bag, and an ugly purse from the back seat.

She walked to the front door of a random house and pretended to look for her keys as the cab pulled away from the curb. Once it had driven down the street and disappeared from sight, she hefted the carseat again and headed for the sidewalk. Strolling in the thin light of dawn, Marissa couldn't help but compare this morning with the gray November one in Kerm's parking lot.

The act was the same, and the players, but nothing else. The hour was earlier, the grass was greener, and her outlook had changed. When she'd left David at Kerm's nearly six months ago, he hadn't been a person. She hadn't known him, didn't love him. She'd left him to an uncertain future, abandoning him for her benefit, not his. Then, she'd left him with a stranger, half hoping to be caught. Now, she was leaving her son with his mother, and she prayed to God she'd get away scot-free.

Libby's house was nicer than she remembered. The whole neighborhood was. Maybe it was just the comparison to Chicago's streets and her apartment. Didn't matter. He was nearly home now.

Tulips crowded the brick planters around the base of two budding maple trees. They were huge trees that would produce mountains of leaves come fall. Leaves David would crawl through. Marissa smiled.

He'd have a good life with Libby. There was no way he'd remember Chicago, the lousy day care, the horrible apartment, or the fire. There were no burn marks on his tender skin, no scars of any kind. She hadn't kept him long enough. Not like her mother. Her finger brushed the round scar on her arm.

He wouldn't have nightmares.

"I love you, David."

He slept, oblivious to the tears that coursed down her cheeks.

She pinned the note to his blanket, kissed his cheek one last time, rang the bell beside the door, and then she was gone.

§

Inside the house, rich black coffee was beginning to drip into the pot. Libby pulled on her jogging clothes, wishing she hadn't agreed to go jogging so early with Jeff. It was Sunday, for heaven's sake. She could sleep in and still go to Mass.

Ah, well. The exercise was good for her. She'd be in shape for the wedding.

Who was she kidding? Two weeks wasn't long enough to get in shape.

Her engagement ring sparkled as she admired it. Two weeks. A smile stretched her face. She'd never thought she'd be a bride, yet tomorrow, Monday, Jeff was going to the courthouse to get the license. She was calling the church secretary to book the small chapel. Mark, Carrie and the kids, and Jeff's family were coming, and that was it. Two weeks. Two weeks to order flowers, book a weekend honeymoon, get a dress. She was half-afraid to find out what size she was now. Never mind. That's what jogging was for.

The only thing missing was David, but she'd resigned herself to that. She and Jeff would make other children, but those babies would never have the part of her heart reserved for David.

The doorbell rang.

Libby looked at the clock. Jeff was early, or he must have forgotten his key. She had half an hour yet. Time for coffee. Or had she gotten the time wrong?

Oh, well. The sooner they got started, the sooner they'd be finished. Coffee could wait until later.

She grabbed her running shoes and carried them to the door with her.

The lock was stiff. It took several seconds of fumbling before it finally disengaged. She yanked the door open. An apology for making him wait died on her lips.

No one was there.

Hmm. She snorted. Strange. Then, Libby looked down and her heart stood still.

"David?"

She put her hand to her chest and rushed out to hoist the car seat from the stoop.

It was a different car seat, larger and well used. David was bigger, too. His face was Gerber-baby round and slightly flushed from the morning chill. He'd grown enough that she wouldn't have recognized him if he'd been anywhere but on her front step.

"David." He was heavy. "Oh, my gosh. David." Tears pooled in her eyes. She scanned the area. She looked carefully, but like that morning nearly six months ago, she saw nothing. But she couldn't trust it. She knew Marissa was out there—somewhere—watching.

"Thank you!" Libby called into the early morning chill, as joy bubbled up inside her. "Thank you for bringing him home."

She lugged the seat into the house and set it in the entryway. "Thank you."

There was so much she wanted to say. Apologies she needed to make. She stumbled outside, looking right and left.

Marissa stepped out from behind the corner of the house and pressed a finger to her lips.

Libby's heart ached. Marissa looked older and leaner. Her clothes weren't as nice, and her hair was shorter and less stylish.

"I'm sorry." Libby hadn't meant to speak, but it came out anyway.

Marissa smiled sadly and mouthed, "Me, too," and stepped back around the corner.

Libby didn't follow. But she wanted to. She stood on the step staring after the woman who'd twice left her beloved son. "I'll take good care of him," she called into the yard. But Marissa was gone.

Back inside, she locked the door. Locking it against…against… what? Another change of heart? No, this time Marissa had freely given her David.

Libby couldn't wait to have him in her arms again. Ignoring the note, she pushed off the blanket. Her fingers fumbled as she tried to loosen the straps and lift her son. He was so much bigger and heavier now, and his clothes were different. He smelled of stale cigarette smoke and cheap air-freshener. He had worn the hair off the sides and back of his head, but the thick dark thatch on the top remained. He looked like Friar Tuck. The thought made her laugh.

Libby laughed and cried, hugging and kissing her son. The jostling and overt affection startled David awake. He cried out, but he was immediately comforted by the warmth and security of the arms that held him. His hazel eyes opened, and he gazed at the face that hovered above his. His lower lip quivered.

Libby smiled and spoke in the high-pitched tone babies like. Her loving gaze touched every inch of him before returning to his eyes. She smiled, though tears dripped from her nose.

She meant to call Jeff, to tell him about David, about Marissa, but his car pulled into the driveway before she finished kissing David hello.

He unlocked the door and let himself in. "Sorry, I'm early. I thought—"

She turned to him with tears streaming down her face and David in her arms. "She brought him back. Marissa brought him back."

"You saw her?" Jeff picked the blanket off the floor.

Libby nodded. "A minute ago." She explained everything as she carried David into his bedroom. The initial shock of having David home had waned enough for Libby to take inventory. She undressed him, ostensibly to change his diaper, but really to see that he was whole and well. He had changed. His limbs were stronger, and he had more control of them. His messes were smellier and larger, too. And while he didn't seem to recognize her, he apparently decided that she was okay, because he smiled at her.

Jeff brought the diaper bag, handing Libby the necessary supplies. "There's a note on the blanket."

She froze for a moment and then purposely finished the job at hand before speaking. Her tension sat like a lump above her breastbone.

"Did you read it?"

"No. I thought we could read it together."

She took a deep breath and picked David up. He was so much heavier than she remembered. She pressed him close. He felt wonderful.

"Let's get David a bottle first." David was all that mattered. The note could wait.

He pulled an empty bottle from the bag. It was dirty. There were two others equally as dirty, equally as empty. It had taken Marissa a while to bring David home.

Libby handed David to Jeff. "It'll be faster if I make one."

She hadn't ever emptied the cupboard of the bottles or powdered formula, just as she hadn't taken down the crib. She'd never believed Marissa would bring him home, but apparently she hadn't given up hope, either.

It took only a moment to run hot tap water and mix a bottle. As she shook it to mix the formula, she looked at Jeff and the squirming child in his arms. She watched as David grabbed Jeff's hand and pulled it to his mouth. He gnawed contentedly, soaking Jeff's hand. She looked at Jeff's face for a negative reaction to the drool. There was none. He was a natural dad.

They sat on the couch in the living room. Jeff unpinned the note while Libby fed David.

"Do you want me to read it out loud?"

She didn't. Not really. Words carried more weight when spoken aloud. "O…kay."

He cleared his throat and unfolded the piece of paper.

"Love him."

The clock ticked.

"That's it?" Libby asked. "That's all it says?"

Jeff nodded. "That's everything."

Libby nodded, as well. "That *is* everything."

They sat in silence as David emptied the bottle.

"What do we do now?" Libby asked.

They stared at each other as if the answer might be written on one of them somewhere.

Jeff shrugged. "I don't know." He shrugged again. "Do what the note said, I guess."

Libby lifted David under the arms and smiled at his belch.

"Do we tell the police he's back?" David wiggled in Libby's arms as he gnawed on his hand. She looked at him. Two tiny teeth poked through on his lower jaw, and the gums on the upper were swollen. Big hazel eyes. Like hers. Marissa's were brown, weren't they? She tried to remember.

He was so big, so strong. It hurt that she didn't know him. Didn't recognize him. It was almost as if he were somebody else.

"Let him roll around on the floor. See what he can do," Jeff suggested, spreading out David's blanket.

David's blanket. The one Marissa took the night she'd stolen him. David.

She placed the wiggling child on the floor by her feet, wiped her drool-dampened hand on the leg of her jeans, and reached for the letter.

"Love him."

She watched David roll onto his back and pull off his sock. Her hands itched to touch him, to stroke his soft cheek, to rub his fat little belly. She set the note on the cushion and bent down to caress her son. "I do." David's image began to blur as tears once again filled Libby's eyes.

Jeff's arm rounded her shoulders and pulled her close.

"I'm so tired of crying," she sobbed. "David is home, and I just want to…" Her voice cracked. "He's so big. I missed so much. M-m-marissa…" She pressed her face in his shoulder and released the emotional floodgates.

"I know." Jeff smoothed her hair and held her close. "Give it some time, sweetheart. Marissa obviously thought he'd be better off with you."

David chewed on his foot, oblivious to the emotional upheaval above him.

When Libby finally regained control, she wiped her face with the back of her hands and reached for a tissue.

"I can't believe Marissa gave him back. I know I should tell the police he's home, but I want to give her a chance to get away."

"I don't want her caught either." He hugged her close. "And we will call the police, but I don't think we'll do it just yet."

On the Run

Marissa saw the curtain flutter in a window across the street. Damn. How ironic that she should be caught giving David away the second time.

The sun rose as Marissa ran through the streets. She had no doubt that the police had been called. Tired from the interminable bus ride from Chicago, she went where her feet took her. She wasn't surprised to find herself nearing campus on her usual route home to her dorm. Crossing the Chippewa on the deserted footbridge, she stopped to stare at the water. School would be over soon, if it wasn't already. Her stomach growled. If school was still in session, maybe she could use her food ID to get something from the cafeteria in Davies. She patted her pocket to be certain it was still there.

A small branch spun a circle below her before disappearing underwater. Pulled under. Marissa thought briefly about her grades. She hadn't officially withdrawn from her classes and was sure to be failing all of them. A smile curved her lips. She'd always been so proud of her grades. She'd always been able to keep her head above water in even the toughest classes. It seemed fitting that her life had become the classic stress nightmare. The one in which she dreamed she walked into a class on the day of the final to take the test, but she had never been to the class before. Cold sweat broke out on her palms and under her arms.

She shook off the thought. Grades were the last thing she should worry about. It wasn't as if she would be going back to school any time soon. She should be worrying about the police. Returning David would get the charges dropped. But admitting she was David's biological mother wouldn't yield a happy ending. Her life was out of control and had been, it now seemed, for quite a while. Since Valentine's Day a year ago.

Fate had taken control and turned what had been a life filled with promise to one filled with despair. *Hubris.* That was the Greek term for it. She had been excessively proud of her life and accomplishments, and now she was paying for that pride, that happiness.

Or maybe this had all become inevitable when Mora had dropped her off years ago. Kim didn't seem to think so. *"Leaving you was the best thing she ever did. Leave it at that, Marissa. Forget about her and go home."*

The water raced under the bridge. Flotsam and foam swirled in the current. Flotsam. She was flotsam swirling out of control on the rushing river of life. *Drivel.* She was tired, that was all. Her eyes burned with the need to sleep. But she had miles to go before she slept. She shook her head. Wasn't there a poem that went like that?

Flecks of foam in the water caught her attention. The river seemed higher than usual. She recalled stories of college students who attempted to swim across the Chippewa when the water was high like this. Those stories often ended in tragedy.

There were countless snags in rivers like this. Leaning over the rail, she focused on a tangle of brush caught against the bridge's pilings. Sometimes it took months for a body to surface, and by then it might be way downstream. On occasion, just personal artifacts would be found: part of a shirt or jacket, maybe part of a limb. And sometimes, nothing at all.

It was a tempting thought.

She shrugged out of her mission jacket and tossed it over the railing, watching as it fell fluttering. The pale pink-and-white-striped garment landed with a small splash and was instantly swirled under the water and under the bridge.

She dashed to the other side, silently cursing. She'd left her college food ID zipped in the pocket. Searching the water, she thought she spotted it as it tumbled down-stream. There'd be no recovering it. No breakfast sandwich to go from the Davies cafeteria.

Returning to the other side, she weighed the benefits of following the jacket downstream. She wouldn't have to deal with police who would certainly want to press charges for David's abandonment. Her grades would no longer be an issue. But most importantly, she wouldn't have to see the hurt and disappointment on her parents' faces. And she wouldn't have to face Paul.

Marissa closed her eyes and summoned David's grin. With it came guilt. She'd made mistake after mistake with him since the day of his conception. Leaving him with Libby this morning was the best thing she could have done. Like Mora. Abandoning her child was the only good thing she'd done. Until today, her love for him had been a guilty love, a love out of obligation, not an honest love.

She watched the water boil over the rocks below. One quick jump and... certainly, suicide couldn't hurt any more than she hurt now.

She hoisted one foot on the railing and stopped. Her parents would blame themselves. Could she really do that to them?

§

Late that afternoon, David fussed as Libby buckled the car seat into the back of her car.

"I know, honey, I want to be home, too. Just one more stop."

Jeff opened the passenger door for Libby. "I can drop the two of you off and do the grocery run by myself. He's been through a lot today." They all had. Since David's return, they'd talked to the police, called relatives, and had David checked out at the walk-in clinic at the hospital. Libby wanted nothing more than to be at home with her son, getting reacquainted.

"That would be wonderful."

Jeff started the engine and the radio came on. Music gave way to a newsbreak as they negotiated the streets back to Libby's house.

"Marissa Fleming, the university student who allegedly kidnapped David Armstrong while baby-sitting for his mother on February 5th, was last seen going onto the university's pedestrian bridge this morning shortly after dawn. Her purse and a note to her parents were found on the bridge, but officers who had been searching for her at either end of the bridge were unable to locate her. Suicide is strongly suspected. Authorities are looking down river for the body."

When the music resumed, Jeff flipped off the radio.

Libby's eyes filled with instant tears. "Suicide," Libby repeated in a stunned whisper. She looked at Jeff and then into the back seat where David slept in his car seat. Had Marissa dropped him off and then committed suicide? Libby regretted not following Marissa around the corner. She didn't know what she could have said or done that would have changed anything. She didn't understand Marissa. Couldn't comprehend leaving David once, much less twice.

Now, she regretted that they hadn't called the police right away. They hadn't called the police at all. A neighbor had seen Marissa leave David on the doorstep and called with her description even before Libby spotted her. Marissa had left a note on the bridge.

"What a waste." She swallowed hard and looked back at Jeff. If

Marissa were dead, then David was hers with no one to gainsay. There was guilt associated with that relief. She couldn't help wondering if that had been a motivating factor in Marissa's decision.

"I guess we just need to be extra thankful that David is okay. That she took such good care of him as she did, and that she dropped him off before she jumped."

They rode in silence.

"I don't believe it," Libby announced as Jeff parked the car in her driveway.

Jeff stared at her. "Why not?"

"It doesn't make any sense." Libby shook her head. "Why would she kill herself? She had to know that I wouldn't pursue charges. She knew that David wasn't…mine." It hurt to complete that thought aloud. "She knew I wasn't his natural mother." Her eyes filled with tears. "It doesn't make any sense. Had she wanted to, she could have proven he was hers and sent me to jail. She was free. She never even had to bring him back."

"Unless, he wasn't hers."

Libby shook her head. "He had to be. Why would she take him otherwise? It's too much of a coincidence. I find a baby—she steals him. I just can't believe she'd kill herself. She was free. She could have started over. It just doesn't make any sense."

Case Closed

The hot, late August wind was like a furnace blast after the air-conditioned chill of the restaurant. The postponed wedding meant a longer honeymoon trip and a smaller size wedding dress.

Libby and Jeff were greeted by their six nieces and nephews armed with handfuls of birdseed. Jeff's mother held David as she supervised the assault.

Libby held her train aloft, lowered her head, and dashed to the car. "Aren't they supposed to throw those outside the church?"

"Father Ryan said no." Jeff tried to shield her, but a handful hit her chest and sent millet trickling into her cleavage. "Too much mess in front of the church."

He opened her car door and helped pile the bulk of her wedding gown into her lap before closing the door.

"We could have just told them throwing rice or bird seed wasn't necessary."

"Why ruin their fun?" He started the car.

Libby looked out the window. Jeff's mom was waving David's hand at them. The wedding ceremony had included an adoption ceremony, too. "It seems like we should be celebrating with David, too."

"No way." Jeff patted her knee. "He'll be fine. Mom watches him almost every day, anyway."

"I know." She forced a smile. "It's just…"

He shook his head and shifted the car in gear. "No one is going to take him. Marissa's dead, honey. There's been no sign of her. The police think she's dead. The district attorney thinks she's dead. I think she's dead. Everyone thinks she's dead, but you."

"Her family doesn't."

"They do, too. They're just waiting for official word before having the memorial service."

Libby shrugged. "I still don't get how they can claim she's dead when they haven't found a body."

Jeff shook his head. It was an old argument. "They haven't found her body because of how high the river was when she went in. They may never find it. You *know* that. You have to trust the police and believe she's dead."

"I know," Libby replied. "But…"

"But nothing. We are going on our honeymoon. David will be fine. Mom and Dad will watch him the entire week. And you won't worry about Marissa. Right?"

She was thinking about the look on Marissa's face the last time she'd seen her. She'd looked tired but not depressed. Not that Libby knew what depressed looked like. It wasn't like it had a color or appeared written in bold letters on a forehead.

"Right?" Jeff repeated. "You are going on our honeymoon, and you are going to focus on me alone, right?"

"Right. But just for the record, I don't believe that Marissa's body is wedged under a rock somewhere south of Eau Claire."

§

They were still on their honeymoon when a fisherman pulled a filthy pink and white spring jacket with Marissa's university food card zipped in the pocket and a woman's tennis shoe from the river more than a hundred miles downstream.

"Well, Lib, there's your proof." They'd only turned on the television because of Ann's phone call. "The police are certain that she was going back to the dorm the day she dropped off David, but changed her mind. She left a suicide note, remember."

"*Mom, Dad, I'm sorry*, isn't necessarily a suicide note. It could just be an apology for all she'd put them through and would continue to put them through because she was disappearing again."

"It's a suicide note," Jeff insisted.

Libby still believed otherwise.

§

From her desk at Tucker and Associates in Boston, newly hired secretary Ann Davids Mather spent her lunch break thumbing through the *Eau Claire Leader Telegram*. Her short, light brown hair curled about her face in a carefree, cosmopolitan style. Her deep brown eyes scanned the paper. An article on the lower right hand corner of page three snagged her eyes—"College Girl Kills Self after Botched Kidnapping." She closed her eyes for a moment, willing her heart to beat normally.

Finding the article shouldn't bring tears to her eyes. She'd been scouring the paper for it since she'd hopped the ride out of Eau Claire that May. She'd longed for it; dreaded it. The article was a symbol of the end, like a period at the end of a long, drawn-out sentence. Seeing it at long last should have been a relief.

And it was. But it wasn't. There was a strange tightness in her throat. She waited for the weight to lift from her shoulders, but it didn't move.

The newspaper called the death, "tragic and avoidable."

The reporter hadn't a clue.

David's face filled her mind's eye—the memory of the snapshot in the Bible beside her bed.

He was better off with Libby.

It was the truth, but being the truth didn't make it easier to embrace. Knowing she'd been stupid from the start didn't negate the stupidity or erase the guilt.

Tragic and avoidable.

There was no changing the past.

She resolutely turned the page.

THE END

ABOUT THE AUTHOR

Laurel Bradley believes prayers really do get answered. After many years of writing, Bradley has finally achieved her dream of seeing her stories in print. Her CRĒME BRŪLĒE UPSET, a contemporary romance novel, was released in early 2008. A WISH IN TIME, her time-travel romance novel, was a 2008 ForeWord Magazine's Book of the Year Award winner in romance and TRUST NO ONE, a romantic suspense, was published by Storyteller Publishing in June 2012. Laurel lives in Wisconsin. She graduated from the University of Wisconsin-Eau Claire with a Bachelors of Arts in English. When she isn't reading, writing, or painting with watercolors, she's cross-country skiing or decorating Ukrainian Eggs.

Please, visit Laurel online at
www.laurelbradley.com.

Made in the USA
Charleston, SC
05 September 2012